SIN & SANCTUM

SIN & SANCTUM

GENE GROSS

Copyright © 2025 by Gene Gross. All rights reserved.

No portion of this book may be reproduced, stored in a retrieval system, or transmitted in any form or by any means—electronic, mechanical, photocopy, recording, scanning, or other—except for brief quotations in critical reviews or articles, without prior written permission of the publisher. Requests to the publisher for permission or information should be submitted via email at info@bookpresspublishing.com.

Any requests or questions for the author should be submitted to him directly at ggross@isunet.net.

This is a work of fiction. Names, characters, businesses, places, events, locales, and incidents are either the products of the author's imagination or used in a fictitious manner. Any resemblance to actual persons, living or dead, or actual events is purely coincidental.

Published in Des Moines, Iowa, by:
Bookpress Publishing
P.O. Box 71532
Des Moines, IA 50325
www.BookpressPublishing.com

Publisher's Cataloging-in-Publication Data

Names: Gross, Gene Francis, author.
Title: Sin and Sanctum / Gene Francis Gross.
Description: Des Moines, IA: Bookpress Publishing, 2025.
Identifiers: LCCN: 2025905381 | ISBN: 978-1-960259332
Subjects: LCSH Crime--Fiction. | Murder--Fiction. | Iowa--Fiction. | Iowa Great Lakes Region (Iowa)--Fiction. | Okoboji Lakes Region (Iowa)--Fiction. | Mystery fiction. | Thrillers (Fiction) | BISAC FICTION / Mystery & Detective / General | FICTION / Crime | FICTION / Thrillers / Crime
Classification: LCC PS3607 .R67 S56 2025 | DDC 813.6--dc23

First Edition
Printed in the United States of America
10 9 8 7 6 5 4 3 2 1

For Dr. Zora Zimmerman,
who helped to turn a wish into reality.

1

Looking back from where he stood in the wheelhouse, Bart Farley could see a few chunks of the diver's styrofoam float and a tinge of pink in the wake's froth. Problem solved, thanks to the help of *Maximilian the Magnificent*, excursion boat extraordinaire! It was risky but serendipitous—an opportunity too good to pass up. This time of day, the worker bees were not home, tourists were mostly busy elsewhere or not up yet, and fortunately, there was little boat traffic in the bay. He was confident his little murderous event had gone unnoticed. Besides, a rented boat and some gear gone missing were common enough and did not necessarily imply a serious crime, at least nothing nefarious. If body parts did begin to show up, the assumption would be that there was a horrible accident brought on by the victim and no one associated with the *Maximilian*. The only possible witness was Charley, but he was below deck fine-tuning the engine, clueless of the hit-and-run drama playing out topside.

He thought ahead. *When we get to the State Pier, I'll have time to check the stern for any loose ends. I'll need to use my mask and fins to check the drive shafts and props, but I can do that later.*

He had to laugh at "loose ends." There certainly were loose ends, or rather loose parts, but nothing that would point to him.

Momentarily reconsidering the matter, Farley decided that, unless someone asked, it would be better not to report the "discovery" of any pieces of float or scraps of rope wrapped around the propellors and drive shafts. They might be explained away as discarded or lost from a passing boat, a dock, or even from one of the constructions sites that dotted the shoreline this time of year, but to be on the safe side, if there was anything to be found, it was better to personally dispose of it in the county landfill or, better yet, any of the ubiquitous dumpsters throughout the area campgrounds.

A good deal was riding on *Maximilian's* success, and any negative association, implied or otherwise, was to be avoided. The whole matter was either unfortunate or fortuitous depending on one's point of view, but better to stay ahead of any potential trouble.

Thank goodness Loren had alerted him. Thinking about the call, he had to laugh. *Nothing like having a staff member at the Lodge who likes to gamble and owes me money. It makes him a good spy. My spy!*

Loren Price intended his call this morning as an update but confirmed the diver had rented a boat from the Sports Shop and, according to its owner, was planning to dive not far from shore a few hundred yards south of The Lodge On Okoboji. Loren may not know the consequences of his latest report, but if he developed suspicions, he would be complicit and would have to keep his yap shut. Besides, Farley would be sure Loren was generously rewarded for his information. It was worth it.

Still, it was all a bit puzzling. According to Loren, the guy had been asking questions and flashing pictures of a missing girl. A brief surreptitious rummage through room and vehicle by Loren were inconsequential, but a search on the internet was disquieting. The guy was retired FBI. He may really have been staying at the Lodge for a vacation trip, but the coincidence was facile at best, and there was too much riding on their enterprise to ignore even the slightest possible threat.

Whatever the authorities might learn could point in several directions, and certain people wanted none of them investigated. Still, as retired FBI, the guy couldn't have been that naive. He must have known his questions would draw attention. If that was part of his calculation, it worked, but not in the way he intended. Fortunately, his interest in SCUBA diving had provided an unexpected solution.

Farley was looking forward to this evening's onboard party. Besides providing transportation for vacationers and guided tours about the lake, *Max* was well designed for private events, large and small. The excursion boat also served the needs of special clients whose business or entertainment was strictly confidential, a service that came with benefits. One very special client was on tonight's list of guests, and Farley was hoping for good news.

Good news following the elimination of a serious potential problem would make this a successful day, but he did consider one additional task. *Loren said the FBI guy's wife was to join him Saturday. Before she gets here, I better have a thorough check made to see if he left anything incriminating in his room or car. And with Loren's help, I know just the person to call.*

He pulled out his mobile phone and dialed her number.

***

While Farley complimented himself on his good fortune, his part-time engineer and maintenance man, Charley Chen, was below deck puzzling over what had caused the RPM on the port drive shaft to drop for several seconds and acquire a slight vibration. After checking everything obvious, he climbed the short ladder and made his way to the boat's stern. He watched while they passed by Fort Dodge Point and entered Smiths Bay, listening, until finally the vibration ended. Pulling his cap lower to shade his eyes, he saw a length of rope commonly found on boats around the lake float away in the wake, a light westerly breeze already pushing it and a few other bits of flotsam toward shore.

Charley was a mechanical engineer, retired from Iowa State University, who had moved with his wife, Lily, from Ames to Okoboji. His passion for fishing was second only to anything mechanical, but after two years of what his wife called "lazy life," found fishing was not enough to fill his days. He missed his students and opportunities for design and hands-on work in his field. He did not know how this fellow, Farley, had learned about his skills, but Charley had immediately accepted the offer to "tinker" and refine the performance of the new excursion boat.

As he made his way back down the ladder to the engine bay, Charley considered, as he had when he was first hired for the project, the viability, if not the suitability, of the large boat on Okoboji. On first sight, the *Maximilian* was impressive. A good deal of effort and money was put into appearance and accommodations for passengers and special events. The mechanical parts, less so.

Max was rebuilt from components of several boats transported to the Iowa Lakes by train, then truck. Resting in a makeshift dry dock near the West Shore Resort this past winter, the catamaran-style hull sections had been welded to the steel frame. For a smoother ride in rough water, a third smaller hull was added to the middle of the craft. The multi-hull design made the craft's ride stable but its maneuverability sluggish. To Charley's way of thinking, the middle hull was superfluous, and its main contribution was to resist efforts to control the craft.

A drive shaft and propellor drove each of the outside hulls and required the pilot to use control levers to slow the speed of one prop while increasing the speed of the other in order to execute a reasonably short turn. It was a throwback in design and took a deft touch and good judgement to know how and when to execute any maneuver. Everything depended upon a finely tuned motor, balanced drive shafts and propellors, and a smoothly functioning control system. Charley's skills as a retired mechanical engineer were continuously required to keep the boat functioning.

As much as he enjoyed the work, Charley felt sorry for *Max*. He considered the regenerated, overly ornate excursion boat closer to a waterborne Frankenstein's monster than *"Maximilian the Magnificent,"* as advertised by its owner. To Charley, *Max* was a living creation but one whose design and character was deeply flawed.

2

"This is not how to run a business! Three times in as many days rented equipment has not been returned. I don't mean late. I mean not returned. That's over two grand! And now a boat and motor is missing." Jerry Strand, assistant manager of the Sports Shop adjacent to the The Lodge On Okoboji, was dependable, hard-working, and great with customers, but a nervous-Nelly when things didn't go as he expected. "It was supposed to be rented for one day, and it's been two days and nights since it should have been returned! I called the marinas, the resorts, and the lake patrol, but no one has seen it. It's as if the lake swallowed it up! I thought we had a quid pro quo, a symbiotic relationship, but everything is at the whim and demand of the Lodge. We're not here to subsidize the Lodge!"

Owner-manager Nigel Waterford, to whom Strand was unloading his concerns, both appreciated and dreaded his employee's intensity. It wasn't so unusual for rentals to be returned late. That's why there were deposits, but in spite of his retail business experience, Jerry seemed to have trouble grasping this concept. Admittedly, his initiative to locate the missing craft was sound, but with all the canals and docks around the 3,825-acre blue-water lake, any attempt was only slightly better than picking the winning numbers in a lottery. If history was prescient, one day soon, the boat would be returned by a penitent renter, or they would get a call reporting an abandoned boat with their name on it.

"Are you sure the boat was checked out by someone from the Lodge?"

"Yes. He said so."

"Did you call to confirm?"

Strand hesitated.

"I'll call now."

"I'll take care of it. I have to go to the weekly meeting later this morning anyway."

As he walked to his office, it occurred to him that Strand's timing was inconvenient. He had enough issues to address at today's meeting. What did she call their group? Ancillary Enterprises! Fancy title for an ass-chewing session. But as busy as he'd been, he may have been remiss in following details as thoroughly as he should have.

Turning back to his hyperactive colleague, Nigel said, "Just to be on the safe side, would you run off the record of rentals, with names, for the past 30 days? Be sure to list everything up to today including anything still out, whether delinquent or not. The computer should tell us who on the list claimed to be a guest at the Lodge. I'll take it with me to the meeting."

Walking into his small, cluttered office, he paused to blow a kiss, as he did every day, to the loving picture of his parents, prominently displayed on the wall behind his desk. Taken somewhere in Oxford, they appeared so young, happy, and in love. Nigel's father grew up in Terrill, a small town near Okoboji, and his mother was from a suburb of London. They had met and married, in England, at the end of

World War II.

Following the war, his family had divided time between Washington, DC and London. His mother worked in some capacity for the British government, and his father owned and successfully managed a private business dedicated to research and consultation in international investments.

Nigel had gone to college, done a stint in the American military, and enjoyed a long career as an analyst for the CIA. His parents were deceased, but his brother soldiered on in the family business, and two sisters were happily married, one to a Brit and the other to an American. It made for interesting though infrequent family reunions. Nigel's wife had been a correspondent for the AP but was killed while reporting from Kosovo, one of several risky and deadly conflicts she had covered abroad. That was many years ago, and Nigel had never gotten around to another relationship. His excuse: If you've been blessed with the best, don't expect a reprise. He still carried in his wallet the first picture ever taken of them together.

Though amenities in large cities still held some allure for him, Nigel had had his fill of government bureaucracy. Owing to his father's family, Nigel had visited Okoboji many times. His vague dream to retire in the Iowa Great Lakes Area was hastened when a realtor he had met years before called to tell him about this nice, quiet little business perfect for someone interested in semi-retirement and with a passion for fishing. On an impulse unusual for him, he bought it.

But now, as Nigel sat at his desk transferring onto his laptop thoughts earlier scribbled on scraps of paper, he could feel himself sinking into that dour mood that clouded his recent days. His discontent was like a failed knot on a hooked trophy walleye. Before the Lodge, this sleepy little business was a paid-up path to part-time retirement. He had looked forward to a gradual slide into leisure with plenty of time to fish and read and do or not do whatever he pleased.

Now, thanks to an affiliation with his revitalized neighbor, business was booming but with a mortgage to finance expansion, 14-hour workdays, and a bellyache.

The money was good, but frankly, he didn't need it. On a particularly stressful day, he had spoken to his assistant manager to see if there was interest in taking over the business, but Jerry had turned down the offer. Still, there was no reason why Nigel shouldn't covertly think ahead if he could find any time to do so. Where was that business card? Opening the bottom left-hand drawer, repository of all that indiscriminately crossed his desk but lacked clear purpose, he dug through the snarl until he found his objective.

She had approached him more than a year ago about working with the newly resuscitated resort as an independent contractor or see if he wished to sell. He wasn't ready to sell, but he was impressed. As a partner and co-owner of a long-established area realty and development company, her reputation as a business professional was understood to be beyond reproach. She had an affiliation of some sort with the Lodge but assured him she was discreet and would not reveal to anyone his intentions until if and when he had made a decision.

Tapping the edge of the card against the desktop, he announced to no one, "I think I should have another little consult with Ms. Janneke Sanderson."

Remarkable how it seemed he was dealing with more women in business as well as outdoor sports. Perhaps it shouldn't matter, but it did, at least for those with whom he worked. While not yet at parity, it was clear to him that the women he dealt with often attended to business more quickly and more dependably than their male counterparts. That was certainly true of the owner of the Lodge and newly widowed, Lucia Sandoval. Annoying or not, she was so good, it was scary. And she was gorgeous, to boot.

Less impressive was the new assistant manager, Tom Bland. What a contrast to both Mrs. Sandoval and her late husband! Short and round in stature, prematurely bald, with a permanent pinch etched into his face, and less-than-charming people skills, he could be a major pain in the bum. Granted, he was earning a degree of begrudging respect for his hard work and sound business judgement. Rumor was he never slept, and to some of his detractors was known as "The Owl" for his oversized glasses and frequent night prowls about the resort. Nigel's rumination was interrupted when Bonita, his newest employee, tapped at the open door.

"Yes, Bonita. What is it?"

"I'm sorry to bother you…"

"It's no bother. Please come in."

Bonita was a young Latina whose family had instilled in her the importance of respect for others, in particular those of an older generation. She was quick to learn, and her care and sincere interest in helping customers had impressed him. For someone so youthful, her respect for him was refreshing and a bit humbling. "The new bait supplier is here and would like to know where you would like him to place your order."

Where to place his order sounded like a slippery slope. One that Bonita may misunderstand. "Thank you, Bonita. Please tell him I'll be out in a minute."

This was a continuing problem. Since the recent demise with extreme prejudice of the previous vendor, Jolly Holiday, Waterford had been pressed to find a dependable replacement. Holiday's bait and supply business had been a cover for drug distribution, though Waterford had to admit that while Jolly was a thug, he always delivered the live bait fresh and on time. Why Lucia's husband, Anthony, was in the drug business with Holiday instead of in bed with Lucia was beyond him. Talk about bad choices! Great business, beautiful wife. Anthony Sandoval was a fool and now a dead fool! Investigators had determined Sandoval's murder was the result of his involvement in the drug business. His killer's identity was unknown and the case remained unsolved.

With bait safely stowed and his laptop in hand, Nigel made his way to the meeting at the resort.

***

Lucia Sandoval was at a critical moment in a heated discussion with her new assistant manager, Tom Bland. Certainly not her choice, Bland's appointment had been a compromise between the board of directors and her extended family. This enterprise was now owned and managed by Lucia after Anthony, her husband and business partner, was killed. Her feelings for the loss of her late husband did not extend to forgiveness. His poor judgement and short-sighted greed had nearly destroyed their business plans for the Lodge. Only the backing of her family and the faith the board had in her abilities had allowed them to provide her more time to succeed.

It wasn't Bland's fussy attention to detail, or obsessive prioritizing and reprioritizing the day-to-day business, it was the lack of empathy for employees and overly blunt communication skills that created friction, with Lucia and everyone else on campus. He was so different from Anthony, who was good with people and a positive image for the Lodge. True, she could hold her own on those accounts, but it was easier when she could focus on Human Resources and the business office and less on development and PR. Now she had to attend to much more and bridge the problems that her new assistant created with staff.

His latest complaint had to do with an AWOL guest. Everything remained in the room, and the car was still in the lot, but there was no guest to speak of, and the wife had shown up this morning to join her absentee husband for a little vacation time. According to housekeeping, he'd been gone two days.

"What do we tell her?" Bland asked.

"Are you sure he's missing?" Lucia replied. "Maybe he's trying to avoid his wife."

"No. He's been here a week, since last Thursday, and she's listed on the room reservation to arrive this Saturday. They have a 7 p.m. reservation for dinner at the Blue Wave Restaurant Saturday evening to celebrate their wedding anniversary. She said she changed her plans and arrived early to surprise him. Needless to say, she is extremely upset."

Lucia hated the phrase "needless to say," especially coming from Bland. He always said whatever it was anyway. "There has to be a simple answer. He's probably out doing the tourist thing. We certainly cannot expect our guests to clear their daily agendas with us. Did she suggest any possible reason her husband wouldn't be on hand?"

"No, she did not, and it's not my place to interrogate her. She insists upon arranging a time to meet with the person in charge."

"That would be you," Lucia said.

"Not according to Mrs. Smith."

"Smith? Please don't tell me his first name is John."

"No, it's Howard. Howard Smith. She is Helen Smith."

"Very well. What did you tell Mrs. Smith?"

"I told her I would speak to the owner and report back to her in short order."

"Where is she now?"

"In room 210. Mr. Smith's room."

"Are you sure it's his wife? Did you ask for confirmation?"

"The registration desk confirmed her name was Helen Smith. The desk did not see a need for further identification."

Lucia bit her lip at the characterization of the Owl's reference to employees as inanimate objects. Maybe a subtle hint: "Who was at the desk?"

"Registration Manager Loren Price."

"Okay. Would you please inform Mrs. Smith that we are about to start a scheduled meeting, but that I will meet with her immediately after, likely around 11:45? In the meantime, she's welcome to have brunch or early lunch gratis at our Pier Cafe."

"Very well. However, now I'll be late to the meeting."

"I realize that, but the first few minutes will be spent on the agenda and announcements you and I worked on together. I'm sure with your exceptional talents, you'll have no trouble getting up to speed on anything you may miss." The words were no sooner out of her mouth than Lucia mentally reprimanded herself. *That was snippy. I hope his attitude is not rubbing off on me, or more importantly, affecting the staff.*

Bland made the conference in good time but thought it peculiar that when he knocked on room 210, Mrs. Smith would not open the door. "This is very inconvenient," she said through the peephole. "I'm about to shower."

He delivered Lucia's message from the hallway, and she agreed to meet Mrs. Sandoval in the cafe at 11:45.

But by 11:45 a.m., Helen Smith was gone, replaced at 4 p.m. by yet another Helen Smith.

3

Lucia's call to the local police department was redirected to the Dickinson County Sheriff's Department, and after a brief account to the receptionist, Lucia found herself explaining in more detail to Sergeant Trudy Weisser the issues of two Helen Smiths and the missing husband, Howard. "I first called the Okoboji police department, but they said they depend on the Sheriff's office to provide investigative support for missing persons."

"That's correct," Weisser said. "When did this Howard Smith go missing?"

"I'm not sure. He checked in last Thursday. Housekeeping says his bed hasn't been used for at least the past two nights, and nothing in his room has been disturbed during that time. I checked his bill, and he was charging meals to his room, but there's been no charge since breakfast and a box lunch he ordered on Tuesday."

"You say there are two women claiming to be his wife?"

"Yes."

"Are they both still at the Lodge?"

"No. The first version arrived this morning, checked in, and since has disappeared. The second woman claiming to be his wife arrived around four and is still here. When the second Mrs. Smith turned up, we made some phone calls to verify identity, and we believe the second woman is the real Mrs. Smith. We have no idea who the woman who checked in this morning really is. Our registration manager working the desk insists the first Helen Smith used her driver's license to confirm her identity, and he felt there was no need for anything further."

"Is it possible the first Mrs. Smith was, to put it delicately, a 'special friend' who was outed?"

"Possible, but hard to say. She was only here a few hours and rudely complained to our staff about Mr. Smith's absence. There is a note on the registration that his wife was to join him Saturday. The second Mrs. Smith said that she had been unable to reach him since Tuesday and that he hadn't called her. She said that was unusual. They speak with each other every day. She was concerned and left work to arrive early. Evidently, he's retired but she isn't. She said she works for Wells Fargo in Des Moines."

"Okay. Well, be sure the second Helen Smith stays there. We'll send one of our deputy investigators over to question her. He'll also want to question any of your staff who may have had contact with Mr. Smith and the first Mrs. Smith. It would be helpful if you could list them and arrange to have them available for interviews."

"Yes, of course." There was an awkward silence as Lucia hesitated.

"Was there something else?"

"It may be useful for your investigator to talk to the owner of the Sports Shop."

"Why is that?"

"I have meetings scheduled every week with the managers of

businesses that provide related services for our guests. We had a meeting this morning, and Nigel—that's Nigel Waterford, the owner-manager of the Sports Shop—reported Mr. Smith had rented a boat for Tuesday. It was all due back the next day, but this is day three, and the boat has not been returned. His assistant manager called Lake Patrol and various businesses, but at this time, no one has seen the boat."

"And that's relevant how?"

"The second Helen Smith said her husband is an experienced SCUBA diver, and he told her he was going to do a little diving. He had all his own gear, including a spear gun. She said the spear gun was only for rough fish, like carp."

"Did he have a diving partner?"

"I don't know. Maybe Nigel can answer that question."

"It's not a good idea to dive alone."

"Mrs. Smith said her husband knew better, but when he was young, he served in the Navy as a recovery diver. He probably considered Okoboji to be like diving in a bathtub. She said, and I quote, 'Sometimes, I think he's part fish!' Unquote."

"Well, even skilled divers can get into trouble. I'll pass this on to Sheriff Conrad, and he'll send a deputy to investigate."

"Thank you. If they stop by the registration desk, I'll personally escort your deputy to Mrs. Smith."

"Will do. Someone from the Sheriff's Office should arrive at the Lodge in twenty or thirty minutes. If it's going to be longer, I'll call you back."

***

Deputy Jack Donahue was one of two experienced homicide investigators for the Dickinson County Sheriff's Department. He, along with Sheriff Conrad and Deputy Navarro, had just finished a briefing via videochat with Homeland Security concerning immigration and human trafficking. He was seated back at his desk when Sheriff Conrad's PA knocked lightly at the open door to his office.

"Delores, come in, come in. You don't need to knock." He had told Delores this before, but the invitation still went unheeded. Delores practiced a respectful protocol for everyone in the close-knit Sheriff's Department.

"I'm sorry to bother you, but Sheriff Conrad would like you to check on a call we received from the owner at the Lodge regarding a missing person. The missing person is a Howard Smith. The caller reported that his wife was to join him at the Lodge on Saturday. Mrs. Smith became concerned when she was unable to reach her husband, so she left work and drove up from Des Moines today. No one at the Lodge has seen Mr. Smith since Tuesday. Sheriff Conrad asked that you stop by his office before you leave."

"Will do. Thank you, Delores."

Closing the folder on his desk, Jack puzzled over why Connie would assign him a missing persons case. Was there something exceptional about this individual?

Jack walked the short hallway to Sheriff Conrad's office. "You wanted to see me before I headed over to the Lodge?"

Sheriff Conrad, Connie to his family and friends, was seated at his desk and appeared to be filling out some sort of form. "Yes. Please come in. Shut the door. Have a seat." Setting his pen aside, Connie traveled down the page with his index finger. Satisfied, he turned the form over and directed his attention to his deputy. "Damn paperwork. It never ends."

"Better you than me. What's this call about a missing person? After the big mess they just had a few weeks ago at the Lodge, is the owner overreacting?"

"Maybe, but I wanted to share some information. Do you know

Howard Smith?"

"No."

"Howard Smith is a retired FBI agent. I first met him at Langley. He was teaching one of the courses I attended. We never worked together, but we've seen each other off and on at various conferences and workshops. He's an Iowa boy who became a highly respected investigator of human trafficking. He lives in Des Moines but has a place in Arizona. He once told me that when his wife retires, they would split their time between Iowa and Arizona. I never met his wife, but my impression is the couple has a strong, loving relationship."

Jack nodded, then asked, "So you think there may be more to this than missed phone calls and an anxious wife?"

"Could be. Anyway, I wanted you to be informed before meeting Mrs. Smith."

"I appreciate it." Jack paused. "Ironic, isn't it?"

"What's that?"

"We just sat in on an update from Homeland Security about immigration and human trafficking, and now we have a retired human trafficking investigator who may have gone missing."

"Understood, but let's get the facts first and save the irony for later."

"You got it."

"Before you leave, check to see if a crime scene deputy is available. After you get to the Lodge, if you think a more thorough inspection of the room, car, or whatever is warranted, call in a CSI."

"I think Terry the Tech is in house."

"Good, and also check with Sergeant Weisser. She took the call from the owner at the Lodge and may have a few more details."

"Will do."

"And Jack."

"Yes?"

"Give me an update when you return."

"You got it."

As he walked across the parking lot to his Interceptor, Jack considered the earnest demeanor Sheriff Conrad conveyed as well as his specific instructions. The detective appreciated the confidence the Sheriff had in him, but it was clear he had a greater interest in Howard Smith than a casual professional acquaintance may warrant. Jack was too good an investigator not to recognize that there was more to Howard Smith and his disappearance than Sheriff Conrad was sharing.

4

She had no idea what to do with Carla Rodriguez. It happened so fast, there was no time to think, only to react. She had worked late into the evening at the Sports Shop, and on her way home, as a favor to Mr. Waterford, she had gone out of her way to drive around the northern end and down the western side of Okoboji to deliver an order of tackle and fresh bait to the West Shore Resort. As she continued home, Bonita was distracted, worrying about the fuss between Mr. Waterford and Mr. Strand. She understood a boat had not been returned on time. It happened once in a while, but the boat and renter always showed up eventually. Bonita did not mind working with Mr. Strand, though at times he could be very particular. Mr. Waterford seemed better when he came back from his meeting with the Lodge owner, but after the phone call and visit late this afternoon by the Sheriff's Deputy, Mr. Waterford was uncharacteristically moody, distressed about something.

And then it happened. Something dashed out from the ditch near the entrance to the Ridge Top Nightclub driveway. Bonita slammed on the brakes and swerved to avoid a collision. There was a bump against the side of her car, and looking back, she could see a small figure by the side of the road. Immediately she thought, *Oh no! I hit a baby deer!*

Bonita stopped, leaped out of the car, and was shocked to see the figure of a young woman stand and stagger toward her. Suddenly the woman frantically charged toward her and wrapped her arms around Bonita, nearly bowling her over. In a hoarse whisper, she begged, "Ayúdame. Dios, ayúdame; help me. Por favor, please help me get away from here."

The small, slender woman was trembling hard, but she squeezed Bonita so tightly, she nearly lost her breath. "Are you hurt?"

"No. ¡Sí! Yes! Take me away from here. Hurry, before they come after me! ¡Por favor, please! I beg you! I need your help!"

Bonita helped the young woman into the car, and as they drove off, her passenger kept looking back, desperate to see if they were being followed.

Bonita stared at her passenger for several seconds, long enough for the car to drift onto the rumble strip in the center of the road. She noticed that she wore only a light summer dress, and though the evening was muggy, she had her arms wrapped about her body, and she was shaking as though she were chilled. In the ambient illumination from the dash, Bonita also noticed scrapes on her knees and what appeared to be a stain of blood on her dress. "May I ask, what is your name?"

"Susie."

"Susie?" Bonita had her doubts.

"They said I would be called Susie, Susie Sweetie Pie, like, do you want a piece of Pie? It was supposed to be a joke."

"What is the name your parents gave you?" There was no response, so she tried Spanish.

In a barely audible voice, she answered, "Carla."

"Carla what?"

Bonita could hear Carla's rapid breathing. The girl was terrified and trying to decide how much to say. "Carla, it's okay. My name is Bonita. I'll help you, but I need to know your name." From the corner of her eye she could see that Carla was staring at her. Reverting to Spanish, Bonita asked, "¿Eres inmigrante?"

There were a few seconds of silence, then Carla responded, "Sí."

"Do you have family here at the lakes?"

Again, there was a pause, then, "No."

"I'm Latina; Mexican-American. Soy mexicana-americana. You can trust me. She paused to let this sink in. "Carla, I see you are afraid, but you are also injured. Let me take you to the medical clinic."

"No. No, I cannot go there." Suddenly, Carla pulled on the passenger door handle. "Let me out."

The doors automatically locked at 15 miles an hour, and Carla's several spastic jerks to open the door were futile, and her panic only increased.

"Carla, it's okay. You're safe with me. Give me a few minutes to figure out what we can do."

From Carla's reaction to the medical clinic, the police, at least for the time being, were out of the question. Bonita tried again, first in English, then in Spanish. "What is your last name? ¿Cuál es tu apellido?"

Carla nodded her head, "Rodriguez."

"Are you badly hurt?"

"No mucho, not bad, some scrapes, maybe a bruise. Mostly my knees."

"Carla, tell me the truth, and it's okay, I can keep a secret, but if I'm going to help you, you have to tell me the truth. Are you illegal?"

Bonita was aware Carla was softly crying.

Carla sniffled, wiped her nose with the back of her hand. Softly she replied, "Sí."

For a long minute, the only sound came from the tires on the road. Suddenly, Carla burst, "Mi rosario!"

"What?"

"My rosary! I dropped it when I was hit by your car. We must go back."

"What if they see you?"

Carla's soft tears turned into a torrent. "It is the rosary of mi madre, my mother. I must get it back. Please, take me back."

"Is it so important you would risk getting caught?"

"Sí, yes! Por favor, please. I have to try. It must be right where I fell. I had it until then."

Pulling into a field access, Bonita carefully turned around and drove past the spot where Carla and the car had connected. Bonita could see no one, turned the car around, and stopped short of the driveway.

Reaching across to the glove compartment, Bonita drew out a flashlight and said, "Stay down, out of sight."

Stepping out into the night, Bonita walked in a zig-zag pattern, using the car's headlights to guide her. She saw nothing, but using the beam of her flashlight, slowly repeated her search pattern.

"Hello, there. Can I help you?"

Engrossed in concentration, Bonita had not noticed the man who approached and stood just outside the beam of the headlights. Startled and sharply aware of possible danger, she raised the beam of her flashlight to the man's face.

"Do you mind? Lower your flashlight. I just wondered if there was a problem." The voice was soft and calm. He sounded sincere but his slicked back hair, large ears, close-set eyes, and pointed nose, reminded Bonita of a rodent.

Bonita backed up toward her car, her mind racing, trying to form the words. "No. No, thank you. I thought I ran over something, but I was wrong. Thank you anyway."

"Wait. Is this what you were looking for?" The voice held out a hand, and dangling below, sparkling in the headlights, was a rosary.

Bonita sucked in a breath. Her hands were shaking. She tried to steady the flashlight as its beam danced on the rosary. She had to answer. She had to get away. "No. Nothing like that. It was something big. It went bump against my car. I must be mistaken. I probably drove onto the shoulder. I do that sometimes. Thanks, anyway."

Trying not to run, Bonita strode back to her car, jumped inside, and drove off, resisting the impulse to "floor it." Checking in the rearview mirror, the man remained standing at the road's edge.

Bonita increased her speed. She didn't know how far she had driven, but at some point, she pulled over onto the side of the road, turned off the car's lights, and waited. "Did you see the man I talked to?"

"No. But I know his voice. He drives our vehículo recreativo. We call him RV Man."

"RV?"

"It's how we travel, a big RV. How we get here to the Nightclub."

"Why?"

In the dark, Bonita could see the outline of Carla's slender shoulders as she shrugged. "You know."

"I know what?"

"What we do. Our business. What they make us do."

Bonita drew in a sharp breath, slowly exhaled, then said, "There are others?"

"Sí."

"How many are there?"

"Usually six or seven. They sometimes bring new girls but keep the ones who are favorites."

"Favorites?"

"A few men have favorite girls. They pay more." Carla paused before adding, "A big man liked me. He always smelled of drink. Sometimes he was very drunk. Then he would become rough and make me do extra things." The darkness did not hide Carla's shame. "None of us want to do this, but we are afraid they will hurt our families or kill us. They were nice at first. They told us they would protect us and help our families, but they lied."

"He had your rosary."

Carla was still. "I should go back."

"Does the rosary mean that much?"

"They know it's important, that I want it back. If I don't go back, I'll never see it again." Carla was quiet, then added, "I was selfish. I ran away, and if I don't go back, they may hurt the others."

"Then we need to go to the police."

"No! We can't. That will make it worse."

"Well, I'm not taking you back to your RV, or wherever they had you."

"He saw you. Now you are in trouble. If I go back, it will be all right."

"It was dark, and he didn't know me," Bonita said. "He won't find me, and you're not going back."

"What are you going to do?"

Several seconds passed in thought, then Bonita nodded her head decisively and asked, "You are Catholic, yes?"

"Sí, yes. Why?"

"Your rosary gave me an idea."

5

At times, *Frau Nägel* was a pain and so demanding! But Michael Cain had promised his mother. The effort and money needed to maintain the classic Chris Craft Riviera outweighed the practical benefits, but as a 25th wedding anniversary gift from his late father to Michael's mother, such considerations were irrelevant. *Frau Nägel* was his father's pet name for Michael's mother. The boat belonged to her, and she insisted it be kept and maintained in pristine condition, a prerequisite for Michael taking over the family's lakeside home. The fact was he had little reason to complain. Marv's Marina had done everything to prep the boat for the summer season, and all Michael needed to do was polish it a little, gas it up, and occasionally take it for a cruise about the lake.

His widowed mother was happily retired in Arizona with her sister Louise and enjoying an active social life that included Fred, a widower and retired stock broker she'd met at dance club. But Michael Cain's family had been a part of the Lakes Area for generations, and as a recent repatriate to Lake Okoboji after years of absence, Michael was rediscovering that there were social niceties and expectations associated with local families of long standing.

The message from Michael's sister, Madge, left on his outdated answering machine, was a reminder he was expected to cheerfully and energetically do his part to uphold the family reputation by participating in the upcoming annual Okoboji Regatta. He'd forgotten all about the Regatta and would have preferred to leave it that way, but her message also included a request for his nephew, Jeremy, and Jeremy's girlfriend, to ride along on the promenade of classic wooden boats.

Michael was sandwiched between his two living siblings, older sister Melanie and younger sister Madge. Melanie lived out of state, but Madge remained in the area and was married to Michael's best friend, Dickinson County Sheriff Mark "Connie" Conrad. It was Connie who reminded Michael that Melanie may be the brains of the family, but Madge was the heart, and what the heart desired, Michael was well-advised to grant. Of course, he agreed to Madge's request and knew he would enjoy himself.

On an impulse, Michael used the Regatta as an excuse to call Janneke and invite her to ride along. The renewed relationship between Michael and his high school lover was another welcome surprise upon his return to his childhood home. Unfortunately, the recent attempt on their lives, thanks to drug dealers, had put a pause in their renewed bond, and she had turned down his invitation. It was not hopeless, but Janneke remained badly shaken. She had made it clear to him that their friendship prevailed, but she would need more time to recover from the shock of recent events before possibly continuing a closer relationship.

Sitting on the broad screened-in porch of what was again his home, Michael nursed his second generous pour of Glenfiddich and watched the evening calm descend on the lake. Life was all so different from what it had been just a few months earlier. One of his favorite recordings, the Dennis Brain performance of the four Mozart Horn Concertos, accompanied by the Philharmonia Orchestra conducted by Von Karajan, drifted to him from his stereo in the front room. A skilled amateur jazz pianist, Michael had also played the French horn in high school and during two years of university. The horn still held a strong place in his musical memories.

As important as music was to him, his dalliance at the University of Iowa with a major in piano performance had been done mostly to rebel against his father's expectations. Given time to find his own way, Michael had switched to pre-law, had gone through the Iowa Law Enforcement Academy after graduation, and had served a short time as a Deputy in the Story County Sheriff's office, until finally turning to the family business and earning his law degree from Drake University.

Appointed a federal prosecutor for the Southern District of Iowa, he had been on the fast track for bigger things when his life was shattered by a series of misfortunes beginning with the dismissal of a high-profile case, prepared and prosecuted by the book—the book he'd written on the relationship between law enforcement and prosecution. Soon thereafter, the prime witness in the case and her small daughter were murdered by the defendant, who had then made an attempt to assassinate Michael and his wife. In an exchange of gunfire that the news media had reported "worthy of the old wild west," Michael killed the assassin. With that, any hope Michael may have had of reconciliation with his philandering wife had been aborted by the attempt to terminate not only their marriage, but their very existence. But the final blow was the sudden death of Michael's beloved father in a plane crash, and his father had been the pilot.

On extended personal leave, Michael had returned to the family home on Okoboji. With professional help and the support of family and long-time friends, he had found his way back from the abyss. Contrary to Thomas Wolfe, Michael found he could go home again.

The deep blue lake had much to do with his recovery. Okoboji, the source of so much joy and many happy memories of his past, provided a renewal, a second baptism, by its waters. He was at peace for the first time in many years.

***

This was the last thing Farley needed. "What do you mean you can't find her? What do you think I'm paying you for?"

The caller tried to reassure Farley. "Take it easy, man. We're on the same team."

"Are you kidding me? This is a lousy time for one of the girls to make a break for freedom, especially this girl! Where does she think she can go? We're a long way from Guatemala or wherever the hell she came from!"

"I said take it easy! She can't go far. We'll handle it."

Enraged, Farley's voice rose in pitch and volume. "Handle it? This isn't some run-of-the mill John, this is the Big Man, our ticket to a casino! He has particular tastes and expectations, and she's it. If he doesn't get what he wants, neither do we. How the hell did this even happen?"

"Your so-called Big Man got drunk. He passed out, and when he woke up this morning, she was gone. He didn't suspect anything. He thought she'd gone back to her room, so we took him back to his room at the Lodge. The girl slipped away while he slept."

"Slipped away? What kind of a half-assed operation are you running?"

"Hey! Don't blow a fuse! We'll take extra good care of Big Man, and we'll find the girl."

Farley lowered his voice to a growl. "You have until tonight to find her or get a replacement, and not just any replacement! Someone that will make him forget all about the missing girl! Comprende?" The call ended before there was a reply.

In addition to the *Maximilian*, Bart Farley was the owner of the Ridge Top Nightclub, appropriately named in light of the fact it was located atop the highest point overlooking the lake. The property included a small, outdated motel and café located just off Highway 86 next to the entrance and long drive up to the nightclub. The nightclub and motel masked and conveniently accommodated the tastes and desires of people of some importance, people whose support was needed for Farley to achieve his goal of a casino located beside Lake Okoboji, or if he had his way, right on the *Maximilian*.

The vote of Big Man, and equally important, his influence on the other members of the Racing and Gaming Commission, were critical to Farley's plans. Big Man's arrival Thursday, as an extended weekend trip to "explore" the viability of Farley's proposed casino, was really an excuse for free booze and more time to "explore" his favorite girl, but Farley wasn't squeamish about doing whatever was necessary to succeed. This was a complex enterprise that required a certain degree of discretion. Dancers and prostitutes were not an area of his expertise, and he had neither the time nor money to build his own supply of young women. As a necessity he had to rely on others to secure some of his objectives.

Arrangements had been made through a broker he learned of while serving a short term in jail for a second OWI. The "RV People," as they collectively referred to themselves, provided the girls, and the results were beneficial for all concerned, except, of course, the girls. He neither knew nor cared where the girls came from, but the arrangements he had painstakingly worked out for them should be followed explicitly. That, he did care about. And now, something had gone wrong. Things might get messy.

Farley mulled over the situation of the missing girl for several minutes. Finally, thinking aloud, he said, "Maybe I should send Ralphy Boy and some of his biker buddies to make my point. Ralphy would like that."

Ralph Cole was a makeshift enforcer Farley had met at a local bar during his former period of immoderate drinking. They had stayed in touch and formed a relationship of convenience: Farley paid well, and Cole was available and willing to take care of any problems Farley needed solved. Both men shared the opinion that laws were flexible and open to interpretation—their interpretation.

"Yes, Cole would like that, but he might be a little too enthusiastic for this stage in the game. Better to wait and give the RV's a chance to make good on their end."

An involuntary shudder rippled across his shoulders as another thought crossed his mind. Though the girls' manager/driver was slimy and the large woman in charge of the girls was intimidating, Farley had come to the conclusion there was someone or something even more powerful behind their business. In the few months since he had become involved in this operation, with the exception of any he requested for special clients, he rarely saw the same woman twice. The variety of women brought in by different upscale vehicles that parked behind the nightclub and the motel at the bottom of the hill no more than a few days and nights at a time suggested there had to be big bucks and influence to protect an organization like this one.

Still, if anything untoward ever came from it, he could sincerely claim it had nothing to do with him. If one of the clients blew the whistle, he still had deniability. But then, none of his clients would say anything. He had too much on them, and they had too much to lose. None of them wanted to destroy their own reputation and gain all the trouble to follow. Besides, Farley would be their protector. All they had to do was grant Farley a few little favors, and everyone would be happy.

6

Janneke knew she needed to be honest with Michael, but since their shared near-death experience at the hands of drug dealers, Janneke remained badly shaken, more than she was willing to admit. She cared deeply for Michael, yet now felt less confident that their renewed relationship as friends and lovers was sustainable. A pall had been cast over them, and she had deliberately distanced herself from Michael.

While physically and emotionally their interests aligned, their professional (and even some personal) goals were less so. Whatever Michael's expectations, Janneke was committed to her career as a businesswoman. That commitment had led to the divorce between Janneke and her childhood friend, Luke.

Janneke and Luke were part of a group of close-knit friends known as the "Four Apostles"—Mathew, Mark, Luke, and Janni, as described by the nuns at their parochial elementary school. All their families had deep roots in the history and business of the Lakes Area, and when Luke and Janneke were married, the overlords of business believed it to have been preordained. In spite of their surface compatibility, it gradually became clear they had different, irreconcilable expectations from marriage. Luke intended they have children, and Janneke intended to have a career rather than children of her own. Why they hadn't considered this before marriage was puzzling to close friends, but there it was. The divorce may have been a greater surprise to Luke and Janneke than to those who knew them well.

Their separation was amiable, and they continued to work together in their shared business enterprise. Luke had remarried someone agreeable to his needs—his secretary, who in a scant six months after, had delivered a baby boy, referred to by the area wags as the "miracle birth." They were expecting a second child, reported by the same wags to arrive in the less miraculous period of nine months.

Little of this had a lasting effect on Janneke. Rather the opposite. Janneke prospered, and as the promoter/commercial developer for the realty side of their company, found herself deeply involved with one of the area's newcomers, a revitalized resort called The Lodge on Okoboji. Business was good, and personal considerations were set aside. Janneke was fine until Michael Cain, the golden son of another prominent area family and Janneke's first love, had returned to his family's home on Lake Okoboji.

So on this morning of the Regatta, rather than joining Michael, she stood before the mirror at her condo attempting to repair the effects of stress on her face and setting aside thoughts of Michael. She had to focus on the critical business taking place today.

Earlier attempts to establish a gaming casino in the Lakes Area had failed, but for whatever reason, this time was more promising. It may have been affected by the Supreme Court decision to allow betting on sports. If the country club set and business people with whom she associated were any indication, the Lakes Area certainly had sports fans willing to put down a wager on their favorite teams.

Although not part of the original plan, the long-term goals for The Lodge on Okoboji, locally referred to as the Lodge, would be greatly expanded with the award of a casino license. Besides the Lodge, there were three other competitors, two so weak it was laughable. But the third, represented by someone new to the area and unknown to Janneke, was a serious contender. Today's meeting with the Iowa Racing and Gaming Commission's representatives was critical.

Her auburn hair hung loosely about her face, but rather than complement, it increased the gray appearance of her complexion and the worry lines on her forehead where recently there had been none. The glow that resulted from her alter-ego outdoors girl was missing. She was held captive by her drive for success on behalf of her client, which limited her personal life.

She shook her head, took a deep breath, leaned forward, and slowly exhaled. Her mirrored image blurred behind the fog, but the stress remained. Aloud, she began her ritualistic pep talk, a device her mother had taught her in high school.

"First thing's first! One step at a time. You are prepared. Focus on the purpose at hand. Set everything else aside. You will succeed." She paused, then expressed a cynical afterthought which may have reduced the mantra's effect. "Michael and my complexion will have to wait until after this morning." She began again. "First thing's first! Focus!"

***

Bart Farley was not given to reflection, whether before a mirror or otherwise. Perhaps that was good given his singular purpose to gain, at any cost, a casino license from the State of Iowa. His only real opposition was that Sanderson broad. And as he liked to brag to fellow misogynists, *The day has not dawned that I can't beat the hell out of a woman, business-wise or otherwise.*

To avoid the usual hue and cry of protest by the locals who opposed a casino on the lakes, the presentations were to be pitched privately to a fragment, a so-called fact-finding subcommittee, of the Iowa Gaming Commission, all officially unofficial, of course, thank goodness. It was hard enough trying to persuade the Commission to expand gambling to the Lakes Area, but if the locals who were opposed to the casino knew about this meeting, they would raise holy hell, especially Marianne Thomas. Why the hell did she have such a bug up her ass? She was smart and organized and passionately opposed to a casino on the lakes. But so what? This was business. She really pissed him off.

Thinking aloud, he said, "By the time I get through with her, Thomas and her bunch of bozos will be outmaneuvered and buried so deep in crap, no one will take them seriously."

Early this morning, he had spoken to his Big Man from the Gaming Commission who would be acting as chair for the meeting. "I'm sorry your favorite girl was unavailable. Were you satisfied with the substitute? Was it a good night?"

"Yes, in fact. It was a pleasant surprise. I've never had an Asian girl. Does she even speak English? Didn't matter, she certainly knew what she was doing, and after giving her my special little pill I like to call "Miss Easy," she was more than accommodating." He barked a rough laugh, bragging. "By the time I finished with her, she was bone-tired, if you get my drift, and sleeping like death."

"Excellent. We aim to please. May I assume the meeting will be favorable?"

"I believe that's a safe assumption. I have to give you credit. If your source is accurate, the FBI and local investigators must be crawling all over the place. Considering the shitstorm hitting them, it was either genius or luck to schedule our meeting at the Lodge. There's no way they can look good."

"I'm glad you approve, and here's a bonus. I'm going to park *Maximilian* at their main dock. All you have to do is move the meeting onto the boat. Just say you're changing the location to avoid drawing unwanted attention to the Lodge."

"Man, that is diabolical! I love it. Consider it done. Oh, and here's something that isn't public but will be announced at the meeting. The other two contenders have dropped out, or rather, they've been eliminated due to recently discovered technicalities. Now it's just you and the Lodge."

"That is good news. I won't ask how you came up with the technicalities."

"You still have to make your case. Remember, it's not just about the competition. There is a significant element on the Gaming Commission that doubts the wisdom of opening a casino in this area. Give me what I need to turn the majority of the Commission your way."

"Will do. Anything else I should know before the meeting?"

"There will be three of us acting as a subcommittee. Although he says he's on the fence, Will Brady may already be in your camp. Our other attendee is Nick Clark. Nick really is undecided. Both men are dedicated to see that the rules and regulations for gaming in Iowa are strictly followed. You need to emphasize how critical this addition is to the Lakes Area and the thousands of people who live and visit here. Lay it on thick. Emphasize jobs and the financial impact the casino will have on the community. Neither man is anyone's fool, but they do favor promoting businesses and jobs for the state."

"Thank you. That's good to know. Is there anything about the Lodge's representative or her presentation I should anticipate?"

"Hah! Good one. Sanderson and Sandoval don't know it yet, but they're spitting into the wind. We'll hear them out. Gotta keep the little ladies happy. Just do your part, and I'll do the rest. See you at the dock."

Even with his Ray-Bans, the early morning sun reflecting off the water dazzled Michael's eyes as he, at the helm of the *Frau Nägel*, rounded Fort Dodge Point and entered Smiths Bay. Several boats were docked, but a small flotilla of wooden crafts was milling about, white froth from their bows frosting the blue water, the crests of their wakes sparkling in the sunlight. Although not everyone followed protocol, Michael knew from past experience that most boat owners waited for a sign from the event's self-appointed harbormaster, a short plump man in a Panama hat, who stood at the end of the foremost dock holding an enormous flag. Even at this distance, Michael could see the wooden boat association's golden crest set on a field of scarlet. An embellishment of gold fringe, likely a conceit by its designer, did little to improve the banner's design but did add to the slapping sound as the flag was buffeted by wind and the efforts of the signalman.

With a vigorous overhead flourish, then a downward swoop of the flag, the master signaled when a passing boat was cleared to enter a slip among several docks made available for the day's event. Exactly which dock to choose was left to be sorted by the driver of the boat. After each cue, the rotund figure paused to affirm the security of the hat on his dome, precariously set as it was for lack of hair.

"I hope Milo is better organized than he used to be, or someone's boat is liable to end up on the bottom of the bay. Let's make sure it's not us, right *Frau Nägel*?" The acting harbormaster was Milo Leadbetter, the well-known owner-publisher of the local newspaper and another area character. An absolute fanatic about wooden boats, Milo was a board member and outspoken advocate for the Iowa Great Lakes Maritime Museum.

As Michael drew closer, the confusion viewed from the mouth of Smiths Bay took on a different form. Moving counterclockwise, the captains had organized their regal vessels into a long, flat loop, the better to display their boats. By the flag's signal, each in turn (more or less), peeled off to find a chosen space.

"Wow! I wasn't aware how much the Regatta had grown. Okay, *Frau Nägel*, I know. It's been years since we've been a part of this, but it is impressive. I'll give him credit. Milo's really gotten his act together." Such spontaneous self-directed discourse was common to Michael. Friends and family paid little attention, but anyone unfamiliar with his disposition and overhearing such jabber tended to quickly separate themselves from the source. But on such declarations, it was Michael who mentally separated himself from those about him.

As he waited to find a niche in the watery orbit, he was suddenly greeted by a bright, tritone blast. Startled, he looked to his left and was greeted by two elderly women enthusiastically waving to him from the cockpit of a beautiful wooden runabout—the Lawery sisters! With another blast of the horn, they vigorously indicated that he take a place in front of their boat.

Michael smiled, gave a short toot from his boat's single-tone horn, and took his place as directed. Turning around in his seat, he gave the Aunties, as they were known by their friends, a large wave and tooted a corny shave-and-a-haircut on his boat's horn. Faethe Lawery, known by all as the matron of the Lawery family, was driving the boat. She smiled and nodded in patient response to Michael's bit of Tom-foolery.

On the other hand, Hoepe Lawery, the warm, all-embracing counterbalance to her sister, tilted her head back in laughter, then reached across Faethe and punched the correct duple finish--"Two bits!"

Michael was happy to see that the recent unpleasantness with Anthony Sandoval, the late co-owner of the Lodge, and his murderous cohort, Jolly Holiday, had done nothing to inhibit the Aunties' enthusiasm for the Lakes' activities. While Michael knew of their involvement tangent to his investigation in the matter, what he did not know and likely would never, was the responsibility the Aunties had assumed that had saved his life and that of his long-time love, Janneke Sanderson.

It took nearly an hour to berth all the circling boats, and in that time, the shoreline and docks became crowded with onlookers eager to experience the beautiful maritime artifacts on display. Michael remained on board *Frau Nägel*, answering questions and posing for pictures, while the harbormaster went from boat to boat with a schedule and instructions as to how the day's events would unfold. As more people arrived, accompanied by news media, food trucks, and even a pop-up craft show, the affair took on a carefree, carnival-like atmosphere.

"Uncle Mike!" Immersed, as it were, in conversation and the surrounding activity, Michael had missed the approach of his nephew, Jeremy, and the young man's girlfriend, Emily.

"Hey, kids! Good timing. Uncle Mike needs a chance to stretch his legs."

"I brought coffee. I thought you might need refueling."

"I do indeed." Michael accepted the coffee and immediately took a sip.

"Kenya Double A. How did you know my favorite?"

"It's on your Facebook page."

"Facebook page? I have a Facebook page?"

"You do now. Mom thought you should cross over into the twenty-first century and had me set it up for you. I guess she was waiting to surprise you."

This was hardly the first surprise from his sister since his return. "I better have a little visit with your mom."

"Don't worry about it, Uncle Mike. It's very generic. Nothing that isn't in the phone book, and I even put in the wrong birth date, so don't be shocked when you get birthday greetings in September instead March."

"Okay. I'll check on it later. Hang with the boat. I'm going to see someone about a blanket."

Jeremy smiled while his girlfriend appeared confused. "It's a family expression. He means he's going to use the porta potty."

Having attended to his "need for a blanket" Michael joined the crowd, strolling the docks and shore, pausing to visit with those he remembered as family friends. He was not surprised when he saw William DeWeerd, aka Weird Willy, a local character known for his skills as a waterman and a dumpster-diver extraordinaire. Willy was sitting on the nearby grassy hillside with his dog, Boxer, lying next to him. However, Michael was surprised to see an attractive woman, slightly younger than Willy's six decades, sitting next to him. The couple, if that was indeed what they were, was engrossed in conversation, ignoring everyone around them. They looked serious until the woman put her hand to her mouth as if to stifle a smile, then drew a small handkerchief from the back pocket of her tight-fitting jeans, moistened a corner and used it to dab something from Willy's stubbled chin. "Well, now I've seen everything," Michael said aloud.

A bit embarrassed by his outburst, Michael peered sidelong to the young man standing next to him, who smiled, nodded his head toward the hillside couple, and said, "You got that right."

Their shared humorous observation was suddenly interrupted by a shrill screech that issued from the dock directly behind them. Michael turned in time to see an attractive, bikini-clad bottom falling over the bow of a late-arriving boat. The driver had cut the engine, and as his companion had reached out to secure the craft, the boat had struck the dock with force, spilling the woman overboard. A large splash was followed by a profound stream of profanity after she bobbed back to the surface.

The boat's pilot quickly threw a looped rope over a post and moved forward to rescue his overboard companion. Suddenly, the profanity was replaced with a loud scream and a great deal of thrashing as the woman desperately struggled to reach the boat. Her rescuer pulled her into the boat in a single heave, but she continued screaming and pointing at some sort of object in the water.

Jumping up and down, she shrieked: "It bit me! It bit me! Kill it! Kill it!"

"What the hell?" Onlookers were shocked when the boat's captain, alarmed by his soaked companion's panic, reached under the boat's console, drew out a large revolver, and proceeded to blast six rounds into the water between the dock and the boat.

***

While the Iowa Great Lakes encompasses a large area, the village known as Okoboji is relatively small, with a population of eight hundred souls, more or less, depending on the time of year. Located between the lakes of West Okoboji and East Okoboji, the Okoboji community is bisected by state Highway 71 which forms a corridor of businesses and services important to the tourist trade as well as local residents. That year, due to disruptive weather and conflicts with other area events, and thanks to the help of local businesses and private homeowners, the Regatta had been relocated across the bay from Arnolds Park to the Okoboji community's southern shore.

Okoboji Police Chief Bartholomew Dunham, aka Chief BD to his friends, was on hand for the event, less for law enforcement and more to schmooze on behalf of his small department. A heavyset, good-humored fellow, the chief was near retirement and intent on not scuttling his boat, so to speak, or allowing anyone else to, before he'd sailed peacefully into the sunset.

Chief BD was sampling the homemade ice cream at one of the food trucks, but when the sound of gunfire erupted, it was as if someone had flipped a switch. Discarding the confection, he barreled through the throng of people and arrived with his handgun drawn.

"Drop the gun, NOW!" he shouted.

Startled by the appearance of the rotund, red-faced man with gun drawn and aimed in a two-handed stance from a distance of five feet, the offender immediately obeyed and carefully laid the revolver beside him on the dock. "Wait, Officer. I can explain."

"Shut up. Fold your hands and place them on top of your head, NOW! Keep your hands in that position, and sit down!" Then, as an afterthought, he demanded, "You, too, lady!"

Both sat down as ordered, but the young lady remained upset, wrapping her arms around her waist and trembling as though she were chilled, though the morning was a typical Iowa July—hot and muggy.

"Officer, please. Let me explain," the man begged.

"Do you have a permit for the handgun?"

"Yes, and I've had training on its use."

"And you thought it was prudent to open fire, into water, in the middle of a crowd? Do you care that someone may have been shot?"

While he was a part of a growing crowd of gawkers taking in the scene, Michael also found it interesting in how quickly the harbormaster had morphed into the local newspaper's owner, editor, and now reporter on the scene. Milo Leadbetter was already standing a few feet behind Sheriff BD. Milo had drawn his pen and notebook nearly as fast as the Chief had drawn his handgun, and Milo was studiously recording the event as it transpired.

As Milo described later in his newspaper: *The boater was Arthur Rascher, an area dentist who recently acquired a vintage Chris-Craft boat. New to the controls, he misjudged the boat's approach to the dock, struck the dock, and spilled his bikini-clad companion overboard. The newly christened boater and companion, Beverley Jones, said they saw something large and pale in the water and that it had attacked Jones when she'd fallen overboard.*

Using the revolver he keeps onboard for emergencies, Dr. Rascher said he "tried to kill it" before it could get away. Following a salvo of rounds, no creature was found.

Though traumatized, it appeared Jones was physically uninjured. She continued to insist that whatever it was had attacked her, and that "it smelled horrible, was slimy, and slapped me with a big, black fin." Both Dr. Rascher and Jones had been drinking "Bloody Marys, you know, for breakfast and the hangovers," they said.

No one else had seen whatever it was that had caused the alarm, or whether there was even something to be seen. The water clarity was poor partly because of midsummer algae bloom, but more due to the boats and the disturbance caused by the woman thrashing about in the water. Sheriff BD picked up the revolver and marched the boater to his cruiser for a breath analyzer test. Milo left out that several eager young men in the crowd voluntarily came forward to comfort the temporarily abandoned young woman and to assure themselves that her lovely body remained unharmed.

***

By noon, most if not all registered boats and their owners had arrived, and at 1 p.m. sharp, Father O'Brian, standing rather precariously in the middle of a pontoon boat anchored offshore, was prepared to perform the blessing of the boats as they passed by under the traditional spray pumped from the local fireboat. With the onshore ceremonial blast from a small brass cannon, the promenade from Smiths Bay to East Okoboji and back began.

By the end, Michael and his crew of two had returned to the docks where the floating exhibit and festivities would continue long into the evening. Jeremy had demonstrated ease guiding the *Frau Nägel* under the bridge into East Okoboji and showed the same skill on their return. The event itself had been impressive, more notably for the attack by a phantom water creature that had drawn gunfire.

8

What the hell was that about? Janneke couldn't believe it. She'd been blindsided. That s.o.b.! It was a set-up!

The meeting with the three representatives from the Iowa Gaming Commission turned out to be a private event, public not invited. To ensure privacy, they met on the *Maximilian* excursion boat, docked in front of the Lodge. When Janneke objected, stating she'd been informed this was to be an official meeting before the public, the chairman, a great-waisted man with a florid face and a broad nose magnified by a profusion of red spider veins, was dismissive.

"My dear, I'm sorry you misunderstood." He went on to explain that this was simply an informal fact-finding trip by the "Subcommittee for Research," and thus was not considered a public meeting. Only those presenting plans and answering questions were allowed to remain. No one else was allowed onto the *Maximilian* while they were in session. Nodding toward the small group of protesters standing on the dock, the chairman said, "I'm sure you'll do fine without your posse."

As they began, the chairman announced that of the parties originally interested, only two remained, the consortium called "Free To Play," as represented by Mr. Farley, and The Lodge on Okoboji, as represented by Ms. Sanderson. Each was to present an update on their proposals with questions from the committee to follow.

Janneke presented first. There were few questions to field, but the acting chairman did ask about the presence of the FBI and whether the Lodge was implicated in their investigation. The chairman seemed determined to imply the owner of the Lodge might be guilty of felonious activities that would disqualify the application for a gambling license.

The few questions put to Bart Farley after his presentation were far less probing, and the chairman emphasized there was nothing in Farley's background that would disqualify his application. In less than an hour, the chairman ended the meeting, thanked them both for their input, and assured them of the value of their presentations. He concluded by thanking Farley for allowing them to meet on the *Maximilian*, or as he put it, "Your generosity provided the privacy needed for a meeting free of biased influences."

Farley invited them all, including Janneke, to enjoy complimentary drinks and light refreshments. Janneke stayed and nursed a glass of white wine while the members of the subcommittee downed several drinks. She attempted to visit with each man individually, but try as she might, she could not crack the boys' club attitude promoted by the chairman. Frustrated and growing impatient, Janneke expressed her thanks (for nothing, she thought) and left before saying what was really on her mind.

***

Janneke was still fuming when she met Lucia Sandoval in the

Sandoval combined business/living suite.

"We were ambushed. Farley had the so-called chairman in his pocket. I'm not sure of the other two members. They seemed uneasy, even surprised, when the chairman asked questions about the presence of the FBI. But I think the fix is in. I better try to find out more about this subcommittee and what the meeting really was about."

"If the fix is in, as you say, does that mean the Racing and Gaming Commission will vote to approve a license for Farley's Free To Play?"

"I don't know. The last I heard, the Commission wasn't unanimously in favor of approving *any* license for a casino in the Lakes Area. But even if a minority of members vote for no license, the remaining members organized as a single bloc could approve and award it to Farley's consortium."

"Do we have anyone on the Commission who might help us?"

"I can talk to the Administrator, John Harris, again. He's a standup guy and will help within the parameters set for him, but he's not likely to add to those parameters."

"Then how is it three members are free to operate beyond what I believe are the Commission's normally accepted limits? And why were neither of the women on the Gaming Commission at the meeting?"

"I don't know, but those are questions I'll ask of Mr. Harris.

"Do you think the influence of the chairman or whatever he is could be enough to swing the majority?"

"It's certainly possible."

While Janneke was fuming and pacing back and forth, Lucia had maintained her composure, an attribute honed by recent experience. "Let's keep our perspective. A casino license may not even be approved. Others have tried and failed. And even if someone else is granted the license, it does not need to change our goals."

"I know, but it seems so much is at stake."

"Perhaps, but Janneke, maybe this is a distraction we could do without. You've done a fantastic job representing the Lodge. I couldn't have done it, and even if we don't land the casino, awareness of our organization has grown, and our Lodge brand has been promoted more than if we hadn't thrown our hat into the ring. You don't know how important you are to me, professionally and personally."

Lucia's eyes glistened as she stood, walked around her desk, and took Janneke in her arms and held her in a long warm hug. Separating but holding close, Janneke wiped a tear from the corner of her eye, smiled, and admitted, "I hate to lose, I guess, especially when dealing with a cheating bastard like Farley."

Lucia laughed. "Your passion is one of the many things I love about you. Regardless of what the future holds, I think we are beautiful together." Their eyes merged and they stood together, silently sharing a lingering smile. Finally stepping back, Lucia took and released a deep breath. The soft smile that lingered was replaced by another expression, as though Lucia's thoughts were elsewhere.

Janneke noticed the change. "What is it? What are you thinking?" But there was no response.

Janneke reached out and lightly adjusted an errant curl of dark hair that had fallen over Lucia's forehead, then spoke softly. "Lucia, we are more than business associates. We've become close friends. You don't need to explain anything, but if it would help to talk, I'm here for you."

There was a long pause, then Lucia slightly nodded her head in acceptance. "It's been a struggle. I thought if I admitted what it was, if I shared it with someone, maybe I could better deal with it. If you're willing…"

"I'll listen and help any way I can."

Lucia's voice wavered as she began. "It's about Virginia Lawery's murder last spring and her involvement with the Lodge. It seems like a strange dream, like it didn't happen. But I can't get past it. It haunts me. It was big news, but there was much more to it than was reported in the news."

"How so?"

"I can't explain it, but over the two years she worked at the Lodge, she became important to us. It was organic. She just gradually insinuated herself into our lives, and we accepted without understanding. I think she had decided that her future was with Anthony and me. We were to become her solution to a life without a mother and the unresolvable challenges she'd faced as a child. We were going to be her new family."

"But she was a grown woman with friends and two loving aunties. Why would she need or even want to replace the family she had?"

Lucia's voice grew stronger. "Ginny was complicated. She did talk about her childhood, but we don't know everything. Whatever happened affected her deeply. She was close with her mother, and after she died, Ginny kept thinking and acting as though her mother were still alive. It sounds bizarre, but Ginny seemed to become her mother or at least to behave like her. Maybe even mimic her."

"She mimicked her mother? Why would she do that?"

"Ginny wanted to please everyone. I think it was a survival tactic. She was to everyone what she thought they expected, and she was so sincere about it, no one considered that it was manipulation. That's how she survived and even prospered. She was beautiful, personable, and highly intelligent. I think in her mind she believed she was honest and sincere. Her mother's behavior and personality were so ingrained, there was a unity that even seemed to overcome separation by death. It was like she was caught in this emotional net created by her mother, a net so powerful it could even ensnare others as they came to know Ginny."

Lucia walked over and sat down on the large leather couch that once sported the Matador Throw, which had played a part in the recent drama at the Lodge. Wrapped around the body of Ginny Lawery, the beloved niece and adopted daughter of the Lawery sisters, the throw had provided an essential clue to Ginny's murder and the drug distribution operation perpetuated by the late Anthony Sandoval, co-owner of The Lodge on Okoboji, and his partner, Jolly Holiday, a biker thug.

Janneke crossed the room to join Lucia, sat down, took her hands in hers, and asked, "But what did Ginny do to so deeply affect you and Anthony? You two were good at business together, and I wouldn't consider either of you gullible. There had to be more."

"There was. I believe that Ginny deliberately got pregnant by Anthony. The last night she was here, Ginny told me that Anthony and I had become her new family. She said we had grown close, so close we could even raise a child together as a family if we had to, like it was a permanent relationship. In the past, when Ginny and I talked, it was often about her ideas or fantasies for her future, and I thought she was just being Ginny, sharing fantasies and big dreams. Neither Anthony nor I knew she was pregnant, and I didn't take her seriously. She slept over that night, like a child with her mother or at least a big sister. We talked until I fell asleep. She was gone in the morning. Anthony said he saw her leave. I never saw her again."

***

Farley was elated. He counted three solid votes. Big Man had been very helpful.

With a wink and a big toothy grin, Big Man said, "A successful meeting if I do say so myself. We should celebrate. Your treat! What say we meet at the Ridge Top around six, and later, maybe I can 'bonerfy' as to Miss Asia's talents again." He slapped Farley on the back and laughed out loud at his coarse pun.

"Great idea. I'll call ahead and plan to have our van pick you up. Just let me know what your fellow subcommittee members prefer, and it'll be arranged." An experienced practitioner, Farley was used to working with slimeballs, but Big Man demonstrated a lack of conscience and empathy that gave even Farley pause. He appreciated the firm handshakes, the boisterous manner in which Big Man filled a room, but after several months up close, Farley knew it was a facade, a thick veneer that disguised a malevolent intelligence, a self-serving evil, subtle but darker than anything he had ever experienced.

Farley watched the three men walk across the grounds and into the Lodge's lobby as the *Maximilian* was pulling away from the dock. Big Man was still talking, emphasizing whatever point he was making with finger stabs and wide arm motions. Not for the first time, Farley wondered if there was something chemical besides the booze contributing to Big Man's behavior.

The breeze blowing through open windows on the main deck was refreshing. For a man who preferred his own judgement, it felt good to leave behind, even temporarily, the anxiety he felt due to dependence upon the advice and action of others. Then the burner phone inside his blazer vibrated. It was RV Man.

9

"You've got a problem."

Not the salutation Farley was expecting from anyone, especially RV Man. "What now?"

"You know your big-shot on the Gaming Commission, the one who likes them young and treats them rough?"

"Yeah, what about it?"

"He likes to choke them, sometimes with a silk scarf, sometimes with his bare hands. He likes to see how close he can come before they pass out while screwing them."

"So?"

"Last night he got too rough."

"What are you saying?"

"She passed out permanently."

"What? He bragged to me that he wore her out and said when he left the room she was sleeping. Are you sure she's not just stoned?"

"I'm dead sure."

"He likes to slip them some sort of pill, something he calls 'Miss

Easy.' You think it was an overdose?"

"Could be. We give some of the girls a soother to loosen them up before entertaining a client. She was wound pretty tight, very young, not fully trained. I'll check with Pauline."

Farley was dumbfounded. Seconds passed in silence until RV man finally asked, "Are you there?"

"Yeah! Yeah, I'm here. I was just thinking it would be better if it was an accidental overdose."

"Well, I'm no pathologist, but the blunt fact is she's dead."

"Does anyone else know, besides you and me?"

"Just you, me, and Pauline. When she didn't return to her room this morning, the roommate reported it to Pauline. When Pauly went to check, she found her dead and called me. We locked the room."

"What about the roommate?"

"Not a problem. She didn't see the body, and she'll believe what we tell her. Now what are you going to do about it?"

"What do you mean? She's your girl."

"We only deal in live ones. This was your guy and your responsibility."

Farley was enraged. If they had been in the same room, he might have killed the arrogant pimp bastard. "Let me make this clear, if I go down, you go down, and Pauly, and everyone else in your organization."

"Wrong! The way I look at it, you're the guy in the middle. You're the one who made the big promises and borrowed big bucks. Pauly and I are just hired for a service. You're the one the authorities will go after, and if they don't, the people I work for, your investors, will."

Farley knew he had to keep it together. All the pieces fit and were in play. He couldn't afford a break in any part of the plan.

"So what do you wanna do?"

He didn't want to, but it felt like there was only one thing he could do. "Okay. Listen closely, and do exactly as I say. Do not move the body. Do not touch anything. Leave everything as-is. Keep the room locked. Nobody is allowed in. You will get a call. Listen to what is said, and again, do exactly as you are told. Follow the instructions to the letter, and this will all go away. Do you understand?"

"Yeah. How soon?"

"Soon. Tonight at the latest. You're using the burner, aren't you?"

"Yes."

"Good. Keep it on you until you get the call."

"What about reimbursement?"

"What the hell are you talking about?"

"Reimbursement for the merchandise. My people will expect compensation for our loss."

"Tell your people this is part of doing business. If they're really in it for the long game, like we planned, this will be nothing but a blip on their balance sheet. Now be sure that door stays locked. And wait for the call."

With that, Farley felt his fear and rage build up inside him. He poked several times at the dot before finally disconnecting. He felt like he was going to vomit, head spinning, nearly blacking out. Realizing he was hyperventilating, he did his best to slow his breathing. As he regained control, he began to mentally tick through his options. It was a short list. "Time for Ralphy Boy," he said to himself.

Ralph Cole was a risk unto his own. He was effective but could be too enthusiastic. Farley would need to lay down limits, keep it simple, make the problem go away without making it worse.

Farley had met Cole at the Spokes and Suds. Both had been overserved while seated next to each other at the bar. They talked, Farley shared a pitcher, they got on well, and following that, the two men stayed in touch. The last of a nascent motorcycle gang disrupted by the breakup of their drug business and the death of their leader, Jolly

Holiday, Cole and a couple of hardcore followers were all that remained. Rather than friendship, a similar deficiency of character, a lack of empathy for others, and a taste for booze kept Farley and Cole in a warped sense of kinship. Ralphy and his boys were rough and reckless. They sorely tried his patience, but Farley knew that for the right kind of job, they could be indispensible.

The call went as well as could be expected. It took all he had to keep from verbally throttling him, but Ralph was eager to take up the task.

"Farley, baby, no worries. I'll get the boys together, we'll pick up the problem and make it go away, permanently, no trace, no witnesses."

Farley thought, *No witnesses! Just Ralphy and his boys, RV Man and Pauline, and of course the Big Man!*

"Fine. I don't care or want to know how you do it, but get rid of that body and then lay low until you hear from me. You got that? Keep your mouths shut!"

"Hey, chill, bro. Me and the boys know what we're doing."

Farley gave Cole the phone number and emphasized, "This is not a social call. Arrange to meet, be discreet, and do the job."

"You worry too much."

Farley wanted to scream but managed to limit his rage to a final order. "Just do it!"

"Hey, just like Nancy Reagan!" Ralph laughed at his own humor and ended the call.

Staring at the phone, Farley screamed. "It's 'Just say no!' you dumb son of a bitch!"

He couldn't believe Ralph Cole would know or remember anything about Nancy Reagan. It was beyond ironic. Cole had to be stoned. He was conflating Reagan's mantra about the war on drugs with Nike's tag line. Farley hoped Cole would have more success than Nancy Reagan in waging her war on drugs.

After his little hissy fit, Farley felt better and began to consider how he might regain control. Maybe this could work to his advantage. Big Man would have to do as he was told or be charged with murder of a minor, whom he had raped. He called RV Man back.

"I spoke to my fixer. He'll call you. Do everything exactly as he tells you to, and do not ask questions. One other thing. Did you video record them?"

"Who?"

"The Big Man and his woman."

"Of course, like all the other times."

"Good. Save the video. Treat it like gold. If we have any trouble, we'll show it to him for a little come-to-Jesus moment. He'll be begging for our help. Oh, and save the sheets. Both of their DNA will be all over them."

After ending the call, Farley considered calling Cole back and asking him to wait so Big Man could see the body before disposal. There would be traces of his DNA all over her. Mentally, Farley rehearsed the scene and effect on Big Man. *He'll insist she was alive when he left and that someone else killed her to set him up. It will be his word against the RV People, not the most honorable witnesses. The video will be enough if it comes to that. I need the Big Man to be focused on the casino license. Better to keep him in the dark for now and dispose of the body as soon as possible.*

10

Although new to the priesthood and parish, Father Jim had established a relationship of trust with the area's Latino community, the majority of whom worked in hospitality, construction, or agriculture in the Iowa Great Lakes region. Many were naturalized citizens and some second and even third generation residents. He understood their concerns about immigration, was privy to their news and even gossip, but he was not naive enough to think all immigrants attending Saint Theresa were documented or held green cards allowing employment.

Consequently, Father Jim had a dilemma. "Talk about a taste of purgatory!" (Or was it limbo?) A parishioner, likely a young Latina, had just left the confessional. She admitted to a sin of breaking the law but refused to disclose details, even to a priest under the sanctity of the confessional. She asked if breaking the law for a good reason was a sin. She finished the Act of Contrition, but before leaving the confessional, she asked, "Does the Church still give sanctuary?"

Father Jim was careful with his response. "It may, but that depends on the reason."

"What if it is to protect someone from danger and save them from sin?"

"That may be possible, but there are different ways to protect someone. Law enforcement and social services may be better." As soon as Father Jim uttered law enforcement, he knew he'd misspoken. The Latina abruptly stood and left the autonomy of the confessional.

Father Jim had grown up in rural Texas among Mexican and South American immigrants and had worked a short time in San Antonio. He had several casual friends who were Tejanos— Mexican-American citizens living in South Texas, descendants of Spanish-speaking settlers who had colonized the area prior to the arrival of Anglo-Americans and long before Texas had achieved statehood.

Father Jim was fluent in Spanish, and the slight variations in her use of Spanish, as well as her accent, sounded to him like she could be possibly of Tejano descent. Father Jim knew there were two families of Tejanos in the local parish. They were American citizens, but it was not a stretch of his imagination that a "sin of illegality" had to do with harboring an undocumented alien.

It was an educated guess, but Father Jim had to consider that this concerned someone who had been trafficked or abused. He had far too much experience with the damage inflicted by criminals on those who were only seeking a better life for themselves and their families. If Father Jim felt he was between a rock and a hard place, what would it be like to be an undocumented immigrant, abused and isolated and fearing that the consequences of seeking help from authorities could be equally bad or worse?

With Saturday's mass and the social niceties completed, Father Jim and his fellow priest and mentor, Father O'Brian, better known to those close to him as Father Barney, were about to enjoy what had become a Saturday evening ritual, a brief chat about parish concerns, then a toddy (or two) and a movie on a rather decrepit VCR/DVD player.

"You're quiet tonight, Jim." Quiet was unusual for the man, who at times could be a bit officious in his observations. He typically exercised a cheerful and exuberant manner that fortified Barney's tolerance for the younger priest's talkative nature.

"I'm sorry," Father Jim said. "I'm not very good company tonight."

"Is there something troubling you?"

Father Barney waited patiently while his colleague considered a reply. "Father, have you ever heard a confession that conflicted with the law? Biblically speaking, I mean the law of Caesar rather than the higher law that we represent?"

Barney pursed his lips and took his time. There was a standard response they had learned when studying for the priesthood, but Barney, from long experience, understood what Jim was seeking required more than a platitude. What he could say would inform but may affect Father Jim's perspective in ways unintended. But it was an earnest question in need of an earnest answer. What he would do with the answer would be up to Father Jim.

"Is someone in danger?"

"I don't know, but I assume that is a possibility. She also asked about sanctuary."

"Is it possible she was just curious?"

"I suggested that a better solution may be to go to law enforcement or social services. That was a mistake. As soon as I said it, she got up and left."

"I can understand that. Do you have an idea who it was that took confession?"

"I'm pretty sure it was a Latina woman from one of the Tejano families. But there are several young ladies in both families, and I can't approach them without breaking the sanctity of the confessional."

Father Barney sat quietly, appearing untroubled and thoughtful. In spite of the decidedly conservative disposition of voters of Northwest

Iowa, there was a need for workers and thus a degree of tolerance, at least in the Lakes Area, when it came to immigration.

"Jim, there is little time for you to change your sermon before tomorrow's evening service in Spanish, but perhaps you could add something about sanctuary, about how the church welcomes all and that we are of one family. Encourage them to come forward if there is a need. Make it clear that, as priests, we will deal with this need in confidence, the same as if it were in the confessional."

Father Jim nodded. "I could do that. I could refer to, 'I was a stranger in a strange land, and you gave me comfort.' We both often make the point that for the church, there are no strangers. All are welcome in the sight of God."

"Excellent! You might add, perhaps in humor, that young people don't tell their parents everything. They may even know of someone who needs help but still be reluctant to talk about it with their parents. Stress that we welcome everyone, including the youth of our parish, to speak with us, in confidence, if needed. You might remind them that we will both be at the coffee and donut social after mass, and all they need to do is ask to meet in private."

Father Jim continued nodding his head. He smiled. "Thank you, Barney. You are one savvy priest."

"I don't know about that, but if you live long enough, you pick up a few ideas. If this is urgent, we need to act quickly."

A sermon rewrite was necessary, Jim agreed. There would be no movie tonight.

***

As planned, Father Jim's homily to the Spanish-speaking congregation Sunday evening deviated from the prescribed gospel and toward a message of safety and solidarity within the Church. Father

Jim stressed that the church was a refuge even for the challenges of daily life. He explained that through God's presence, there existed an emotional and physical sanctum within the walls of any church, especially this one. Before the final blessing, he added a rejoinder that anyone fearing for their safety or who knew of someone fearing harm, could speak to Father Barney or himself with the same confidentiality as the confessional.

After mass, Father Jim stood outside the church, shaking hands and blessing the infants and elderly. Last to pass was a small group of young women. They were engrossed in happy chatter, but as they walked by, each smiled and dipped her head in respect to Father Jim. One in the group lingered. Stopping before Father Jim and with downcast eyes, she asked, "Father, may I talk to you in private?"

"Yes, of course. Would you like to step inside?"

Bonita cast a nervous glance toward her parents who were walking toward the parking lot. "No, but I thought maybe…"

Before she could finish, her parents shouted, "Bonita! Hurry up. We're waiting."

"Coming, Papa."

"I'm sorry. Thank you, Father." She bowed slightly, turned, and rushed to catch up with her family.

It was frustrating and perhaps futile, but Father Jim called after her. "Please, Bonita. I'll be happy to meet with you whenever you like."

Bonita turned, did a little wave, and was gone.

The body pickup was easy. Disposal, not so much. Ralph Cole had a plan, but first, he needed to call an old on-again, off-again friend, as in, one he called only when he needed a favor.

"Al, baby! Long time, no see."

"Who is this?"

"Hey, this is your old pal Ralph Cole."

"Bullshit. You're no pal of mine."

Ignoring the response, Cole went on. "I just need a little advice. If everything works out, I owe you, and it could mean big money."

"And if it doesn't work out?"

"No foul, no problem. It's just advice."

A brief silence. Then Cole talked fast. "Does that kid that works at the junkyard still like his weed?"

"Why?"

"Just wondered. I know he used to hang with you guys, and I might want to trade him a deal for a favor, that's all."

Again, a too-long silence. "Come on, man. It's no big deal. I just need to know."

Alan Borsch was getting impatient. Ralph Cole was trouble, and since the killing at the Lodge last spring, Al and his loose-knit group of weekend biker friends-cum-stoners, wanted nothing to do with Cole or his fellow hoodlums. "Yeah, he lives for the stuff."

"Great! So does he still work at the junkyard?"

"As far as I know."

"Great! Do you have his phone number?"

"You gotta be kidding."

"Just his number, and we're done. I owe you."

Al knew Ralphy would keep calling if he didn't do something, so he coughed up the number. "Now, Cole, get this straight. You do your thing, and we do ours. Keep it that way. And if you try doing anything with Junkyard Sam, leave us out. He's not about to help us or anyone associated with that pothead kid who works for him."

"I thought you guys were friendly. You know, did a little business together."

"We did until his daughter turned sixteen and gorgeous. We're lucky he didn't turn us all into eunuchs. Don't underestimate him. He's mean and one tough old bastard."

"Maybe his daughter needs a boyfriend. I bet she'd love what I could give her."

Al laughed out loud. "You're nuts, man. Oh, and look out for Percy."

"What?"

Al laughed again. "If you see red, it's too late." Still laughing, he hung up.

***

Late that night, after Fathers Barney and Jim completed their pious task to revise their Sunday homilies, Ralph Cole, on a task less pious, stopped his beat-up Ford—with its bumper sticker, "My other car is a Harley"—in the junkyard drive and flashed the headlights. A tall, scrawny figure stepped out of the shadows and unlocked the gate. Cole pulled into the yard, shut off the lights and engine, and accompanied by his two buddies, Tolly and Joe, stepped out to talk to the creepy-looking gatekeeper. Cole was hardly one to talk. He had met his share of oddballs but couldn't help thinking, *There's something seriously wrong with this guy.*

"Hey, Pete. Thanks for helping us." He could hear a dog barking, a deep, guttural, enraged challenge.

Pete did something crooked with his mouth. Maybe a smile? "Don't worry. I locked him up. You got the weed?"

Cole handed over a quart-size baggie stuffed with pot. "This is primo product. You might want to go easy on it."

Pete opened the bag, closed his eyes, and took a deep sniff. He stood silently, briefly somewhere else, opened his eyes, and closed the bag. "Move your car out of sight, around the corner of that pile of tires over there. I've got an old Chevy prepped and on the fork lift. I'll show you how to drop it in and how to operate the crusher. You can leave it in the crusher when you're done. I'll move it Monday morning when I get to work. Other than that, you're on your own."

The instructions were easy enough.

"Any questions?" Pete asked, but he didn't wait for an answer. "Good. I'm gone. Remember, padlock the gate when you leave. Oh, and whatever you do, don't go into the workshop."

It took all three of them to remove the body from the car's trunk and position it for maximum result in the derelict Chevy. With a couple of false starts and much profanity, Cole's boys managed to get the Chevy into the crusher. With the controls in hand, Cole turned on the mammoth device, and within minutes, the car was flattened into scrap metal ready for transport to a smelter. All three of the men were mesmerized by the machine's enormous power and effect on the scrapped car, so much so that they were unaware Junkyard Sam had walked over from his nearby house to see why someone might be crushing cars in the middle of a Saturday night.

Sam shouted, "Shut that damn thing off! What the hell are you men doing in my junkyard?" Sam was past his prime, but his bald pate and short height were balanced by a broad chest, thick arms, and eyes that even in the dim glow of the yard light, blazed with fury.

While his companions remained frozen in place, Cole was quick to explain. "Hey, Sam. We just needed to get rid of some junk, and the crusher seemed like a good idea. No harm done. We'll even pay for using it."

"Bullshit. I know you. You're part of that bunch that got busted last spring." With that, Sam reached into a nearby pile of scrap metal and came up with a two-foot-long steel rod, sharply hooked at one end.

Cole stepped back and drew out a handgun. "Now, Sam. No one needs to get hurt. We ain't causing no trouble." He slowly raised his pistol. "You know what they say, don't bring a club, or whatever that is, to a gunfight."

Sam gave a grunt and dropped the rod. While Cole kept his firearm trained on Sam, the burly yard owner showed his empty hands and slowly made his way past the three intruders to the side door of his workshop. "Okay. You got me. Finish what you're doing, and get out of here."

Cole flashed a big grin. "Nice doing business with you, Sammy Boy."

All three laughed, but as they turned to walk back to Cole's car, Sam called out, "Hey, boys, before you leave, I'd like to introduce you to Percy." Cole and his men turned as Sam opened the side door to the workshop. With a howl from the bowels of hell and a flash of red-furred fury, the largest hound any of them had ever seen burst out the doorway. The ugly gargoyle with massive, slavering jaws and teeth the size of railroad spikes would be on them in seconds. With a group shriek, they broke for Cole's car. Cole managed to dive inside and slam the door, a split second before the beast crashed against the car, its saliva spraying across the door's window.

Cole ground the starter, the engine caught, he shifted the car in reverse and charged for the exit as the huge, red beast kept snapping at the tires. Passing through the gate, Cole didn't check whether his buddies were in the car, but as he floored the gas pedal, he did catch a glimpse of Junkyard Sam pointing and bending over in laughter.

***

Cole and company drove directly to their safe place, the Spokes and Suds, where it took several shots of tequila and a pitcher of beer before the boys finally managed to get their nerves under control.

"What the hell was that?"

"Hell is right. It was a beast straight from hell."

"Keep it down. I should have asked Al what he meant."

Both boys looked at him. Tolly asked, "What he meant?"

Cole sat staring morosely at his beer. "He said watch out for Percy. He didn't say Percy was a dog."

"Dog! No dog is that big. That was a demon, the Devil's own hellhound!"

Joe rapped his knuckles repeatedly on the table as he said, "I don't like it one bit. It's a sign."

Tolly nodded his head. "Wait, what do you mean a sign?"

"A hellhound gunning for us? It means we're cursed. We're going straight to hell."

Cole looked up, a grin on his face. "Well, you already knew that."

The boys did not laugh. "Maybe, but I never seen a real, live demon."

"Me, neither."

"Quiet. Here comes Shirley."

"How you fellas doing? Can I get you anything to eat?"

Cole forced a smile. "No, we're good."

"Okay, but drink up. Closing is in ten minutes."

Tolly reached out and grasped Shirley's arm.

"Hey! Watch it!" Shirley protested.

Tolly pulled back his hand. "Sorry, Shirl. Can we get another round of tequila?"

Joe added, "Make it a double."

Shirley looked the three over. "What's the deal? You guys look like crap."

Cole tried humor again. "Didn't you hear? The stock market went down." He sat there with his stupid grin while his boys kept silent, watching for any cue.

Shirley shifted her weight to one side, put a hand on a curvaceous hip, and glanced from one man to the next. "Alright. No food, three double tequilas for the gentlemen," she called to her part-time, late-night bartender, Weird Willy. Eyeballing the group, she tapped a well-manicured finger on the tabletop and added, "Then I'm cutting you off."

Tolly and Joe sounded in chorus, "Thanks, Shirl."

If Cole and friends hadn't been so preoccupied by their escape from the hellhound, they might have noticed Shirley step behind the bar to speak to Willy. "Something's up with those guys. I appreciate all their business, but I don't want to be a part of their trouble."

Willy retrieved a bottle of tequila and four shot glasses, walked over to the table, and as if solicitous, "Shirley and I are really worried about you guys. Did something happen?" With that, he sat down and started pouring.

The first round went fast. After the second pour, Joe leaned closer to Willy, trying to focus his watery, bloodshot eyes. "Have you ever seen a real, live demon?"

Willy leaned back. "What?"

"A demon. You know, like from hell."

Willy narrowed his eyes. "I've been to hell. We called it Vietnam." Willy's memories of brutal combat were reason enough for his claim.

"Then you know."

"Know what?"

"You know about demons, hellhounds, curses."

"You need another tequila." All four pounded down their drinks, and Willy poured another large enough to empty the bottle.

Closing time passed, but Cole and the boys remained. In tears, Cole tried to explain he didn't know he had accepted a job so evil that they would see Satan's demons. "Right there! Right there in the junkyard, hell opened up and that beast came to drag us down!"

Willy knew, even when he wasn't high (which was rare), that Cole lived life in La-La Land. But he continued to listen, nodding in agreement, encouraging them as a priest would three supplicants eager to unburden themselves of mortal sin to escape eternal damnation!

It didn't take any effort for Willy to figure out the hound from hell was Junkyard Sam's enormous guard dog. Willy had no problems with Junkyard Sam or his dog, but on the few occasions he'd been at the junkyard, he'd gone out of his way to treat both with respect.

No names were mentioned in the gush of babble, but enough was said that it became evident something serious had taken place that bore some vague connection to Cole's buddy, Farley, owner of the Ridge Top Nightclub and that excursion boat monstrosity.

While not a patron of the Ridge Top, Willy was familiar with the associated rumors about gambling and prostitution. He had seen young, attractive women delivered in RVs or vans and had known shortly after there would be an uptick in the number of men visiting the nightclub and the motel below. Many of the gentlemen would be driving expensive cars. Willy would know. He was recognized as an expert fisherman, dumpster-diver extraordinaire, and professor of gossip for the Lakes Area.

Shirley loudly cleared her throat, and when Willy looked over, she tapped her wrist as a sign to close up.

Willy rose from the table. "Well, men, you don't have to go home, but you can't stay here. The boss just told me it's time."

All three men dug deep into their pockets and threw down enough money for drinks and a generous tip. Cole pushed back his chair, tried to stand, and promptly flopped back down. "Whoops! Got up too fast."

Cole's buddies rushed to help him, but he pushed them away, got up, and fell against Willy. "Oops. Sorry," he said, and gave Willy a big hug. "Thanks, Willy. You're a real pal."

As they staggered out of the bar, all three waved back and thanked Shirley. Stopping at the doorway, Cole turned, pointed, then looked at Willy and announced, "That woman's a beautiful person. She's a saint. Don't ever let some drunk bastard mess with her." At that, he saluted, turned, and ran into the doorframe. On the second try, he managed to make an exit.

"Willy. What if they get pulled over by the police?"

"They won't."

"But what if they do?"

"They won't even remember where they were, and if they do, we'll just say they were fine when they left."

Less than assured, Shirley remained dubious. "What was all that blubbering and moaning about?"

"I think Ralphy and the boys have been up to no good."

"Do you think it's serious?"

"Maybe."

"Should we do something about it? Notify the police? Get a lawyer?"

"No, nothing like that. Don't even worry about it, Shirl. And if anyone asks, Ol' Willy will take care of it. Come here, sweetie." Willy took Shirley into a bear hug, patted her lovely behind, and said, "Let's blow this popsicle stand. Your place or mine? Oh, wait. My place is being remodeled."

While Ralph Cole and his buddies were doing their part, Farley's meeting with the Big Man did not go as planned. The "Subcommittee for Research" had arrived at the Ridge Top where they were wined, dined, and given a private show by the best strippers. After the show, two of the committee members were driven back to their quarters at the Lodge while the Big Man remained, looking forward to his new favorite girl. But first, Farley insisted on a short meeting.

With the body disposed of, or in the process, Farley considered it was time to explain to the Big Man why Farley was his protector and Big Man would be safe as long as he did as he was told. To better set the scene, Farley and RV Man chose to meet him in the same room the Big Man had used the night before. Big Man knew the RV People on sight, but until now had never interacted with any of them.

"Whatta ya mean, she's indisposed?" Big Man was well-liquored and intended to get what was promised.

"Well, not so much indisposed. More like fit only to someone whose tastes lean toward necrophilia." Farley smiled, pleased as much with his clever choice of words as the Big Man's confusion.

"What the hell does that mean?"

"It means you killed her!"

"Bullshit! What sort of scam are you pulling now?"

"No scam. When Pauly went into your room this morning to check on your new favorite girl, she found her in your bed, very dead. You went a little too far this time with the strangling. Your fingerprints are all over her neck. So we—you and I—are going to revise our agreement. You are going to do exactly what I tell you, and as long as you do, your secret is safe with me."

As Farley spoke, Big Man's mottled face turned dark scarlet and sweaty. Breathing heavily, confused, with eyes unfocused from the booze, he managed to croak, "That poor girl. She was beautiful, so desirable, so passionate. We were just having fun. She wanted me to do it."

Relishing his control over the Big Man, Farley replied, "I doubt the authorities would understand it that way."

The Big Man began to sob. Tears ran down his face, and he said in a soft voice, "I want to see her."

Farley declared flatly, "No! You don't get to see her. You don't get anything unless I tell you. She's been taken care of. And now I own you!" With his lips stretched into a grimace and tongue flicking in and out to moisten his lips, Farley delivered his staggering blow. "However, you may watch yourselves perform on video."

There were a few seconds of silence, then the Big Man raised his head and asked, "What video?"

"Our girls are valuable. Surely you don't think we would allow our lovely girls to be unprotected while with their clients. We have a video camera strategically placed in every room. Believe me when I say, we have you recorded in all your glory including the moment you strangled her to death."

There was a change. His face hardened. "Show me the video."

Until now, RV Man had stood a silent witness to the drama. Farley looked over at RV Man and nodded. "Show him the video."

But rather than produce the video, RV Man said to Farley, "Let's talk outside."

Stepping outside, Farley could not believe what he'd heard. "Unbelievable! It's not that complicated!"

"It's more complicated than you think! The camera comes on when the girls use their key cards, but sometimes the keycards don't work or the code doesn't take. Nothing we can do. We aren't going to barge in and say, 'Excuse me while I turn on the camera.' I can't help it if once in a while there's a problem. It's not like any of us are technicians."

"Did you get anything at all?"

RV Man shook his head. "I don't know why, but it was all blacked out."

"Did you check the camera?"

"Hey, we barely had time to move the body and clean up the room. I checked the video just before we met up, and there's nothing on the tape."

"Tape? What is this, the 1970s?"

"That's all we've ever used. We only check it when there's a need, and we've never had a problem before."

"A problem? A *problem*? This isn't a problem. This is a total fucking mess."

Farley stood with his mouth agape, eyes bugged out in rage, silent but screaming inside. Finally, he demanded, "Where's the body?"

"I don't know. Your guys picked her up while we were at the nightclub. They could be anywhere by now."

Farley whipped out his phone and dialed Cole, but the line went to voice mail. "Cole! This is…" Farley paused, then said, "Look, you know who this is. Call me as soon as you get this."

Farley turned to RV Man and asked, "You still have the bedding, right?"

RV Man shuffled his feet. "Ah, no. After your boys picked up the body and we were at the Ridge Top watching strippers, housekeeping went back in and took the bedding."

Hands raised, palms forward to hold back Farley, RV Man said, "Before you go ballistic, think about it. You don't need the bedding or the video."

Farley was beside himself. "Are you out of your *fucking* mind?"

"You've still got him on the hook."

"What do you mean?"

"He doesn't know there's no video or bedding. Keep telling him you make the rules and he doesn't have a choice."

The space between them smelled sour with rage and frustration. Finally, Farley agreed. "I hope you're right. Big Man shouldn't know the difference. He'll have to do what I tell him."

Stepping back into the room, Farley feigned enthusiasm. "Wow! What a performance!"

"Show me the video," Big Man said again.

"Not now, but someday. In fact, someday we'll give you your own copy."

Big Man was seated on the edge of the bed. No longer crying, he broke into a large smile. Pointing at the fire alarm above the bed, he asked, "Tell me, is that the camera that took the video?"

RV Man looked up at the alarm, then at Farley, and nodded. "Yes."

Big Man reached inside his blazer and withdrew a roll of black electrical tape, speared on a sausage-sized index finger. "A camera isn't worth shit if the lens is covered with tape."

Farley and RV Man froze as Big Man stood up, walked over to

Farley and, as he spoke, thumped Farley's chest with the same sausage finger sans tape. "Let me paint a picture for you assholes. You don't have a body. You don't have a video. You've scrubbed all the physical evidence. The only witnesses are either the illegals working for you or citizens of questionable character. And when the people who are backing your enterprise find out you've screwed the pooch, well, I wouldn't want to be in your shoes. Call your driver. I'm leaving."

Pausing at the door, Big Man turned to add, "We'll continue on my schedule unless you decide to deep-six the entire operation, in which case, the Lodge gets the casino. I know I'm pissing in the wind, but I'll say it anyway. Don't do anything else stupid. You take me down, we all go down. You're not the only one with a backup plan."

He didn't bother to close the door.

***

RV Man didn't want to call, but his boss needed to be informed. There was one ring, and a deep voice answered. "You're not supposed to call me unless absolutely necessary. Are you using the burner?"

"Yes, I'm using the burner."

"This better be important. What's up?"

"Farley is a royal fuck-up."

"Yeah, so?"

"You know Farley's big buddy on the Gaming Commission who's supposed to deliver the vote on the casino?"

"Yeah."

"As part of his bargain, we provide young girls he likes, especially non-white young girls. He also likes it rough. He slaps them around and strangles them while they're screwing."

"So? Not the first time we've had a client with particular tastes."

RV Man caught his breath. "Yeah, but last night the client got carried away and killed her."

The sound was muffled but he overheard the boss saying, "Hey, Babe. Do me a favor and refresh my scotch will yah? And get some more ice while you're at it." There was a brief pause, then, "That's not a first, either, but it is a problem. What are you doing about it?"

"I told Farley he needed to get rid of the body. He had a couple of his buddies dispose of it, but then he tried to blackmail his Big Man, and it backfired. That's when it all went south."

"How's that?"

"Farley told the Big Man we videotaped the killing, only we didn't. The Big Man found the camera and covered the lens. Blew us off. He said the vote on the casino would go on as planned, and he said not to screw with him. He said he had a back-up plan, but I think that was a bluff. Do you want to pull the plug?"

"Do you have it contained for now?"

"I believe so. Everyone wants the same thing, and as far as I can tell, no one will connect us to the murdered girl. We brought her in special, and the Big Man was the only client who had been with her. He probably doesn't believe she's dead, or he thinks we killed her to frame him."

"Good. Let's give it time to play out. We've got too much invested to pull out now. The decision on the casino should be up for a vote by next week. Then we'll decide how to proceed."

"We have one more problem, thanks to Farley's Big Man."

"You gotta be kidding me! Just a minute." There was the clink of ice dropped into a glass followed by a muffled voice. "Thanks, Babe. Why don't you get us a bag of chips and some salsa? There's a new bag in the kitchen and the salsa's in the fridge." Removing his hand from the receiver, he asked, "What's the problem with Farley's so-called Big Man?"

"The Big Man came on Thursday, a couple days early, to finalize arrangements for the so-called subcommittee meeting with Farley and the Lodge. It was just an excuse for free booze and to screw his favorite girl, Carla. He planned to spend the night with her but was so bombed, he passed out. She took advantage of the opportunity, slipped out of the room, and escaped. Pauly was doing rounds to check on our girls and saw Carla run across the parking lot. Pauly called me, but before I could stop Carla, some good Samaritan picked her up. I'm sure she's hiding and considering her background, she's probably more afraid of the police than she is of us. I can find her, I have a lead on the car, but we need someone with the expertise to take care of this particular type of problem."

The silence hung heavy like a body from a noose. Finally, his boss said, "So we have no control of the Big Man, a body, supposedly disposed of, a missing girl that needs to be found and eliminated, and an accomplice in over his head. Anything else to add to the list?"

"No, Sir. That's it."

"Does the Big Man know Carla escaped?"

"No. He thinks she got up during the night and went back to her room. We let him believe that and told him she wasn't available the rest of the weekend because of her time of the month. And that's why we had to bring in someone new. Someone special for him."

"I see. Do I need to show up, or can you still handle the operation from your end?"

"I can deal with everything except eliminating Carla. Like I said, I can locate her, but she needs to be taken out, and I need some talent to do the job."

There was a pause while the boss downed the scotch and began crunching on one of the ice cubes. "I have someone. We'll try to get the asset back but if we can't, we'll eliminate her. Either way we buy some time. I'm not worried about the local hicks. My concern is the Feds."

"The Feds are sniffing around because of the dead former agent. Farley's spy at the Lodge has kept us informed, and there's been nothing to suggest a connection to our enterprise."

"All right. Find the girl, then call me on the burner to let me know where she's hiding and who's helping her. I'll let you know when and where to meet our specialist. Do everything exactly as instructed. This should be a quick in-and-out, done before anyone knows what happened. Is there anything else I should know?"

"Not if we deal with our missing girl."

"Stay with the plan, but as soon as the Gaming Commission announces their decision, we roll up this operation with the girls. After we get the casino established, we'll move back in. In the meantime, Mr. Farley will have an unfortunate accident, we'll collect on what he owes, and we'll have a casino. If Big Man or any others are loose ends, they'll be eliminated."

Standing alone in the dark parking lot, in spite of the heat and humidity, RV Man began to shake. He could only hope he and Pauline were not loose ends.

***

Farley reached Cole mid-morning the next day. "Do you still have the body?"

"Ah, no. We got rid of it like you said."

"How?"

"She became one with a Chevy."

"Damn. All right. You and the boys stay out of sight until you hear from me. Got it?"

"What about…"

"No questions!" Farley barked, and the line disconnected.

13

Michael loved to be around people. His sisters accused him of being gregarious to a fault. Whether to argue, exchange information, or just gossip—especially to gossip, although he'd never admit to it—he nearly always found something interesting to enjoy when in the company of others. As a result, people enjoyed talking to Michael, sometimes with surprising candor. Professionally, he recognized and exercised limitations, but on his return to the Lakes, he had gradually spent more time schmoozing with family and long-time friends. Consequently, he had become less vigilant in setting priorities and boundaries for demands on his time. So it happened that, smitten with the overly expressed enthusiasm of some of his colleagues at Iowa Lakes Community College, Michael found himself early on this sunny, overheated morning, standing on the stone pier jutting from the grounds of the Lodge as a volunteer for the annual Okoboji Triathlon. (Two events in two consecutive days! He was on a slippery slope!)

Madge was excited to learn he was assisting. Jeremy was competing in the race, and for Madge, this was another chance for

Michael to support his nephew.

"Aren't you and Connie going to be there?"

"Sure will. The kids and I will be at the finish line, but Connie is on duty. I worry about Jeremy, especially the swimming part. I feel better knowing you'll be there to help."

Normally, the Regatta and Triathlon would not have been on the same weekend, but the Triathlon had been postponed from the weekend before thanks to persistent thunderstorms. With the summer season passing quickly and a full schedule of special events, the best date remaining for a possible make-up was today.

The first leg of the race was the swimming event, and as Michael stood with the group of volunteers getting final instructions, he saw his nephew standing on the beach next to the pier. Jeremy had teamed up with his girlfriend for the three-pronged race. She would bike and he would swim and run.

Not for the first time, Michael marveled at the striking resemblance of Jeremy to his father. Only 18 years of age, Jeremy was already tall and broad at the shoulders. Thanks to his mother, Jeremy's stature was tempered by a gentleness in manner, yet in his eyes could be seen the intelligence and stark intensity of his father, the same characteristics that made Connie exceptional in his duties as Sheriff Mark Conrad of Dickinson County.

The swimmers were to swim out to a buoy and back to the sandy beach that fronted the Lodge. As part of his duty, Michael would pilot *Frau Nägel* at a safe distance alongside the swimmers as a precaution in the event someone would need to be rescued. On the side opposite from Michael, sharing in the precaution was a Lake Patrol boat driven by tough-minded Department of Natural Resources officer, Richard Piccard, known to his detractors as "Picky Piccard." Michael knew Piccard, and thanks to Picky's help with a criminal investigation this spring, held a grudging respect for the Officer.

The swimmers entered the water with a great deal of thrashing, and the strongest quickly took the lead while the various skills of those who followed resulted in a long procession. Jeremy was a strong swimmer, and as he rounded the buoy, took a slight lead over the best of the competition.

As Michael took in the buoy-seeking swimmers being lapped by those stroking for shore, he saw Piccard turn his boat and carefully approach a struggling swimmer. From the corner of his eye, he saw Jeremy break from the lead and sprint to the swimmer who was now desperately fighting to stay afloat.

Jeremy secured the distressed swimmer, a young woman, as Piccard carefully drew alongside. With a push from Jeremy, Piccard pulled the swimmer into his boat and was rewarded with a gush of vomited lake water. He encouraged her to hang her head over the boat's gunwale while he reached under the console and withdrew a landing net. He'd seen something while helping the swimmer. With a deft scoop into the water, Piccard netted what appeared to be a large, dead fish.

Momentarily impressed by the Conservation Officer's skill at multi-tasking, Michael's attention returned to his nephew, who had struck off for shore. With powerful strokes, Jeremy gained on the leaders and was among the half dozen or so who first hit the beach. Jeremy tagged his partner with a high five, and Emily, tucking her head low over the handlebars, powered off on her leg of the race.

With the stragglers accounted for, Michael docked *Frau Nägel* and joined a small group silently gathered on the pier alongside Piccard's boat. The rescued swimmer was safely seated in the front of the boat, wrapped in a bright orange blanket and shivering in spite of the heat. But the focus of attention was not on her, but the contents of the fish net.

Stepping closer to the boat, Michael spoke up. "Looked like a trophy from where I was. How big is it?"

Piccard looked up, his jaw clenched and his eyes hard. "This is more in your line of business, Counselor." Lifting the net, he revealed what had been obscured by the side of the boat. Rather than a fish, it was a human arm, raggedly severed above the elbow with a large, battered diver's watch hanging from the bloodless wrist.

Early Monday morning was sunny and bright, and Junkyard Sam was pissed. His brother-in-law had not shown up for work, was probably hung over again, and the harebrained pothead who worked for him, if he remembered to show up at all, was here late and higher than a kite.

"Where the hell have you been? The truck will be here this afternoon and we still have two cars to prep and crush."

"Hey man, I was up late. Gimme a break."

"I'll give you a break, starting with your face. And what did those guys want the other night?"

"What guys?"

"Ralph Cole and the rat pack he brought with him Saturday. Remember? Man, you need to lay off the weed while you have any brain cells left."

"Hey, my brain cells are fine."

"Yeah? What did I just ask you?"

Pothead Pete stared at Sam, unseeing and unknowing.

"Cole and his buddies. Saturday night?"

"Oh, that. Cole said he had some junk he wanted to get rid of, probably old bike parts."

"So why didn't he come during the day and drop it off?"

"I didn't ask. Maybe he's a busy guy."

"Bullshit! It was something hot, and they thought they could get rid of it here."

"Nah, nothing like that. I showed them what to do and left. They didn't hurt nothing."

Sam stared at the crusher with the recently flattened car. "Put that car on the pile, then get busy tearing apart those other two. Get at it, or you're fired!"

"Again?"

"Just get at it! I need to see if my wife has the scrap permits and paperwork ready."

Sam went into the workshop and walked back to the small office where his wife was working. "Are those scrap certificates ready?"

While Sam took care of everything in the yard, Wanda handled the finances and record-keeping end of the business. "Right here, big guy. What's going on out there?"

"Pothead Pete is stoned, and your brother didn't show up for work again."

"So what else is new? How's Percy? Ever since I let him out this morning, he's been whining and crying. Is he sick or something?"

"Not that I noticed."

Pete was at the office door. "Boss?"

"Yeah? Now what's wrong?"

"It's Percy. Every time I go to get that car out of the crusher with the forklift, the damn dog goes berserk. He starts growling and snapping at me. You'd better tie him up if you want me to get anything done."

Wanda got up and headed for the yard. "I told you something was wrong with him. Here, Percy! Good dog. How's my sweetheart? Are you okay?"

Percy ran to Wanda and began to bark and jump about.

"Good Percy. Good dog." Wanda made a sweeping motion with her arm. "Go, Percy. Show Mama what's wrong."

Percy turned and ran to the crusher. Turning around twice, Percy froze in place, whining and staring at the wreck.

Sam, with Wanda and Pete right behind, followed the dog. Reaching down to stroke the massive head, he asked, "What is it boy? Is it the car?"

Percy looked up at Sam, barked once, then began frantically pawing the ground next to the crusher.

Sam saw what was bothering the dog. "Damn! Good boy, Percy!" Sam pulled him back by the collar. "Now, sit! Stay."

A crushed car might leak residual oil or lubricants, but when Sam bent over and drew his finger through the stained dirt, the fluid was not oil. Sam moved over to the controls and lifted the crusher's plates off the car.

Wanda turned her head. "Oh, my God!" She began shaking, taking deep breaths, trying to gain control. Percy had moved to her side, whining and rubbing against her, nearly pushing her over.

Sam went to Wanda and wrapped his arms around her. "Let's go inside. I'll call the police. Percy, come, boy!"

Pothead Pete stood staring at the bloody ooze running down the side of the crushed car. "Cool!" he exclaimed.

***

The junkyard was cordoned off as a crime scene. Officers and detectives from the Spencer Police Department were on site waiting for the arrival of Special Agents and Crime Scene Investigators from the Iowa Department of Criminal Investigation. Pothead Pete had managed to pull it together well enough to answer preliminary questions but was ordered to remain so the DCI Agents could question him in more detail.

Pete excused himself to use the restroom inside the workshop. Locking the door behind him, he punched in a call to the number he'd placed on his contact list only two nights before. The phone rang, but no one picked up, and the call went to voicemail.

"Ralph, this is Pete. You need to pick up." Pete paused, thinking for a second. "There are cops all over the place. Call me!"

15

Mid-July was a quiet time at Iowa Lakes Community College. Summer classes were winding down, many staff members were on vacation or, like Michael, working on projects that superseded the standard boundaries of the academic year. Even as he arrived this morning, he noted the nearly empty staff parking lot, and as he passed through the lobby, a different receptionist, likely a temp. After all the weekend excitement, he was looking forward to some quiet time to work in his office.

Soon after his return to the Lakes Area to recuperate, and on the advice of his longtime mentor, Father Barney, Michael had agreed to be a substitute instructor at ILCC. He replaced Pam Schneider, who was about to go on maternity leave for the spring semester. Pam taught courses for those studying for a degree in Criminal Justice. With his background, Michael was an excellent fit and was surprised by how satisfying it was to work with students. The experience was an unexpected positive component to his rehabilitation.

With the end of the spring term, Michael assumed his work at

ILCC would end as would his extended leave of absence. A last-minute request from his department chair and approved by the college president to supervise student interns over the summer had extended his responsibilities. However, by the end of the summer term, he had to decide whether to return to or resign from his position as a prosecutor in the Office of the Attorney General for the Southern District of Iowa.

It wasn't as though he had avoided the issue. It seemed like he had used up a ream of legal pads listing pros and cons and a multitude of scenarios, but this time, his favored approach to sort out a problem had failed him. It gradually became clear he would need to suck it up and commit to whatever he decided.

Fortunately, money was not a personal priority. Thanks to an inheritance and his own investments, he was financially well-off, a status unaffected by the divorce from his promiscuous wife. He had the resources and ability to do pretty much whatever he wanted. But he remained uncertain and unsure of the motives behind his possible choices.

Like so many times in the past few months, he sat quietly attempting to sort out all these matters jumbled up in his mind. Suddenly, he was jolted from this mental quagmire by the sharp insistence of his office phone. When he picked up, he was surprised to hear the voice of Francine Scarlatti, the chair of the Education, Human and Public Services department which included studies in Criminal Justice.

"Hello, Michael."

"Hello, Francine. I thought you and your family were on vacation in Yellowstone."

"We are, but some duties don't end at the border. I need to ask you something."

"Okay."

"Michael, I want to begin by thanking you, again, for your fine work subbing for Pam Schneider this last semester. Personally, I also appreciated your candor at our end-of-year interview regarding whether to remain in the Lakes Area or to return to your previous position. I don't know if you've made up your mind, but I wanted to let you know about something that just came up."

"Is everything alright? Is there something you need done?"

"No emergency, just something unexpected. Last week, one of our colleagues, Galen Manders, was offered an opportunity he feels he must accept. He resigned as of Friday. I spoke with my superiors and associates within our department. You know what wonderful people we have on staff, and to a person, they agreed to adjust class assignments to accommodate a last-minute hire. I'm calling to offer you Galen's position. I know this is unexpected, but welcome to my world, so to speak."

The silence that followed grew in length. "Michael, are you still there?"

"Oh, sorry. Yes, I'm here. I have to say, Francine, I'm beginning to think you're becoming a harbinger of surprise in my life—first the offer to substitute teach, then to supervise summer interns, and now this."

"I know. I apologize, but there it is. I might add that Galen is, or was, a valued instructor and was the one who proposed you be offered an opportunity to continue as a member of our staff. And, to quote Pam Schneider, 'You'd have to be fricking nuts not to hire Michael Cain!' Think it over, but I need an answer very soon, like by yesterday." They disconnected with a promise that Michael would decide by Wednesday.

There it was, D-day, decision time. Should he turn down Francine and this new opportunity and return to the stress and rigorous work with the Feds? He thrived on the demands as a federal prosecutor, but his life was changed. Instilled early by family, he was imbued with a sense of service, but there were different ways to serve. If he remained at ILCC, he could teach, write, do research, consult, and still have time to enjoy family, friends, and the blue waters of Lake Okoboji. There was a way to make an impact on the future of law enforcement and create a better future for himself.

Was it wrong to have a personal life, to have the flexibility to enjoy family and friends? His recently rekindled romance with Janneke could be reason enough to remain. In addition to being his first romantic love, Janneke was one of four longtime and dearest friends who remained in the area.

He smiled as he recalled the time Father Barney shared with him that the nuns in their parochial school had noticed the close relationships and as a play on names called them the four apostles—Matthew, Mark, Luke and Janni. Matthew was now a physician practicing in Spirit Lake and the Dickinson County Medical Examiner, Mark was Michael's foster brother and Dickinson County Sheriff, Luke was a successful area businessman, and Janneke was a successful businesswoman in her own right. The nuns had a special regard for Michael and had elevated him to archangel, not only because of his name, but for his willingness to do battle, intellectually and physically, for what he thought a just cause.

As he sat in his office, trying to force the agitation from his mind intensified by this latest complication, a stillness slowly descended about him. Gone were the voices and footsteps beyond his office. No ringing phones, bells, or whistles. He experienced the deep calm that came over him at the oddest times. He'd not shared this peculiar phenomenon with anyone, even with his therapist. As an adult, it had occurred when Michael found himself in a life-changing moment, in special need, or on those rarest of occasions, faced with danger. It was as if someone had placed an unseen hand of assurance on his very soul. Even Michael thought it sounded loopy. He blamed Gabriel.

His older sister, Melanie, had related to Michael the odd behavior she'd seen while Michael was a toddler, how whenever he was playing alone, it was as if he was playing with an unseen playmate. Gabriel, Michael's twin brother, had died at birth, and Melanie told of hearing their parents say, "Gabriel and Michael are playing together." Perhaps it was delusional, but Michael preferred to blame Gabriel for these eccentricities.

Softly thinking aloud, "But this is not life or death. Must life only have value when compared to death? Can I simply choose life?"

Michael did not take up pen and pad to resift through pros and cons. Not this time. Michael listened, and with a deep sigh, embraced what he would do. Retrieving his mobile phone from his book bag, he dialed Francine.

***

While Michael was considering his life choices, Sheriff Mark Conrad was dealing with flack due to a bizarre discovery. The news of the recovered limb was on the front page of the local news sheet with a picture of the young woman who had "bumped into" the offending limb while swimming the first stage of the triathlon. Coincidently, she was also the newspaper's summer intern, Stevie Carson. An accompanying editorial by the paper's owner/provocateur cited repugnant possibilities for death on the Lakes, and several proposed fantastical avenues for investigation.

As he glanced through the editorial, Sheriff Conrad muttered, "Way to go, Milo. Why report the news when you can declare the sky is falling? I hope he gets crap from the business community. This will be in every Iowa newsroom by this afternoon." But there was one suggestion in the editorial that had already been acted upon with a surprising result.

News among members of the area's law community traveled fast. Having learned of the recovery of a severed arm, the Okoboji Chief of Police, Bartholomew Dunham, had called to confirm whether Sheriff Conrad knew of the odd incident during the Regatta involving gunfire and the unsubstantiated attack upon a young woman. He went on to suggest that perhaps some of the volunteer divers for the Dickinson County Sheriff's Department could be called in to search about the docks used during the Regatta to confirm there was no danger from a water creature lurking nearby and to search for other possible "items of interest," as labeled by Chief BD. Subsequently, the afternoon of the Triathlon, Sheriff Conrad had dispatched two of his volunteer divers to the site.

It was an easy dive and was concluded in less than an hour. The divers retrieved a variety of fishing gear, a liberated boat anchor, some bottles, and one item of significance—a leg, severed below the knee, with a ragged diver's fin still attached to the foot and a twist of rope wrapped tightly around the ankle. Of additional interest was what was likely a large bullet hole through the calf muscle.

16

Monday evening, as Michael was deciding whether to microwave hot dogs or mac and cheese for supper (he had both), Jeremy called to invite him to a victory party of sorts. In spite of a few minutes lost when Jeremy stopped to help the struggling swimmer, he and Emily had placed first in their division.

"Mom told me to tell you she was making fried chicken, real potatoes and gravy, and cherry pie. She said it was a chance for you to have a great meal rather than your usual 'swill,' whatever that is—her words, not mine. But I'd really like you to come over so I can thank you for the Regatta and helping with the Triathlon. And to introduce you to Emily's parents."

The words cascaded from Jeremy in such a rush that Michael's first thought was, *Looks like his father but sounds like his mother.*

"Okay, sure. What time?"

Upon his arrival Tuesday, the first words from his sister were, "I called Janni, but she had a conflict and couldn't come. Is everything all right between the two of you?"

Michael was only slightly annoyed. *Maybe I'm getting used to this.* "Not now, Madge. Maybe later. Besides, I have some other news."

"Emee's folks are out on the deck with Connie. Go say 'Hi' and tell them we'll be ready to eat in ten."

Michael knew Emily's father, Glen Novak, but had not met her mother, though he knew she was the Spanish and German teacher in the local school district. As he stepped out onto the deck, Glen stood and greeted Michael with a solid handshake. Short and burly, Glen had what Michael considered Popeye forearms and farmer's hands— the thick palms and calloused fingers of someone accustomed to manual labor.

"I don't believe you've met my wife, Candace. Candace, this is Michael Cain."

Before she could stand, Michael reached over and shook her hand.

Candace smiled. "Good to finally meet you. I saw you in church earlier this summer, but we didn't have a chance to talk."

Connie piped up. "That might have been Michael's annual visitation to the family pew."

The inside joke between Connie and Michael about the word "pew" could have turned awkward but fortunately, Glen was eager to share his news about Michael's truck. The 1959 GMC pickup he had lovingly restored and customized when he was in high school had been unintentionally abused in Michael's haste to rescue Janneke from the threat against her life at the Lodge this past spring. Glen was a master at the restoration of classic cars and trucks, and his work could be seen at a locally owned collection that remained available to the public.

"I'm sorry it's taken so long. We have a backlog, but I've spent some personal time on your truck and finished the body work a few days ago. Our paint guy will do his thing, and it should be ready sometime this week. Next week at the latest."

"That's great news, Glen. My car is fine for everyday use, but I miss my truck."

"Let me know when you'll come by, and I'll give you the nickel tour. You'll be surprised to see how much the collection and the workshop have grown."

The patio door slid open, and Madge called, "The kids are here! Let's eat!"

Jeremy had picked Emily up from work, and as they ate, they entertained everyone with their excited descriptions of the Triathlon. It was a great meal. Michael wasn't one for overindulgence, but tonight was an exception. The cherry pie and Connie's homemade ice cream were to die for.

While the older kids volunteered to clear the table and wash the dishes, the younger kids went out to play in the back yard, and the adults moved to the deck to finish their coffee and enjoy the cooling air of evening. It did not take long until the compliments about the meal and easy chit-chat turned to more serious discussion and questions about the morbid discovery of body parts floating in the lake.

Although measured in what he was able to divulge, Connie did share what was or would soon be publicly known. "Fingerprints revealed that the victim is our missing retired FBI agent. Mrs. Smith also identified his wristwatch. We've sent the leg and arm to Ankeny for analysis, and we're waiting on DNA confirmation. I've contacted the Iowa Lakes Fishing Club to ask its members to watch for any additional remains, and our Dickinson County Volunteers are walking the shoreline and using their boats to check around the docks. So far, nothing else has been discovered. As you can imagine, the FBI folks are going bonkers. Whether we want their help or not, the FBI is now a part of the investigation. I think my phone number is on speed dial with major national and area news media outlets."

Glen was the first to ask questions. "Why not let the Feds deal with it?"

"The victim was not an active agent, so the Governor insists Iowa Law Enforcement has primary responsibility. Since it happened on our patch, the Dickinson County Sheriff's Office has the lead with the assistance of the Iowa Division of Criminal Investigation. In spite of that, the Feds are all over it. They're engaged in what I would politely call a parallel investigation. They insist we keep them apprised of everything we learn but are reluctant to do the same for us. They're holding something back, but I'm not sure what it could be."

Curious, Glen continued to press. "Wasn't it an accident, or is there more to it?"

For the first time in the conversation, Connie appeared uncomfortable and took his time to answer. "It's too early in the investigation to make a conclusion. At this time, we're trying to determine how the victim died and learn as much as possible about the circumstances surrounding his death."

"But isn't it likely that he drowned and his body was hit by a boat's propellor?"

Connie nodded but added, "We may know more after we get the pathologist's report."

Michael recognized that Connie had gone into "news media mode," and there would be no further specifics to share, if there were any. But Michael did notice what he considered an anomaly.

"Connie, why would the Governor have an interest in this?"

Connie leaned back in his chair, a tight smile edging into the corners of his mouth. Before answering, he thought to himself, *Yes, Michael, you would pick up on that.* "The Governor is interested in and committed to all aspects of law enforcement in our state."

Michael blinked but understood. Something's up. *The FBI isn't the only one holding back.* Though unrelated by blood, Michael and Connie were brothers by temperament and commitment to the law. They shared everything about law enforcement, and Michael understood what Connie was implying. *This will wait until we can talk privately.*

While Candace sipped her coffee and listened, she considered a connection that even she thought remote. "I have a question, Connie. The word all over the school this spring was about a casino coming to the Lakes Area. I know I'm thinking outside the box, but I wondered, does what happened to the retired agent have anything to do with the proposed casino? I read in the newspaper that the victim was staying at the Lodge, and everyone knows the Lodge is one of the organizations competing for the casino. It also may be why the Governor is interested."

As she spoke, Candace intently scrutinized Connie, as though she were dealing with a recalcitrant student.

Connie drained his coffee cup before answering. "That is an interesting thought, but I'm sorry to say it's too early to theorize."

For Madge, that was enough of the dismal subject, and whether for concern or disinterest, she redirected the conversation by asking Glen and Candace if Emily, who had received several offers of acceptance, had decided which school to attend in the fall.

As dark closed in, Connie lit the tiki torches around the deck's edge. The glow added to the ambiance, and with Madge's encouragement, conversation remained about families and the difference they would feel in their home lives with Jeremy and Emily gone away to university.

It was an enjoyable evening, but as the shadows turned to night, the Novaks expressed their thanks and rounded up their share of the younger crowd. Before leaving, Glen assured Michael he would call as soon as the truck was finished.

Sitting on the deck while Connie and Madge saw their guests to the door, Michael mentally rehearsed how to announce his decision to remain in the Lakes Area. He was excited but remained a bit apprehensive, likely a remnant of concern over such a significant decision. He wanted Connie and Madge to be among the first to know he had resigned from the Feds as of today and had accepted Francine's offer to teach at ILCC and remain at Okoboji.

Connie was the first to rejoin him. "Can you stay for a few minutes, Michael? Madge and I have something we'd like to talk over with you."

"Sure. Hopefully it's nothing too serious. I have something to tell you both, too."

Madge soon returned and sat down on her deck chair, the only chair with a cushion embroidered with the word "Mom."

"It really was a great meal, Madge, and I enjoyed getting to know Emily's folks. Thanks for including me."

"You're welcome. We're glad you could be here."

As eager as he was to tell his news, there was something about Madge's demeanor that gave him pause. He decided to defer. "Connie said there's something you want to discuss?"

Madge bit her lower lip and pushed her glasses up higher on her nose, a ritual she had begun at an early age and which meant she was reluctant to speak out, a trait rarely observed. She glanced over at Connie, who was watching her expectantly. He nodded and accepted Madge's reluctance as a need for help.

Clearing his throat, Connie spoke to the task at hand. "Listen, Michael. Madge and I think highly of Emily and her family. She and Jeremy are happy and make a good couple, but we have concerns. Worries, I guess, like any parents might have."

"What kind of concerns?"

Madge interjected, "Concerns that they are too young to have a serious relationship."

Michael waited, then offered, "They seem happy together and mature for their age. Is there something else that could be the problem?"

"No," Madge said, "but their whole life is spread before them. We want them to take their time and make good decisions."

In a flash, it came to Michael. It had to do with the intense relationship he and Janni shared at the same age as Jeremy and Emily, the resistance they'd met from their families, the professional expectations both clans had held for their futures, and their excitement and bewilderment when he and Janni had gone skinny dipping that hot summer night and fully experienced their love for the first time. And finally, the painful end. Whether due to family or their separation due to attending different schools, Michael had never really known. "With Jeremy and Emily, life doesn't have to be the same as it was with Janni and me."

"We know, but Emily's parents have the same concern we do. Connie's spoken to Jeremy, and I know Emily's parents have spoken with her, and both kids insist there's nothing to worry about."

"Well, I'm hardly the one to ask for advice. Adults I can usually manage, but children? I'm one degree from clueless."

Connie looked over at his wife and then to Michael. "We're not asking for advice."

"What is it, then?"

Connie took a deep breath, then got to the matter. "We would like you to sit down with both of them and talk about your experience and what it meant to you."

Madge pitched in. "I had hoped Janni would have come over tonight. We think it may be even better if you and Janni both would talk to them."

The tiki torches were burning low, and the encroaching darkness allied with the change in Michael's mood. Maybe he should be flattered that Connie and Madge would take him in their confidence on such an important family matter, but this was a big ask. This would require reflection on memories he preferred to leave buried. Surely, they knew that.

The silence begged his reply. "Look, I'm not even sure if Janni and I have the answers for ourselves. There are some things we should have discussed long ago, things we never talked about, maybe even avoided. I don't see how this could help."

"That's what you could share with the kids. In itself, it's a powerful message. And please don't take this the wrong way, but it might be an opportunity for you and Janni to work out some of the things you left undone."

The evening ended on less than a high note, but Michael agreed to a half-hearted "I'll think about it." When Madge suggested she call Janni, Michael disagreed and said that was something he would do.

On the drive home, it occurred to Michael he had not shared his big news to remain in the Lakes Area.

17

Lucia didn't understand. Yes, as they now knew, a retired FBI agent staying at the Lodge had gone missing. Preliminary tests of body parts recovered from the waters of West Lake Okoboji indicated they were the missing agent's. Lucia knew this much due to the local news, gossip, and several interviews with the detectives and FBI agents assigned to the case. And why the FBI? They said they always followed up on their own, but the agent was retired and on vacation. Shouldn't the case be up to local or state law enforcement? What did that have to do with murder? Was this even a murder? He could have had an accident or a medical crisis.

And why all the questions about illegal immigrants and trafficking? Prior to her husband's death, one of her responsibilities was human resources, specifically hiring and firing. Owing as much to her own Hispanic heritage, Lucia had been insistent that everything was in order when hiring immigrants, to the degree of even working directly with federal immigration authorities. Now the sole owner and principal manager, the policy had not changed, and her new assistant manager, "the owl," and the new human resource director were both in complete agreement.

So, what was really going on? The staff was on edge, an unusual number of cancellations had been called in, and it seemed the FBI was encouraging the news media to believe the Lodge was the nexus of evil. The Lodge was recovering from the trouble this spring but this could be a serious setback.

While Michael spent the evening with family, Janneke was at the Lodge. She had turned down the invitation from Madge, perhaps in part to avoid a possibly awkward situation with Michael, but more in response to an anxious call for help from Lucia.

"Lucia, I've reviewed your numbers," Janni said, "and the business at the Lodge has rebounded nicely. However, we don't know what these recent events are going to do to the bottom line. I needn't tell you we're in the middle of the high season for vacationers. This is make or break time."

An astute independent businesswoman, Janneke was also the treasurer of the board of directors for The Lodge on Okoboji, and at Lucia's request had just reviewed the current financial position of the Lodge. Lucia Sandoval as its owner/manager was answerable to investors, which included her family in Arizona, and she shared the board's concern about the effect on business due to this latest disruption.

"I know, but it all seems out of control," said Lucia. "I don't understand why the FBI is asking all these questions about illegal immigrants. Yesterday, my assistant manager overheard two agents discussing human trafficking. Earlier today, the FBI handed me a warrant for employee records. I saw to it that there was a thorough background check on each of our employees, but this is the FBI. With their resources, who knows what they'll claim to have found?"

Janni frowned and asked, "Human trafficking?"

"That's what I was told."

"Besides the missing retired agent, that's a good reason why the FBI might have gotten involved."

"Janneke, I know I can continue to be successful, but after all the money and hard work, I feel like everything is slipping away. I can manage the business, but I have no idea how to deal with the FBI."

"You've done a magnificent job with the Lodge. This too shall pass. It may take a little longer to accomplish your goals, but you'll get there."

Lucia's weak smile expressed her appreciation for Janneke's support, but she still lacked confidence. Janneke had a good deal of influence with the board of directors, and it was her suggestion that Faethe Lawery be added to the board. It was a smart move. Faethe had a wealth of experience and success as a businesswoman earned in a time when women were expected to stay home and let the men do the "real" work. After the disaster of murder, drug dealing, and money laundering perpetrated by Lucia's late husband, Faethe's advice and reputation had helped to restore the board's confidence in Lucia.

Janneke had played a part in the discovery of Anthony Sandoval's scheme and subsequently felt a responsibility to help Lucia in any possible way. But there was someone else close to Janneke who had a major role in the investigation. Someone who might be able to untangle some of the present confusion.

"Lucia, what would you think if I were to ask Michael Cain to help? Investigate the investigation, so to speak? He has experience in law enforcement and knows nearly everybody. And there's a reason why people refer to his many friends and colleagues as 'Michael's Marauders.'"

"My husband nearly murdered him. And you. After all that, why would he want to help?"

"Michael's funny that way. He has this overdeveloped sense of justice. If you agree, I'll give him a call. I'm sure he'll meet with you, and you can decide then whether to have him sort things out. At the very least, he may learn whether there's more to the investigation than we've been told."

Janni was thinking to herself again. *I haven't been fair. I know he wants to reconcile. I've been avoiding him, and it's time we talked.*

18

Having recently reread *The Old Man and the Sea*, Michael was thinking of the opening line of the novella as he descended the nineteen steps from his home to the dock. Whereas Hemingway's elderly fisherman "had gone eighty-four days now without a fish," it had been years since Michael had sailed, or in his case, motored forth alone for a complete day fishing the waters of Okoboji. So, it was early on a sunny morning in mid-July, with a light southwest breeze to wrinkle the water and cool the skin, when Michael loaded his sixteen-foot Lund Rebel with gear, bait, and ample provisions, and set out to reclaim a summer tradition.

Still smarting from the request to speak with Jeremy and Emily, he had decided to wait for a more opportune time to share his decision to remain in the Lakes Area. He had called Connie the night before to share his plans to spend the day fishing. Connie had cautioned that Okoboji in July was not the same as it had been a generation earlier. Indeed, the number, the variety, and the size of boats were far greater when compared to the recall of their youthful adventures.

Undeterred, Michael had assured Connie that he would safely use all his navigational skills while applying his exceptional knowledge of stalking whatever finned species were careless enough to fall for his sneaky wiles. His intent was to have a calming, soul-renewing day on the deep blue waters.

Connie had actually laughed out loud. "Do you even look at all the boat traffic going by your place? I'm not worried about your skills. I'm worried about other boaters' lack of judgement. There's a lot of stupidity out there. Think less about renewal and more about self-defense. Seriously, stay away from high-traffic areas at the mouth of the bays and off the points. Better yet, put your special day off until this fall."

"Sorry, no can do. I plan to hit every point and every bay, on this, my special day.

Connie snorted. "Look, there's a reason the old-timers do most of their fishing on West Okoboji before Memorial Day and after Labor Day. At least go to East Okoboji or one of the smaller lakes."

Michael went on as if he were talking to himself. "I thought I'd try off of Gull State Park first and go around to Emerson Bay, then Pocahontas Point. If that gets too busy, I'll head back to Millers Bay or Pikes Point. I'll end my day off Pillsbury and Fort Dodge Points, maybe fish the reef."

"If you want to fish Pillsbury and Fort Dodge, I'd recommend starting there early. The greatest boat traffic going into or out of Smiths Bay is from noon until mid-evening. The wakes, especially from the larger craft, are so big, you'll have trouble controlling your boat, and the fish will not be interested in what you have to offer. Better yet, stay away from Smiths Bay."

"Aye, aye, great captain! This mariner will consider your command."

With concern but resignation, Connie said, "Just be careful. You need to be as watchful for other craft around you as if you were flying your Cessna near a busy airport. By the way, Madge says you're not going to regain your youth by acting like an idiot. Just thought you'd like to know."

"Tell my sister I love her, too, and remind her that she comes from the same gene pool."

There was an exchange muffled by Connie's hand, and then Connie was back. "Madge wants me to inform you that you came from the shallow end of the gene pool, the end that was dry. Do you want to speak with her?"

"Nope. Gotta go. Bye!"

Connie was laughing as Michael ended the call. Michael loved both his sisters, but even with all good intentions, proximity to his younger sister could be quite taxing.

Accepting some of Connie's advice, Michael began by pointing the bow of his fishing boat toward the mouth of Smiths Bay, then across to the rocks and reef off Pillsbury Point. He knew from past experience he could probably entice a few smallmouth bass in this location even if he had no success elsewhere on the lake. That was why he had planned to end his day here.

Maneuvering above large rocks on the edge of the reef, Michael shut down his Mercury and dropped anchor. Speaking aloud, as though Connie were present, he said, "Okay, Sheriff Conrad, let's consider this the warm-up instead of cool-down." Reaching into an oversized, less-than-organized tackle box, Michael selected his favorite smallmouth lure—a pink-headed jig with chartreuse twister tail and homemade stinger made of a single #10 Mustad hook on a snell. With several rods at hand, he selected the medium Fenwick with the classic Cardinal Four spooled with 8 pound Berkley Trilene line and tied on the jig. Opening his worm box, he picked out a lively inhabitant, hooked the head of the fat nightcrawler to the jig, and threaded the homemade stinger through the worm's tail. It was ugly but whimsical, and Michael knew it worked on aggressive smallmouth.

His first cast was toward the shore. Successive casts fanned out to progressively deeper water. About mid-depth, he was rewarded with a hard, wrist-snapping strike. The rod bent sharply, throbbed, then relaxed as the fish burst to the surface and jumped repeatedly. Michael netted the bass, carefully removed the hook, and briefly paused to admire the green and bronze that shimmered from the smallmouth's sides and back. When he slipped the fish carefully into the water, there was a small splash when the bass defiantly flipped its tail and streaked to protective depths.

Michael caught and released several bass, pulled anchor, and maneuvered about using the electric trolling motor, repeating his success as he made his way further out into the mouth of the bay. Concentrating on line and rod tip, he was startled by the loud blast from an air horn. With his back to the main lake, he was unaware of the huge craft approaching the mouth of Smiths Bay. He was not in danger of being run over but was alarmed by the large wake pushed from the bows of the excursion boat.

Michael immediately turned the electric trolling motor to full power to maintain control of the boat. When the wake caught up to his boat, water splashed over the transom, and the Lund Rebel Sport was in peril of being pushed up onto the rocks near the shore. Desperately punching the starter, the forty-horse Mercury responded on the first try. Simultaneously shutting down the electric motor and shifting the outboard to reverse, Michael back-trolled his boat against the large waves. While water continued to slosh over the transom, Michael managed to turn the boat in the direction of the main lake. Shifting gears, he opened up the motor and sprinted out of harm's way.

Angered by the indifference of the larger craft and its pilot, Michael executed something he seldom did in public. Harmonized by some exotic lingo, he flipped off the boat, passengers, crew, and especially the boat's driver.

Looking back, he had a greater appreciation for Connie's warning. Smiths Bay was starting to churn with competing wakes from an increasing number of crafts of all sizes, most moving too fast for conditions unless the intended purpose was to create mayhem.

Disgusted and a bit shaken from nearly being forced onto a rock pile, Michael continued across the lake and was soon approaching Gull State Park.

The beach of the park was already overrun by boats, swimmers, and whatever people carried onto the sands to enhance their fun in the sun. Sharply turning, he directed his Lund to Emerson Bay.

For an experienced fisherman, Emerson Bay was like a lake unto itself. Due to the variety of structures, all species of desirable game fish could be found in abundance in or near Emerson Bay. Unfortunately, like Smiths Bay, Emerson was churning, too, and in a state of fluid turmoil. The most promising spot appeared to be along the southern shore.

Watching the fish finder, Michael guided his boat to a depth of ten feet and cut the engine. Rigging another rod with a diving plug, he began to troll at a moderate speed while directing the boat back and forth between depths of ten and fifteen feet. As he approached the mouth of the bay and Pocahontas Point, he was presented with a remarkable sight. Two fishing boats, one larger and newer, were anchored within a few boat lengths of one another. A single man was in each craft and appeared to be casting large, spooned lures in an attempt to hook the other's anchor rope. One of the combatants succeeded but as he hauled back on the rod the fishing line snapped and he nearly tumbled backwards into the water.

As the fallen man reached into a tackle box and began tying on another large lure of some sort, his competitor continued to thrash the water in an attempt to hook the other's anchor rope. With the replacement lure secure, the man who'd nearly fallen into the water changed his technique and cast at the other boat, hooking the gunwale while just missing the occupant. With a roar of profanity, the technique was replicated by the second contender who managed to also hook his opponent's boat. With rods pulled back and reels straining, the boats began to converge on one another. Their efforts finally brought the boats close, and Michael was aghast to see two elderly men stand and begin flailing fists at one another. In one of the boats, adding to the confusion, was a large dog loudly barking and trying to stretch over the gunwale to snap at the opposition.

Each time a man would swing and miss, he would fall over but regain his balance by grabbing the side of his boat. When the boats finally drifted together, the men stopped swinging and seized each other in a mutual bear hug, the effect of which was to gradually force the boats apart. Refusing to give in to the other man, they remained locked in a desperate embrace in spite of the growing gap between the boats. Michael watched in fascination as the boats continued to separate until the men, in an act of mutual destruction, were suspended over the water; then they weren't. With a large splash, they both fell into the lake.

Neither man was wearing a life preserver and what appeared to be a comedy was turning into a tragedy. Reeling in his line, Michael put his electric motor on high and headed for the belligerents. He was still a long cast from reaching the men when suddenly from behind him there came the short, sharp shriek of a siren, and a Lake Patrol boat roared past him and into the fray.

The man at the controls was none other than Michael's "favorite" Department of Natural Resources Officer, "Picky" Piccard. As the patrol boat slowed, easing into the gap left between the receding fishing boats, Piccard's partner bent over the bow to retrieve the now waterlogged but still thrashing combatants.

Gripped by the neck of his shirt, the first warrior within reach was yanked free of his adversary's clasp only to have the contender slip below the water. Ripping free of the rescuer's grip, the first miscreant swam several hard strokes, dove underwater, and brought the sputtering co-combatant to the surface.

Once safely in the patrol boat and shrouded in orange blankets, the semi-drowned rats re-engaged in their argument. Piccard sat banging his forehead on the top of the steering wheel while his partner, a huge grin spreading across his face, stood next to Piccard in the boat's cockpit.

As the argument, sprinkled liberally with obscenities, increased in intensity, Piccard lifted his head and audibly sighed. Rising from the captain's chair, he took a deep breath and bellowed "SHUT THE HELL UP!"

Both men, as well as waterfowl bobbing near the shore, fell silent. Michael was impressed by Piccard's capacity to affect change and thought it likely anyone out-of-doors between Pocahontas Point and the nearby community of Milford had also followed the edict to "Shut the hell up!"

***

Michael followed the DNR officers with one boat in tow and the other behind Michael. Even as he followed, he could see Piccard gesturing and berating the two semi-drowned hooligans. He had recognized one of them as Weird Willy, but did not know the other man.

As they approached the Gull Point Lake Patrol Station, Michael watched a Dickinson County Sheriff's Interceptor park in the lot and the driver step out and stroll down to the long T-shaped dock that formed part of the Lake Patrol facility.

Michael waited until the patrol and the boat it was towing were both secured, then slowly eased up alongside the dock. Piccard's assistant tied the second confiscated boat to the first and helped Michael lash his boat to the dock. Pointing at the boat Willy was using, he said, "That doesn't look good."

That was when Michael first noticed "Property of Sports Shop" emblazoned on the bow.

Both men could have been ticketed and released with a possible admonition of "go home and no more fishing today," but Michael was surprised to see both men put into handcuffs and loaded into the Deputy's Interceptor.

The exchange completed, Piccard strode the dock to his boat, leading Willy's dog, Boxer, on a makeshift leash. Michael pointed at the Interceptor and asked, "What is that about?"

"It seems Willy took some liberty with a missing boat he said he found in the slough by his place this morning. He claims it must have drifted in overnight, and he was on his way to return it when he got into an argument with Charley Chen. Those lame brains are going to kill each other if someone doesn't do something."

"Handcuffing and hauling them to the Law Center seems a bit much."

"Normally, that would be true, but the FBI wants to question them both. It seems the boat Willy was using has some connection with that missing retired FBI agent. I've been ordered to leave the boat tied up to the Lake Patrol's dock. I expect someone with more letters in their title will want to go over the boat with a fine-toothed comb."

"Sounds serious."

"Above my pay grade. I'm just trying to keep those lame brains from killing each other or endangering other boaters."

"To borrow a phrase, 'What's the beef?'," Michael asked with a corny smile.

"Willy's complaining Charley always poaches his best fishing spots. Charley works on *Maximilian*, that big, ugly beast of an excursion boat, and Willy says *Maximilian* is bad for fishing and the environment. He calls Charley a pervert because he goes to the Bikers' Bar, Spokes and Suds, and orders what he calls fairy water. Daiquiris. Willy claims Charley wants to talk up the owner, Shirley, and admire her charms, front and back, when he's got a perfectly good wife at home. Now, Charley complains that Willy doesn't own the lake and isn't the only one who knows how to fish, accuses Willy of using live bait instead of lures, and is a dirty old man who thinks the Bikers' Bar's owner and manager is his girlfriend. I get the impression that Willy and Shirley may be an item."

"I never considered Willy to be so possessive."

"Territorial, as in fishing, yes, but a girlfriend is a new one on me."

"So what happens now?"

"I'd say that is up to the FBI and whether they believe Willy. Funny thing, as much as Willy gossips, most of what he blabs about has some truth to it."

"Yeah, I remember our experience with that."

"So, what are you doing out in a fishing boat among all the summer daytime nut jobs?"

"I had a funny notion that I could relive a tradition of my youth, enjoy a relaxing day of fishing by myself, anywhere I wanted to fish."

"Ha! Better to wait until after Labor Day."

Michael smiled. "That's what Connie told me. I won't tell you what my sister said."

Piccard smiled, a rarity during business hours. "Good advice. By the way, Willy wants you to take care of his dog while he's inconvenienced." With that, Piccard handed Michael the leash, and the dog leaped aboard, sat down mid-ship, tongue lolling from its mouth, and stared at Michael. Michael could have sworn Boxer was smiling.

"Stay safe, Counselor." With that, Piccard untied and climbed into the Lake Patrol boat. He hit the starter, backed from the dock, turned the bow toward the northern shore, opened up all 115 horses, and went from hole to plane in seconds.

19

Whether a coincidence or an unappreciated sign from the poltergeist of his twin brother, Gabriel, Michael decided with a dog on board, the spectacle of two older men trying to walk on water to duke it out, and the general risk extant by the profusion of competing boaters, it was time to head back to his home port. But first, he turned to the dog. "Hey, Boxer, are you hungry?" The large, mix-breed Labrador passenger barked sharply, eagerly wagging and banging his tail against the side of the boat.

"Me, too. Let's pick up something at the 5Bs and chill out on their deck."

The funky old 5Bs was a throwback to a simpler place and time. From the ancient out-of-use gas pump at the dock and the rickety steps up the hillside to the unimproved exterior, the 5Bs was a stubborn dissenter to the surrounding veneration of fast and temporary.

Billy Cass was the building's original owner, but since he couldn't run the business in his usual drunken state, he had sold half-interest to his part-time girlfriend, Betty. Considerably more the entrepreneur,

Betty had remodeled the malodorous dump into a diner that sold beer and bait. When Betty changed the name to Bill and Betty's Beer, Bait, and Bagels, it was more than Billy could tolerate, and he sulked off to a liquor bottle except when he occasionally sobered enough for carnal visits.

The enterprise was a huge success. Besides a prime location, it was the only place on the Lakes where one could stop for bagels, locally-sourced cream cheese, great breakfast and lunch fare, handmade hash browns, mouthwatering gravy, and still get fresh bait and cold beer to go.

Billy and Betty were retired, and their daughter, Veronica, ran the business. The fruit had fallen near the tree, and Veronica's only deviation was to take down the original hand-painted sign and replace it with "The 5Bs." Below was a smaller sign that read: "Don't mess with perfection!"

At the counter, a blond, scraggly, bearded young man took Michael's order for two cheeseburgers, a side of hash browns with gravy, and a glass of beer. With his glass of beer in hand, Michael led Boxer out to a table on the deck.

Thirsty after his morning adventures, he was interrupted mid-sip by a familiar voice. "Hey, Michael! Here's your order. Two burgers, one with extra patty, and a bowl of water for your dog."

Michael broke into a broad smile. "Hello, Veronica. Wie gehts?"

Familiar with a game of greetings used by Michael and his friends, Veronica responded, "The gate's fine, but the fence is down. How ya doin', and who's your friend?"

"I'm good. I'm dog-sitting. This is Boxer, whose owner is temporarily a guest compliments of the Dickinson County Sheriff. Long story. How are your folks?"

"Still ornery, but as long as Billy stays away from the booze, they live together in a state of truce."

"And your daughter?"

"Growing up too fast. Hey, Michael, you get around. What's up with the missing FBI agent, the one that was staying at the Lodge? Was he the one who showed up in pieces?"

Michael, hardly for the first time, was impressed with the speed at which gossip traveled and morphed as it was shared. "I don't know. What have you heard?"

Veronica appeared disappointed. "Oh, not much. Mostly what I read in the paper. Couple customers were talking about it earlier today, and one of the local cops came in for coffee. He said the FBI was all up in the Lodge's business but said he didn't know why."

Michael had a good idea who had the loose lips, but before he could ask, from inside there was a loud shout. "Order up!"

"I swear, sometimes I think that blond dork thinks he owns the place. If he wasn't so cheap, I'd fire him. Gotta go. See ya soon, I hope."

He caught himself watching her lovely beam sail away.

Michael and Boxer snarfed down their burgers, Michael's dressed with onion and pickles, hold the lettuce and tomato, and Boxer's with double meat, no trash. Boxer washed it down with the bowl of water—thank you, Veronica—while Michael enjoyed his rare noontime glass of beer.

Glad for the oversize umbrella shading his table, Michael was content for the moment to sit and watch the spectacle of varied watercraft that motored past and under the nearby bridge that spanned and marked the divide between West and East Okoboji. He was slightly annoyed when his mobile phone vibrated for attention. Michael recognized the number of the Sheriff's Office, and Boxer spread out in comfort under the table, managed to raise his ears when asked, "Now what?"

"Hello. Michael?" said the voice on the other end of the line.

"Speaking."

"This is Delores, Sheriff Conrad's PA. The Sheriff asked me to let you know Willy DeWeerd claims you are his lawyer and demands that you be called before he answers any more questions."

"Well, that's news to me. Has he been charged with something?"

"No, but an agent from the FBI is here and very interested in how Willy came by the boat that was missing from the Sports Shop. Detective Donahue was interviewing Willy, but when the FBI agent showed up, Willy expressed his opinion on Federal Law Enforcement in terms disagreeable to the agent, and Willy is now cooling his jets in a holding cell."

Michael sighed. Having dealt with Willy in the past, he understood there was a thin line that divided agreeable and angry. "Okay. What does Connie want me to do?"

"Sheriff Conrad believes Detective Donahue can still have a productive interview with Mr. DeWeerd if you are present and without the agent in question."

Silence lingered following Delores's pronouncement. Whatever Connie had in mind, Delores's message was clear. Sheriff Conrad was not only her boss, but to Delores, he was also atop the pyramid of respect in law enforcement. Michael was expected to react at once.

Tempting as it was to leave Willy on his own, it occurred to Michael that he was idling in the shade watching boats go by and would soon be bored with the repetition. It was not a great imposition to see what Willy expected. Michael tolerated Boxer, too, but had no design on extending this responsibility. Besides, Michael was curious to know what Willy had to say about the missing boat and perhaps learn why, besides loyalty to its own, the FBI was so intensely interested in the case.

"Michael, are you there?"

"Yes. Sorry, Delores. I just finished lunch at the 5Bs. Tell Connie and Detective Donahue I'll be there shortly."

Willy had finished lunch provided by the jail's kitchen staff, and with Michael's arrival, he agreed to an interview with Detective Donahue. Donahue shared that Charley had been questioned and released, but the FBI was interested in Willy and the boat he said he'd found. Willy was still damp, but his hygiene improved through his unplanned dip in the lake.

"I'll talk to Jack but not that twelve-year-old twerp from the FBI." Even to Michael, the federal agent disparaged by Willy appeared unusually young, likely someone new to the Bureau. Confronted by Willy's agitation and adamant refusal to cooperate, the agent agreed to observe from outside the room.

Michael sat in as Donahue conducted the interview and was impressed, not for the first time, by Donahue's skill when interviewing a subject. By the end of the interview, Willy's answers to Jack's questions were credible and Willy had become chatty. Further questions posed a risk of Willy spinning off into one of his many conspiracy and philosophical orations on the decay of western civilization and on the increase of debauchery that damned the human race in general.

Before Willy could catch a verbal tailwind, Jack concluded the interview with a reminder there may be more questions, but for now, Willy was free to go pending charges by the Sports Shop.

"No problemo. Ol' Nigel and I are good buddies. Just remind him I was on my way to return his boat when 'Charley Chan' attacked me."

Donahue just shook his head. "Ah, yeah, whatever. Just stay out of trouble, and if you find another unclaimed boat, leave it where it is and call Lake Patrol or the Sheriff's office."

Ignoring the warning, Willy turned to Michael. "You got my dog?"

"We shared lunch. He's in your holding cell enjoying whatever snacks the staff has been feeding him."

"Good. You can give us both a ride home."

***

Michael's time in the car with Willy, as they drove to the ramshackle shack he considered his little slice of paradise, was another chapter in what had become a bizarre day. The long dirt driveway with its jarring potholes and teeth-rattling washboard did little to interrupt the flow of near-sighted philosophy, factually challenged opinions, and profanity directed at politicians and their moneyed overseers, whose mission, if Michael could sort it out, was to destroy the republic and weaken the greatest military force in the world, all for their own gain. Who it was and how it would be to their gain, was not addressed. Knowing a bit about Willy's recreational habits, it occurred to Michael that his talkative companion might be in need of something calming. But on arrival, Willy declared, "Well that's enough about uncivilized civilization. Come on in, Counselor, and we'll talk serious. How 'bout a cup of Kenya Double A?"

A bit of a coffee-hound, Michael had not had a cup since early morning and his thermos was still in his boat. Michael remembered the excellent coffee Willy had served him on a former visit. Besides, after his latest rant, he wondered what Willy considered serious. Turning off the engine, Michael answered, "I'd like that." But Willy was already climbing out of the vehicle and with Boxer trotting alongside, striding to the cabin. Stopping on the porch, he turned, gestured, and called out, "Well, come on. Don't be shy."

Seated in the same wobbly captain's chair as on a previous visit, Michael observed that the cabin's interior remained as he recalled, a varied, resplendent collection of discarded living brought back to life for Willy's modest needs. A kerosene lantern rested on the well-worn wooden table while a light bulb dangled by its cord from the ceiling. Hidden in the nearby woods, the source for the long line of sagging electrical wire was suspect, but not a curiosity Michael wanted to explore. The leaky hot water heater, no worse nor better for wear, remained in the utility/mud room, and a well-used speckled blue-and-white coffee pot rested on the ancient iron stove. The room was overly warm and stuffy, made more so by the pungent olfactory residue of the host's attempts to self-medicate the effects of service in Vietnam.

In spite of his long limbs, Willy moved about with a smooth purpose born of early habit. His face was out-of-doors, with a burned, leathery appearance, splintering into innumerable creases when he laughed or grew enraged. A scar high on the forehead made more prominent as black-gray hair receded, suggested a question that would go unasked. Willy was wearing his usual attire of faded overalls, today accompanied by a t-shirt that declared, "Kilroy Ain't Here." He stood tall, with no concession to time, his bony shoulders easily bearing the straps of his overalls and history. Congenial for the moment, there was a rough presence about him, a potential hardness better left unchallenged.

Michael thought it interesting they shared a coffee preference and watched as Willy, in spite of broad hands and fingers like sausages, delicately filled the small, white grinder and milled the beans to his liking. He filled the spotted pot from the leaky faucet, and perhaps with some consideration for his guest's time and comfort, he lit a propane-fueled cooking ring rather than the wood stove. In anticipation, Willy took two "4K Construction" gimme cups from hooks on the wall, blew off possible dust, and placed them onto the table as he sat down across from Michael.

Willy bowed his head and went silent for a few seconds. When he looked up, his face appeared doleful and moisture formed at the corners of his eyes, threatening to fill the adjoining crinkles. "Some people think I hate Charley, but I don't. He's a good man. Charley's too good a man to be messing with that god-awful boat and the slimy bastard who owns it. Charley should be fishing and hunting and with his woman, not screwing around with stuff that destroys our beautiful lakes. That Farley fart-head…Sorry, I usually use worse words, but I respect your tender ears. …that shit-head Farley *(oops)* doesn't care about the Lakes or about people. He just cares about money."

"Who and what boat are we talking about?"

"You know, that oversized casino boat disguised as a cruiser for tourists."

"I don't think anyone has a casino license in the Lakes Area, on or off a boat."

"You just wait. You can bet the fix is in and that scum bag is kissing every fat ass from here to Des Moines to get that license."

"I'm confused. Are we talking about Charley or someone else?"

"Both! Charley is one hell of an engineer. He likes to tinker with stuff and *Maximilian* is the biggest new toy on the lake. Charley takes care of the engine and drive train for that beast."

While they talked, Boxer patiently sat on his haunches, moving his head back and forth from one speaker to another, acting as an interested observer. He stood, crossed the room, and laid his head on Willy's lap. Willy gave Boxer's head a gentle stroke and addressed his canine companion with a tenderness in contrast to the day's earlier events. "I'm forgetting my duties, ain't I, old pal?"

Willy stood, retrieved and filled Boxer's food and water bowls, and set them in their intended place near the doorway to the mud room. Boxer eagerly began lapping water and although recently fed, soon shifted his attention to the accompanying bowl of dog food. With that task complete, Willy recovered the coffee cups.

"Let's check the coffee." Pouring a small amount into a cup, he proclaimed, "Close enough," and filled each cup near to overflowing. With the first sip, Michael found the flavor as he remembered. Smiling at Willy he said, "Ambrosia."

Willy gently blew across the surface, then took a tentative taste of his cup of coffee, sat back with satisfaction, and returned Michael's smile. "I do like my coffee."

They sat silently, sharing a pleasant moment. Finally, Willy set his cup down and inhaled, held, then released a big breath, as if he had come to a decision.

Willy began to ramble on about not liking changes and how he had lived all his life around the Lakes except for his government-paid vacation to Vietnam. He knew time brought change but resented the kinds of things he'd seen at the Ridge Top Nightclub, the nearby motel, and now a huge floating monstrosity, the *Maximilian*.

"We don't need the casino people. They just bring trouble. I like that lady that owns the Lodge. She don't need a casino, but if anyone gets it, I hope she does. She'll do it right. She needs a break after that drug-dealing s.o.b. she had as a husband. And now the old FBI guy goes missing, body parts start showing up, and you know it's him."

"How do you know?"

"Early morning, me and Boxer were checking out the dumpsters by the Lodge and saw him load a bunch of diving gear into one of the Sport Shop's boats. I was curious, so I watched him until he anchored his boat down the bay just offshore, not far from the Lodge. He put out that funny little flag that divers use. I know it was him." Michael sipped his coffee. "Did you tell the FBI Agent or Jack Donahue what you saw?"

"Nah."

"Why not?"

"They didn't ask, and I'm not going to help them dig me into a hole."

Michael nodded. Looking around the room, he asked, "What else did you see?"

"I don't know." Willy blushed slightly and paused to clear his throat. "I promised my boss I'd help tend bar for the noon crowd, so I left. Last I saw, he was fine, sitting in the boat, fussing with something."

"And today, you show up with his boat?"

"It was the Sports Shop's boat. I didn't know he'd rented that one. Man, you should have heard that FBI piss-ant tie into me about the boat and what had I done and I was in big trouble for screwing up the evidence and all the kinds of bullshit he was going to do to me. I told him to eff off and a few other things. I respect our local law folks, even Picky Piccard on a good day, but the Feds can kiss my bony ass and Boxer's furry ass, too."

Watered and overfed, Boxer had resumed a watchful position, but at the sound of his name, he expressed his opinion with a loud "Woof!" Michael glanced at him and would have sworn the dog was smiling.

"What else did the FBI agent say?"

"Not much. I pissed him off and Donahue dragged me out, well sort of, and put me in the holding cell to cool off. I think he was annoyed at the agent too."

"Why's that?"

"He didn't lock the cell and he asked me if I was hungry. I said, 'Does a bear defecate among the trees?' He laughed, then went to ask that nice young receptionist if she would call down to the kitchen and get me something to eat. You heard most of it after that."

"I did, but I wondered why Jack asked you about the Ridge Top Nightclub? What did that have to do with the boat?"

"Beats me. That was unexpected. I think that was a FBI guy question."

"Why do you think that?"

"Well, Shirley told me all about an older guy who came into the bar one evening. He had a couple of beers and showed Shirl a picture of this foreign girl. Shirl thought she was Chinese and wanted to know if she had seen her before. Shirl told him she wasn't sure but there was only one Asian woman, as far as she could remember, who had been in the bar recently. She came in with some guy. They were having a good time, had a couple of beers, and left together."

"Could Shirley describe the guy the Asian woman was with?"

"That's what this guy asked." Willy took a sip of coffee, and as he lowered his cup, his eyes took on a faraway look. Knowing a bit of his history, Michael was unsure how far back Willy had gone in time but drank a bit of coffee and quietly waited.

After a moment of silence, Willy continued. "Sorry. What did you say?"

"I wondered if Shirley remembered what the guy the woman was with looked like."

Willy nodded his head, stood up, retrieved the blue pot, and recharged their coffee cups. Resettling in his place, Willy was more subdued than usual, taking his time, distant. Michael wondered whether Willy was in a fog and trying to remember or if he was sorting out what and how much to share.

Finally, he said, "Shirley said the guy was young, almost femme, if you know what I mean. Long, blondish hair, good tan, taller than the girl by half a head, seemed quiet but with a nice laugh, and wore a jacket, sorta like you'd wear riding a motorcycle."

Michael was surprised the description was so detailed. Suddenly in interrogator mode, Michael wondered if Willy knew more than he was willing to share. "Anything else?"

"Nah. That was about it. He left a business card and asked her to call if she saw the girl again or heard anything. He started to leave, then came back and asked Shirley if she knew anything about the Ridge Top Nightclub. Shirl asked him what that had to do with the missing girl, and he said probably nothing. He was just curious. He said he used to vacation on Okoboji and hadn't noticed it before."

Michael waited, but Willy seemed to be done. "Why didn't you tell Jack about this?"

"Are you kidding? I'd still be sitting there. Besides, he didn't ask. Now, you can't tell anyone, right? I mean you're my confidential lawyer."

Michael again paused. Finally, he said, "Okay, let's have an agreement. I'll help you, but you have to help me and tell me anything more you may learn that concerns the retired missing agent. I may have to share the info with Jack, but I'll say it was from a confidential source. Will that work for you?"

Willy squinted his eyes, stroked his unshaven face, then broke into a big grin. "I'm a confidential source? Like undercover, right? Do I get paid?"

Michael laughed. "No, but you get an excellent lawyer's help, pro bono."

"All right! Anything more I learn about the retired missing agent. I can live with that. Let me top off these cups one more time."

With cups again recharged, Michael remained silent, in listening mode. As much as he liked to talk, he knew silence often elicited information that might have otherwise gone unshared, and Willy was not prone to long periods of silence.

"I really did find the boat in the slough near my place. It was out of gas, so I gassed it up, and since it was my gas, I decided I could fish my way over to the Sports Shop."

"I heard you say that. Jack asked you if there was anything left in the boat. Between you and me, was there anything you might have overlooked or forgotten about?"

"Nope. Just a boat and motor. I think someone else borrowed it, used it till it ran out of gas, and took whatever was left."

"You didn't tell Jack that."

"I didn't need to. He's a smart fella. He'll figure it out. Besides, the FBI was listening in, and I didn't want to give him anything to use against me."

"Is there anything else I should know?"

"Probably, but that's all for now. I'll let you know if I think of anything. You got my number, right?"

That was one of those curiosities about Willy. An old shack filled with discarded furniture but he had an up-to-date smartphone. That was a surprise Michael learned from an earlier experience. "Yes, I do. And you have mine."

With that, Michael stood, the chair sounding a complaint as it scraped against the rough board floor, and held out his hand. Willy's large mitt nearly engulfed Michael's, but thankfully, his grip was gentle. As he stepped out onto the porch, Michael stopped, considered something, and without turning back, said, "You know, Willy, that FBI agent is probably getting a warrant right now to search your place. I'm not saying there's anything to be found, but should there be something unrelated to the case, it may be better if it was somewhere less likely to be a problem."

With a big guffaw, Willy slapped Michael on the back, and exclaimed, "Why Counselor, I don't know what you're talking about!"

As he climbed into his car, Michael waved at Bess, Willy's beloved old draft horse watching at a rail of the makeshift corral. As he drove out of the driveway, Michael was left smiling over their final exchange but with an uneasy feeling that Willy might have snookered him.

21

With the agreement to continue to teach at ILCC came the need for Michael to organize and prepare for his new classes. Galen had called and arranged to meet with Michael this morning to share syllabi and class notes and determine what else Michael might need to do to prepare. Galen was well-organized, and his notes addressed expected goals and outcomes that were listed in the curriculum guide. The material was familiar, but the educational jargon and tasking—sequence, expected outcomes, documenting progress—was uncharted territory.

In spite of this, Michael's confidence improved as he began to understand what Galen had provided. Galen's course outlines, enhanced by Michael's real-life experiences, suggested an enriched experience for students. Any doubt he may have held faded away. This next step in his life was doable, and Michael felt excited to take on this new challenge. He had a month to prepare, easy peasy, and they assigned him a larger office and a better parking space.

Having completed an overview, Galen excused himself and as he left, promised to be responsive to any questions. Eagerly, Michael began to read through the voluminous material of the classes he would teach. As he read, he wrote down his thoughts on a fresh legal pad. What he wrote would be reviewed, revised, and prioritized several times—standard operating procedure for Michael—before any changes or additions would be considered.

Midway through the first syllabus, his smartphone chimed the opening chorus to "Margaritaville." His annoyance faded when his screen identified the caller as Sheriff Conrad.

"Buenos días, Connie. How's the wide world of law enforcement?"

"The banditos are winning."

"I hope not."

"Have you recovered from your day of misadventures on the lake?"

"You mean day, less by half. My largest catch was two old farts attacking each other while trying to walk on water."

Connie chuckled. "Yeah, I heard about that. I think the FBI agent was considering Willy his break in the case until he listened to a couple of hours of Willy-jabber. Man, Willy has two talking speeds—nonstop or none."

"So I've noticed. Before you ask, I haven't called Janni, but when I do, I'll pass along your request for us to talk to Jeremy and Amy."

"Glad to know that, but I'm calling about another possible conversation."

Connie was plain-spoken, not given to the mysterious, so it was unusual for him to ask to meet at Michael's home at 1 p.m. and provide no explanation. "Is there anything I should be aware of?"

"Not at this point."

"Should I have a lawyer present?"

"You are a lawyer."

"Yes, but you know what they say."

"You do not need a lawyer present. In fact, I would counsel

against it."

"Should I prepare refreshments?"

"Coffee would be appropriate. Nothing else is necessary. This likely will not be a long visit. That's all I can say for now. I'll see you at one."

***

Michael had ground the coffee beans and was at his kitchen sink filling the carafe with water when Connie, in his personal pickup truck followed by a long, black sedan with heavily tinted windows, pulled into the driveway. A large, burly man emerged from behind the wheel of the sedan, donned a dark blue blazer, closed his car door, and stepped back to open the backseat passenger door. A few words were exchanged, and the passenger stepped out.

Michael hardly noticed Connie exit his truck. He poured water into the coffee maker, pushed the button to brew, and rushed to the door.

"Governor Dirksen, what a surprise! Please come in. Hi, Connie!"

While the governor shook Michael's hand, his large driver/bodyguard brushed by Michael for a quick reconnoiter to assure there were no issues, human or device. "All clear!"

"Thank you, Michael. Sorry about the circumstances, but you'll soon understand."

"That's quite alright. The coffee should be ready in a few minutes. Why don't we go to the living room?"

"Great, and if you don't mind, may we sit in the dining room? I have some pictures and information to show you. It might be easier at the table."

"Sure, right in here." Michael extended his hand and greeting to the large man standing next to the governor. His greeting was not shared but evoked a hard stare from the man with a bulge in the blazer from likely a large handgun slung under the shoulder.

"It's okay, Cliff. I'll be fine."

"Yes sir." But Cliff followed a few steps behind and stood near as the governor sat down at the head of the dining room table with Connie on his right and Michael on the left.

"The coffee does smell good. Ate a sandwich in the car—steamed chicken breast on multi-grain bread, light mayo, and some sort of diet fruit drink. My wife's idea. She thinks I need to improve my diet and lower my stress level. We left Des Moines early, made two official stops, and have two more stops besides this one before we return to the capital. Some business is better done in person. You wouldn't happen to have some cookies or something to go with the coffee? Your mother used to make great cookies."

Michael smiled. "Coming right up." Fortunately, sister Madge had made a point of supplying Michael with cookies, homemade rolls, and the occasional pie, all baked according to his mother's recipes. Michael retrieved his sister's cookies from the freezer and hit thaw on the microwave. The coffee was nearly done. *Close enough. The Gov probably could use a little extra jolt of caffeine.*

By the time he had taken down four matching mugs *(thank you, Mother, for leaving hospitable dishes)* and filled an insulated carafe with coffee, the cookies were thawed. He carefully carried the tray of spoons, cookies, small plates, napkins, condiments, and coffee to the table. He filled and passed out cups of coffee accompanied by small dishes. Michael left the tray in the middle of the table and invited everyone to help themselves. Speaking for the first time since his signal of all-clear, Cliff, in a surprisingly high tenor voice, politely declined.

Following polite chit-chat about families and the weather, two cookies and a refill of coffee, the governor spread his hands wide, complimented Michael on his hospitality, and announced it was time for business. Cliff stepped forward and handed Governor Dirksen a tan, soft-sided briefcase. Dirksen withdrew from the briefcase several thick folders and spread an array of pictures out on the table while Cliff stepped back and remained silent and alert.

Looking directly at Michael, Governor Dirksen asked, "You heard of the retired FBI agent who went missing while vacationing at The Lodge on Okoboji?"

"Yes."

"What do you know about the case?"

Michael hesitated, considering whether to share and interpret Willy's ramblings, then decided not to. "Not much. Mostly what I've read in the paper."

"Have you and Sheriff Conrad talked about it?"

Michael looked over at Connie, who was sitting across the table from Michael. He appeared stoic and non-communicative. "Only in passing. No specifics other than Sheriff Conrad is getting heat from both the news media and the FBI."

Governor Dirksen added, "And me."

Michael leaned back in his chair and waited.

Taking and releasing a large breath, the governor continued. "What happened to Agent Smith is on me. Many years ago, I had the honor of meeting and escorting a delegation from China on a tour of our state. What was initially a visit to learn more about agriculture became a long-term relationship between China and Iowa. It was also the beginning of a personal friendship between your governor and several people in the Chinese delegation, most of whom have risen to positions of varying prominence in the Chinese government."

Governor Dirksen hesitated, studied the diminished number of cookies on the tray, then continued. "I recently received a call from one of my friends who is concerned about a young Chinese woman who is attending Iowa State University. Her father is involved in research at the University but is back in China for the summer while her mother remains in Ames with the children. While their daughter visited some university friends in Okoboji, she disappeared. We're considering her a missing person, but she is very independent-minded and may have done something foolish. As you can imagine, the family is very worried, and we are all interested in finding her without causing a major incident. The family is related to someone of importance in China, and the call I received was to ask if it was possible to investigate quietly without attracting attention. Subsequently, I called upon my long-time friend, retired FBI Agent Smith, to spend some time in Okoboji and quietly see what he may learn. Howard has had a great deal of experience and success investigating human trafficking. It would appear Agent Smith may have learned of something or was at risk to learn something others did not want to be revealed. It may be about the missing woman, or he may have stumbled onto something entirely unrelated."

Michael was listening intently. "Something unrelated? Like what?"

The governor grimaced slightly and nodded his head in response to the interruption. "As I was about to say, the FBI has shared that in cooperation with Immigration and the National Security Agency, they have an ongoing investigation in the Lakes Area into a criminal organization dealing with kidnapping, human trafficking, prostitution, and extortion."

In spite of the governor's displeasure, Michael exclaimed, "Here in the Lakes Area? That sound's like something found in a big city, not in rural Iowa."

It was Connie who responded. "Don't kid yourself. Between Memorial Day and Labor Day, we have thousands of visitors. With that addition to our permanent residents, that's a lot of people with money and a thirst for entertainment. There's always someone who will take advantage of the opportunity to provide what some people want and even expect." He tapped a finger on the table top for emphasis. "The sort of crime you may see in Minneapolis, Kansas City, or Chicago, and even in Sioux Falls and Des Moines, are right here in our community. Remember what you just experienced at the Lodge."

The governor stared at Connie with the same appearance of disapproval given to Michael. "Right. Thank you, Sheriff Conrad. If I may continue, right now there is a mishmash of agencies flailing about, trying to determine if Agent Smith's demise is related in any way to the ongoing federal investigation. Complicating matters, and I don't know if you're aware of this, this past Monday, a young woman's body was discovered in a very disturbing state in a Spencer junkyard. Her body has been transported along with the junked car in which she was found, to the state lab in Ankeny. The autopsy is complicated, and it will be some time before it's finished. The cause of death is unknown. What we do know is that the young woman is Asian. My friend in China and the missing women's family have not been informed of this development. The autopsy should determine whether this is our missing person. If not, it may be a victim of human trafficking."

"The Spencer Police and Iowa Department of Criminal Investigation are cooperating and have determined it is likely that the young woman's body was brought to the junkyard last Saturday for disposal. We know who brought the body, so have an APB out to arrest three individuals of interest. You can imagine what a disaster this will become should the body found last Saturday turn out to be our missing woman. And if it is not our missing woman, we still need to find her, and to do so under the radar. Michael, I'm afraid I may be putting you in the same danger as Agent Smith, but this is a personal request. Will you please continue Agent Smith's investigation?"

Before allowing Michael time to respond, Governor Dirksen continued. "The family of the missing woman and the friend and family she was visiting here in Okoboji have been thoroughly vetted and interviewed. They have not been able to shed any light on where she went, but we do know she met some new people her age and one of the new friends, a young man, also is unaccounted for. They met at a local bar and evidently hit it off pretty well. Nothing is known about him—no name, no picture. We don't think he was local. Likely just passing through. If they are together, we don't know where they've gone. Without giving away too much information, we have a nationwide alert and added she may be with a young man, early twenties, tall, blondish hair, and good-looking, according to witnesses. We have a composite sketch of the man, but it's pretty generic. Her friend reported he rode a cool motorcycle. Said it looked old, had a sidecar, and was painted powder blue. Powder blue! Hard to believe we haven't been able to find it."

The governor paused to take a sip of coffee, glancing over the rim to see if Connie or Michael had anything to say. Satisfied his listeners were appropriately subdued, he put down the cup and picked up the largest folder. Handing it to Michael, he said, "This is everything made available to me concerning the investigation into our missing woman and Agent Smith's murder. And I do consider Agent Smith to have been murdered. I knew him well. We went back a long time. He was in excellent health and much too experienced to have a diving accident. You may not learn any more than Agent Smith, but you grew up in the area and know the locals. You also have your extensive network of friends and colleagues, the so-called Marauders. With you and Sheriff Conrad and his deputies working the case, we may be able to sort out this mess."

The governor drew out a small packet of business cards from the breast pocket of his suit jacket, wrote on the back of one, and handed it to Michael. "The name and the phone number I added to the back of my card is the liaison between you and me. He answers only to me, and he will see to it you receive any resources you need. Sheriff Conrad will be apprised of everything that is learned. Let me know if you decide not to take up this task. I understand if you cannot, but I would consider it an important personal favor if you could. I look forward to hearing from you."

Michael had been surprised with the arrival of the governor, but the significance of his request was stunning. "Governor, I can't promise I'll learn anything more, and I'm sure the FBI has a far greater presence in this matter, but I'll do everything I can to help you and assist law enforcement."

"Good. I knew I could depend on you. Now, believe it or not, I'm on my way to visit a cattle yard in Sioux County. As if there wasn't enough manure coming out of the capital! Thank you, Michael. Your father and I were close friends. He often spoke fondly of you and Connie. I know you miss him, and I do as well. Stay in touch. Let me know if you need anything."

Rising, Governor Dirksen shook hands with Michael and Connie, retrieved his briefcase, and took his leave, but not before using the restroom and accepting a cup of coffee to go along with a baggie of cookies.

Michael followed Governor Dirksen to the car, shook hands, watched as Cliff backed the large sedan out of the driveway, and waved as the governor drove off. In the kitchen, Connie was putting dishes and cups into the dishwasher.

"Well, now what?" Michael asked.

"Don't ask me. Your dad was pals with the Gov, and since he's no longer with us, it appears our governor considers you the family proxy."

"I don't do politics."

"Yeah, right! Michael, this is about more than politics, and protestations aside, your principles and many of mine are influenced, if not predicated upon, a good deal of political expediency. In this case, expediency aside, accept Governor Dirksen at face value, and let's do what we can to find this young woman. Who knows? Maybe we'll learn more in the process about why the FBI is up in arms."

"The FBI is frustrated because they lost one of their own and publicly can't blame the governor. Agent Smith was retired and acting as his good friend, and the governor was acting at the behest of his longtime Chinese friends."

"I'm not so sure. I've been working with Special Agent Kaufmann. He's a cut above standard-issue FBI and seems willing to cooperate. If we make it clear our only interest is finding the woman, the FBI may be more forthcoming or at least give us some space. Besides, if we find her, it might help in whatever they're investigating."

Michael paused, and something ticked in his mind. "How much do you know about, as you say, whatever the FBI is investigating?"

Now Connie paused and considered the governor's instructions. "Well, you know how it is—give and take. We give and they take. However, Kaufmann did confirm that the FBI and likely some other alphabet agencies are involved in an ongoing investigation in the Lakes Region. The case of the missing ex-agent provided them a cover to the public for their overt presence but forced them to deal with us in their investigation. If the Gov is right, and the FBI is looking into human trafficking, prostitution, and all the rest, then the disappearance of retired Agent Smith has really complicated matters."

"I don't know anything about money laundering or extortion, but every summer, the same issues reemerge and at the end of the tourist season, fade away again. Why is this different?"

"The difference, again according to Special Agent Kaufmann, is the increase in activity and level of sophistication. The FBI has been following a larger organization intent on setting up a permanent presence in the Lakes Area. It's the early stages, but Kaufmann said the FBI thinks there are plans to use area businesses for money laundering, either by extortion or outright ownership. We certainly saw evidence of that potential with the mess at the Lodge. As I understand it, criminal organizations are looking for smaller markets with less Fed scrutiny, and the Lakes Region may be a prime target. Supposedly, we 'hicks in the sticks' won't notice. Thanks to our nearby highways, the Lakes Region is accessible to just about anyone and already acts as a nexus for the distribution of products and services between larger cities. Tourism and a large number of transients play a part, as well."

"You make it sound like a criminal version of Amazon."

"Sorry, but I agree with the Feds on this. There is a snake in our little slice of paradise, and if we don't do something about it now, it will be a greater problem in the future. Even my department has heard of possible human trafficking in our area. We don't have enough personnel or resources, especially in the summer season, to focus in-depth on one issue. All the more reason why we need interagency cooperation."

"And all the more reason to find our missing Chinese student. Heaven forbid she's been scooped up by some pimp or trafficker. You work your FBI Special Agent, and I'll review the information the governor gave us. After that, I'll retrace as much of the work done by Agent Smith as I can."

"That's a start. Keep me up to date on what you learn. The Gov's guy is going to be on my case every day."

***

Michael's mind was a snarl of competing thoughts. It was time for his version of Organization 101. Going to the study, he opened the bottom drawer of his desk and pulled out several legal pads. On the first page of each, and in no particular order, he wrote a single subject—ILCC classes, Missing Woman/Agent Smith, Jeremy and Emily, Janni, and Governor Dirksen/the Feds. He posted each pad on a clipboard hanging from a nail on the wall behind his desk. It was not an elegant system.

Satisfied, he opened the thick folder Dirksen had given him and carefully read the background information provided on the missing woman, Lei Ming, and her family, followed by the detailed intelligence of a variety of officials investigating her disappearance. Michael was disappointed when he read the reports Agent Smith had sent to the Governor. Smith had found little to add to what already was known. But Agent Smith's notes and memos as saved and downloaded from his computer were impressive. Smith was exceptionally detailed in what he wrote, and as any good agent should, he accounted for everything even remotely helpful he came across, whether it may prove relevant or not.

Among his entries, Agent Smith had a list of people he had interviewed. To Michael, one name stood out by its absence: Iowa State University Chief of Police Barry Seward. Taking up the "Woman/Smith" pad, he began a "To-Do List." Item one was, "Call Barry Seward."

As a prosecutor, Michael had worked with Barry on several cases involving ISU students. Barry brought a balanced understanding of what it meant to work with young people and university staff and was able to navigate the multitude of university guidelines or rules, some of which, depending on whom you were dealing with, seemed to change daily. He underlined, "Call Barry!"

There were some impressions Smith had formulated and added about Lei Ming, but as Michael continued to read, what became evident was an accumulation of information unrelated to Agent Smith's primary investigation. Michael was surprised when the excursion boat, *Maximilian*, was referenced several times, as was its owner, a man named Bart Farley, and Farley's interest in a casino license. Interspersed were unanswered questions about prostitution and gambling and a possible link to the Ridge Top Nightclub.

He said to himself, "What is it Alice said? 'Curiouser and curiouser!'"

He added to his list: Item two—Research Bart Farley; item

three—Research Ridge Top Nightclub; item four—Ride *Maximilian* excursion boat.

His musings on the recent brush with *Maximilian* was interrupted by the landline phone. Annoyed, he allowed it to go to voice mail but dashed to pick up when he heard the voice of the caller. "Hey, Glen. Sorry I didn't pick up sooner. What's the word?"

"The word is your truck is finished, and if I may say so myself, restored to your specifications. It looks good. No sign of any mishap. You're welcome to come by and pick it up. We're open until six. If you get here early enough, I'll give you a personal tour."

"That's great news. Frankly, I need a break, but there's one problem."

Michael's one problem had been needing a ride to get his truck. Glen's response: "No problemo. I'll send someone."

When his ride arrived, Michael was surprised to see his nephew behind the wheel of an older model pickup. He judged it dated back to the '70s. Except for its coat of primer in need of a coat of paint, the pickup was in a remarkably good state. Michael climbed in and greeted his nephew, but had to ask, "Tell me, Jeremy, why were you at Glen's shop?"

"I'm working part-time in the shop, and Glen helps me with my project. Dad and I bought this old pickup truck. Do you like it? It's been slow going, but I've learned a lot. We're almost done. We did the primer coat over the weekend, but we need to wait a few more days before we do the finish coat. Glen is like a genius when it comes to restoring old cars and trucks. He even showed me how to do some of my own body work."

"It looks great, but I thought you already had a job."

"Yeah, but my time is flexible, and I have my evenings and

weekends."

"What does Emily think of that?"

"She's busy too. She's working long hours this summer at Lyle's Deli and volunteers at the Maritime Museum. We both are trying to make as much money as we can for school."

"Has she decided where she's going?"

"Yup. We're both headed for Iowa State."

"Oh? I thought she hadn't decided."

"Emily and I talked about it, and we want to go to the same school. We're serious about our relationship, but we don't know if it'll be permanent. We know you and Janni were together at this age but went to different schools. Emily and I decided we might make better decisions if we stayed close but took our time."

Michael looked over at his nephew and thought, *Who is this mature, thoughtful man?*

"Why are you looking at me like that?" Jeremy asked when he caught Michael's gaze.

"Like what?"

"Like I said something wrong! I didn't mean you and Janni didn't make good decisions. That came out wrong."

"It came out fine. It sounds to me like you and Emily are better at making this decision than Janni and I were. I didn't mean to look at you funny. I was impressed by your maturity."

Jeremy blushed a deep crimson. "Thank you, Uncle Mike. That means a lot."

If not now, when? Michael thought. "With that in mind, Janni and I would like to visit with you and Emily about some of the challenges we had in our relationship when we were your age."

Jeremy glanced at his uncle. He nodded. "Sounds like Mom and Dad got to you. Emily's parents had 'The Talk' with her too. Everyone has been clear they have concerns."

"They just want the best for you both, and I'm sorry to say, Janni and I did not provide the best example."

"I know, but aren't you and Janni back together?"

"I'm not sure what we are, but let's keep this about you and Emily."

"I'm okay with it if you want to get together. Emily will be too. When do you want to meet?"

"Talk to Emily and decide what works for the two of you. I'm flexible, but I'll need to clear it with Janni."

***

The exterior of Glen's building was he same as he remembered, but Michael was surprised with the changes and additions to the interior. The old battered counter near the entrance was gone, replaced by a desk and a receptionist. Gone were the mismatched chairs and end tables, and in their place, new furniture well-suited to represent a successful business. The freshly painted walls displayed large posters of classic vehicles and pictures of cars and trucks that had been restored by Glen and his talented staff. At the back of the spacious room was an office area, restrooms, and what Michael assumed was a break room. Off to his right, a sign above a double door announced the entrance to the workshop.

"Pretty impressive, isn't it?" Jeremy had waited while Michael took in the spacious, newly remodeled room. "Wait until you see the workshop."

Following Jeremy, Michael was even more impressed with the changes to the workshop. It had been greatly expanded and instead of the single bay Michael remembered, there were multiple work bays with a vehicle in each. Tools and replacement parts were organized and filled shelves and nearly every space on the massive work bench. Jeremy led the way. "Your truck is in the showroom."

Glen was wiping away any possible remnants of dust but looked up as they entered. "Well, what do you think?"

Michael circled the truck and marveled at the amazing result. "It looks great! I don't see any evidence of my truck abuse." The damage inflicted in Michael's haste to save Janneke from a murderer was excusable, but he was delighted to see that his old project from high school, his custom, beefed up, and much pampered 1959 GMC, had been so well cared for.

"I'm glad you're satisfied with the repairs. We had to reconstruct some of your work, but it went well. You did a great job, especially for a high school kid."

"Thank you, Glen. Truth be told, I had excellent advice, and your dad gave me a lot of encouragement. Considering that, how is my nephew doing?"

Glen looked at Jeremy and with a big grin said, "He's learning, and he's a good worker. I like having him around. Jeremy's the most positive person I have in the shop. He brightens everyone's day."

Jeremy again blushed and said, "I have a good teacher. I better get back to work."

After Jeremy left, Michael asked, "How is the work on his truck?"

"Great! It's almost done. We prime coated it earlier this week and will paint it next week. If he wants to, he can take it to school this fall."

"That's good. I know Connie and Madge, especially Madge, are going to miss him, but they both work and are busy with the younger kids. Everyone will adjust."

"Yup. That's life. Change happens. Same thing with me and my wife. Do you have time for a quick tour?"

It had been years since Michael had gone through the collection of restored and original collectibles. It was excellent before but had grown impressive! "I can't believe how much it's changed."

"I know. I get calls nearly every day from someone who either wants a car restored or to give me a lead I might find interesting. It keeps me jumping. There's enough interest that I may start offering winter tours. We get a lot of calls from schools, but the word is out, and if there's enough interest, we may open a new venue for meetings and social gatherings. Lyle's Deli would be a natural for food service, and we have the facilities and enough space to accommodate up to a hundred people or more. We already had a couple of weddings and a lot of graduation pictures. We even thought about opening the back warehouse and hosting a rock-and-roll night. Lots of possibilities but we're already so busy we have trouble keeping up with demand."

"Well, I'm impressed. Whether for nostalgia or an appreciation for fine restoration, you've got a gold mine. I'll be back when I can spend more time."

As he drove off, Michael appreciated the smooth rumble of the GMC's engine and the firm suspension that had been such a challenge to add when he'd begun working on the truck. Glen's father had been his shop teacher whose common sense and valued advice solved problems with and beyond the truck. Glen was another example once cited by Michael's father as fruit not falling far from the tree.

24

Enjoying his reclaimed prize, Michael nearly drove by the turn-off from highway 71 to the Iowa Great Lakes Maritime Museum, located in the Arnold's Park Amusement Park. Having just read about the *Maximilian* and its owner as part of Agent Smith's report and recalling Willy's complaints as well as his personal wake-induced unpleasantness created by the large boat, he was curious to get a professional's opinion. What better place than the Maritime Museum and its curator Annabelle O'Sullivan?

Anna and her late husband were native to the Lakes Area and had owned and maintained an excursion boat business that went back decades in Anna's family, earlier than anything Michael could recall. The business and its owners had been featured in news articles over the years and were included in books on the history of the Lakes. Besides history, with all her years of experience plying the waters, Anna was deeply steeped in the design and function of the boats that motored or sailed on the Iowa Great Lakes.

Parking some distance from the museum entrance, Michael was

reminded why he seldom came to the Arnolds Park Amusement Park in the summer—performances in the Roof Garden the exception. Late in the afternoon on a pleasant summer day, the park was packed with tourists. The collective ambiance of sounds from carnival rides and competing sources of music along with a complex aroma of bars, food venders, and vehicle exhaust hanging in still, humid air, had been exciting to a young Michael and his friends. But to the mature Michael, the charms of the popular playground quickly wore thin when combined with the crush of so many sweaty bodies in the park's limited space.

Entering the lobby, Michael was cheerily greeted by a young woman behind the counter and mercifully, the wash of cool air carrying the slight fragrance of a time gone by. With a brochure thrust into his hand and assurance that Mrs. O'Sullivan was in her office, Michael stepped into a space devoted to the past, much of which was familiar having grown up in the region and from the stories told by his parents and grandparents.

He was reminded of the ending passage of *A River Runs Through It* that had touched him years ago: *Eventually, all things merge into one, and a river runs through it ... I am haunted by waters.*

For Michael, the lake replaced the river, and if he was "haunted" by anything, it was the collective memories augmented here by the artifacts and words on display, some of which preserved his own family's deep history in the Lakes Region. Although the great room was unchanged, the amount and organization of history on display had expanded into every possible space since his first and only visit years before.

"Hello, Michael. So nice to see you."

Mesmerized by the display, he was unaware of her approach. With a start, he turned and accepted the hand extended in greeting. "Anna! Thank you. It's so nice to see you. I was so impressed by all this I didn't hear you coming. You've done an incredible job."

Anna tilted her head and smiled. "I had a little help. In fact, if you have time, we could use another volunteer."

Here was another subtle reminder—and there had been several since his return less than a year now—that the golden boy from a prominent family with long history in the area may have been remiss in not paying his respects to another family of equal note. "I'll think about the volunteer part, but I promise to return and take my time going through the displays. I'd heard the museum had expanded under your leadership, but this is amazing."

"Well, thank you, Michael. You may want to take note of the display of old outboard motors. There is a 1932 Evinrude Sportwin, an early twin piston outboard motor. It was your grandfather's, and your dad donated it, along with some other items, when we first opened the museum."

"I didn't know that." A brief reminder flashed through his mind. He needed to call and have a long talk with his mother. He had been absent from home for years, and in recent months, as he had gradually come out of his deep depression, he had become acutely aware of a need that at times seemed visceral, to learn about and perhaps regain something of what he had forfeited.

"I know it's near closing time, but I wondered if I might ask you some questions. It may have something to do with a little help I'm giving Sheriff Conrad."

"Sure. Give me a moment to check on my crew. We're setting up for a private party. I'll meet you in my office."

Michael looked around but could not distinguish between office and display. "Ah, and where may that be?"

Anna smiled and with twinkling mischievous eyes, "Look for the clown. I consider my door as the entrance to the 'Fun House.'"

As the petite woman stepped away, Michael marveled at the contrast between this place that commemorated change and the enduring appearance of its curator. In spite of six decades or more, Anna's hair was black with only a wisp of white among her soft curls. Immutable, her smile animated her face and her bright eyes sparkled with intelligence, a countenance enhanced by a complexion lightly tanned and polished smooth. (The wind and sun had been kind.) A lilt of speech suggested Irish ancestry, and she bore confidence well as the captain of her own ship. In that sense, she had been and remained so.

Using Anna's directions, Michael immediately spotted the designated figure. He had to smile. For decades, the "clown" had been seen by anyone entering the "Fun House." No longer a staple of the Park, the museum maintained a few of the "House" artifacts, possibly none so immediately memorable as the carved wooden figure that had once sat above the entrance, welcoming all to a good time inside.

Michael took out his phone and snapped a photo of the office door and the greeter above.

"Do you approve?" Anna was at his elbow.

"I do. Perhaps you should loan it out to certain chambers in our Statehouse."

"Hah! I'd rather use it locally, if you get my drift."

Michael nodded in agreement. "I can see that." Michael could think of quite a number of other places it would be useful.

"Well, come in. Pardon the clutter." It was a command rather than apology.

"No problem. Been there, done that."

In terms of clutter, Michael had observed worse, but clearly, this was a busy place. Nearly every surface was covered. The large, battered, and otherwise nondescript desk sat in the middle of the room with two straight-backed chairs before it. The surface of the desk was submerged beneath a desk computer, printer, binders, folders, cups, and what was likely leftovers from lunch. In the corner of the room sat a small dorm-style refrigerator with a microwave on top crowned by a coffee machine with a carafe stained a dark brown. Some shelving hosted books and knickknacks while pictures and posters adorned nearly all available wall space. A row of file cabinets stacked high with more binders and file folders was against the wall behind the desk, separated by a large executive chair of a more recent provenance and improved pedigree than the desk. Motioning for Michael to be seated, Anna took her place behind the desk, her small figure sheltered within the large chair.

"May I get you anything? The coffee's a bit stale, but I have some bottled tea and water."

"No, but thank you. Anna, before anything else, I want to say how sorry I am for the loss of your husband. I know it's been a while, but I wasn't aware of it until recently."

"Thank you, Michael. I miss him every day, but my work at the museum has helped to keep the good memories alive. And I want to express my condolences on the loss of your father. I don't know if you were aware of this, but he was a big supporter, a patron of the Maritime Museum. His advice and financial support is part of the reason we exist."

A brief, memory-laden interval of silence was ended by the announcement over the public address system that the museum would be closing in five minutes. Motivated by concern for the curator's time, Michael took up his initial purpose.

"Anna, you are an expert on the history of the Lakes, especially when it comes to excursion boats, I wanted to get your professional assessment and opinion of the newest member of that class, the *Maximilian*."

She reacted as though a lightning bolt had struck. "Excursion boat! That floating chunk of crap is *not* an excursion boat! It's an obvious ploy to establish gambling and who knows what else in the Lakes

Area. It's an abomination, an assault on the aesthetics of watercraft everywhere, a threat to the ecology and welfare of the Lakes, and the darkest cloud on the history of watercraft on the Lakes since the tragedy of 1929!"

Startled, Michael stared at the woman whose bright eyes had turned dark, whose creamy complexion had become mottled, and whose hands had become clenched fists. She appeared prepared to overpower everything and everyone in her reach. Even the large desk seemed diminished by her passion. His facial expression must have reflected his concern.

"Sorry, Michael." Anna paused, waved a hand dismissively, and went on. "I'm just so upset by that damn beast. It's so big and ugly, and every time it passes over the reef between Pillsbury and Fort Dodge Points, I expect it to scrape bottom or damage the reef with its props. It's too large for the lake. Even a minor drop in the lake level could prove disastrous. It's all about money. Screw history and ecology." Anna took several slow calming breaths. "Sorry, Michael."

Leaning forward in his chair, he said, "No, I understand. Do we preserve or exploit the Lakes? It's the same disagreement that has been around for most of the twentieth and now the twenty-first century. I'm not sure there's a solution. Perhaps, at best, maybe a compromise. But I agree, the *Maximilian* is an anathema."

Having reclaimed her normal demeanor, Anna asked, "Why the interest?"

"Besides the fact it nearly ran me over while fishing? I'm assisting Sheriff Conrad with an investigation into a missing person, mostly retracing the work done by someone else. The investigation was not about the *Maximilian*, but the boat and its owner's name keep popping up in the case notes, like a tangent or a sidebar. I don't know why it would be relevant, but I thought if anyone could help, it would be you."

"I don't know anything about a missing person, but I can tell you about the boat and especially its owner, Bart Farley. Farley has been in the Lakes Area off and on for the past few years. I think he came in from the east coast, and rumor has it he's some sort of entrepreneur of questionable repute. I know he's a drinker. I've seen his name in the paper for OWI. He also claimed bankruptcy a couple of years ago, but he managed to hang on to some property, including the old nightclub on the hill west of Okoboji and the ratty motel and restaurant at the bottom of the hill. I think he renamed the nightclub 'Ridge Top' or something like that. I've heard some nasty things about the Ridge Top and about him."

"Like what?" Michael was a bit surprised by the direction and tone the conversation had taken.

"Like illegal gambling and prostitution. It's supposed to be hush-hush, but when the area's Grand Poobahs are seen frequenting a questionable establishment, it gets noticed. Of course, I don't have personal knowledge, and it may mostly be gossip, but I overheard a few prominent museum supporters talk about it casually during some of our receptions and meetings. I got the impression their knowledge was firsthand. We're not exactly flush with cash, so I'm not going to rock a tippy canoe, but it does taint one's opinion of otherwise respectable supporters."

"That must put you in an awkward position."

"It's their choice, and as long as it doesn't affect our business, I hold my nose and don't ask them questions."

"Do you know of anyone else asking questions?"

"Why do you ask?"

"I'm just following the trail someone else laid out."

Anna gave Michael a quizzical look. "Then there must be something in your notes about his visit to the museum."

"So, you met?"

"I'm not sure. Who are you referring to?"

Michael considered her use of "his visit" and decided it was worth sharing information. In the past, he had found that if he shared information, others were more inclined to share something in return. "The person in question was investigating a missing woman but seems to have become interested in 'the *Max*'—his word—and Farley. I don't see the connection, but his interest didn't seem casual, and I would like to know why."

Anna nodded her head. "Yes, I met a gentleman who identified himself as retired FBI and who had questions about the *Maximilian* and Farley. He said he was investigating a missing person for a friend and not making any progress. He said he became interested in the boat and its owner after several locals suggested that if he wanted to investigate something, he should investigate Farley and the kind of business he was up to with the Ridge Top and his crappy boat. I told him the same as I told you. I don't think I was very helpful, but he thanked me and left his business card." With that, she reached into her desk and pulled out Howard Smith's card. She handed it to Michael. It was the same as the card included in the Governor's folder.

Handing it back, Michael observed, "I don't remember seeing the *Max* before this summer."

"You wouldn't have. It arrived by train and flatbed truck before ice out. Marv's Marina helped weld it back together and get it refitted. The state certified and issued a permit and by late May, it was on the lake."

"Marv's Marina is on East Okoboji. How did they get it to West Okoboji?"

"Marv's people did the work, but it was set up on shore and moved into the water near the West Shore Resort. The locals weren't happy, but it took less than six weeks, and those nearby were given free season passes to ride the boat. It docks at West Shore Resort and stops at various sites around the lake, most importantly the state pier at Arnolds Park. It can't stop everywhere because it is restricted by its draft. It has a modified triple hull to accommodate its size and twin screws for greater propulsion, and it needs deeper water to dock. Charley Chen volunteers here at the museum and works part time to keep the *Maximilian* running. He says it's a beast, overpowered engines, oversize screws, and has a drive train that takes skill to maintain and to pilot. He thinks it's too big for the lake and poses a danger to other watercraft. Charley should know. He's retired but has the mechanical engineering degree and experience, to boot."

Michael waited until he was sure Anna had finished, then asked the obvious. "Why?"

"Why what?"

"Why have such a large craft? Is there a need for or any interest in a boat that size?"

"It's no secret that Farley intends to score a casino license and establish state-sanctioned gambling at the lakes. I think the boat is part of a plan. It would be used for transportation between resorts and the Park and could be a party boat for special events or fire up the crowd on their way to the casino."

"But why so big? Wouldn't a more modest craft do just as well?"

"Evidently not. I think Farley is trying to wow the Gaming Commission, make it seem like he's the promoter who can get the job done. He may also have some notion about onboard gambling. I wouldn't trust him any further than my anchor rope."

"Have you met him?"

"Yes. He's been in several times with questions about variations in lake depths and water hazards. It may seem reasonable, but it's all about his boat and not what's best for the lake. Believe me, this will not end well for someone. I just hope it doesn't do harm to the lake's environment."

With her fifty-plus years of experience plying the waters, Anna knew more than anyone about the design and function of the boats, past and present, that motored or sailed on the Iowa Great Lakes. Surrounded by history and committed to preservation, her love for the lake was palpable.

Michael thanked Anna for her time and promised to visit again when he could stay longer. As he walked across the hot parking lot to his truck, he thought about Anna's concern for the lake. It had left an impression. If anyone could understand the threat a craft like the *Maximilian* could pose for the lake, it was Annabelle O'Sullivan. Her parting words weighed heavily on his mind.

25

"I'm worried about her," Emily said in a quiet voice.

After dropping off Uncle Mike to reclaim his truck, Jeremy had finished work and picked up Emily to drive her home from her job at Lyle's Deli.

"She's busy with work and helps out at home," Jeremy replied. "I'm sure she's okay."

"I don't know. We were supposed to go shopping together for school clothes. We planned this a couple of weeks ago. We were going to shop, have lunch, maybe add a movie, have a girls' day out, but now she says she can't go. I asked her if anything's wrong, and she told me to leave her alone."

"Maybe she changed her mind about going to college."

"I hope not. She's a really good student and would be the first in her family to get a college degree. If we both go to ISU, we plan to be roommates this fall."

The empathy she felt toward others was what had first attracted Jeremy to Emily, and if she was worried about her close friend,

Bonita, then he needed to do more than offer trite excuses. He liked Bonita. She was a classmate, and as Emily's friend, he had gotten to know her and her family.

"How about we go fishing?" Jeremy asked.

"What?"

"You know, fishing."

"How does that help?"

"Well, if you go fishing, you need to stop at the Sports Shop to get bait and find out where the fish are biting."

Emily stared at him. Jeremy raised his eyebrows. Emily began to smile. "Aren't you the smarty pants?"

"I try."

"Bonita gets off work at six. We could stop at the Sports Shop a little before six and ask her where people have been catching fish."

"We could ask her if she wants to go fishing."

"Really? What if she says yes?"

"Better yet, we go fishing."

***

Bonita's notion of sanctuary within the church had worked the first night but was untenable during the day. There were simply too many people in, out, and around the church itself. Carla had asked about the adjacent school. Sanctuary was where you found it, and the school was the better choice, all of which was meant to be short-term, but Bonita was struggling to find a more permanent solution.

The night she rescued Carla, Bonita returned to the church with medical supplies and fast food and did what she could to repair the injuries to Carla's knees and hands. Each night since, she had brought food, personal supplies, and clean clothing, anxious that they might be found out and she would be riddled with guilt for lying to her family.

In the meantime, Father Barney thought it curious that so many fast-food containers were collecting in the hallway bin near the parochial school's offices. Most of the work to prepare St. Theresa's Elementary Parochial School for the fall semester was finished. The school/parish custodian, Bert Hagley, worked full-time, but during the summer, much of his time was spent on mowing and trimming the grounds around the church, parsonage, and school. Father Barney and Father Jim worked on parish and school business from adjacent offices in the administrative suite but ate their meals at the parsonage. Eleanor, their receptionist/secretary, still came in part-time during the summer, but she was a vegetarian. Very curious, indeed. Monday he would talk to Eleanor to learn if there was an activity scheduled at the school that he had overlooked.

Father Barney needed to hurry. He was late, and supper at the parsonage was served promptly at six o'clock. He locked the main door to the office area and set aside the growing curiosity in the hallway.

Had he paused outside the school's front doorway, he might have observed a slender young woman in ill-fitting clothing and bandaged knees tiptoeing down the hallway and surreptitiously peeking from the vestibule.

***

Jeremy pulled into the parking lot in time to see Bonita walking out the front door of the Sports Shop and get into her car. Before he could stop her, Bonita backed out and was on the blacktop heading to Highway 71. "Hurry! Turn around. Try to catch up with her."

"I'm trying." By the time Jeremy reached Highway 71, Bonita was traveling north.

"Where is she going? If she's going home, she should have turned south. Keep following her."

"I'm on it."

Jeremy followed at some distance, aided by a large silver pickup truck traveling between Bonita and his truck. They followed as she turned onto a side street and were surprised to see her pull into a McDonald's lot and stop at the drive-through. Jeremy drove past the drive, turned around, and parked. "That's unusual."

"What? You mean stopping at McDonald's?"

"Bonita likes fresh fruits and veggies and home-cooked food. It's not like her to stop for fast food."

"They have onion rings. Does that count?"

Emily smacked Jeremy on the shoulder. "No, wise guy. Let's just wait and see what she does."

They followed Bonita as she left McDonald's and turned south on Highway 71 and drove in the direction of home. As they approached the town of Milford, all appeared normal until Bonita turned onto the side street to St. Theresa Church and Parochial School.

"What the hell?"

Emily again smacked Jeremy on the shoulder.

"Sorry."

"Pull over in front of the parsonage. Let's see what she does."

Bonita drove around the far side of the school, out of sight. "That's weird. I want to see what she's doing." With that, Emily jumped out of the truck and sprinted toward the far side of the school with Jeremy right behind.

Arriving at the building edge, Emily slowly looked around the corner. Bonita's car was out of sight. "She must have parked in back. Come on!" Emily sprinted for the back entrance to the school. She arrived behind the school in time to see Bonita walking through the back door carrying a gym bag and a McDonald's sack.

Calling out, Emily dashed to the door, caught it before it latched, and threw it open. Two astonished people stared at her and stepped back as Jeremy joined Emily.

"Bonita, what is going on? You don't call, you stay away, and now this?"

The young woman by her side continued to back up until Bonita reached out and caught her by the wrist. "It's alright. These are friends." Looking doubtful, the young woman remained behind Bonita. With a furtive glance out the open doorway, Bonita urged Emily and Jeremy. "Come in. Quick! Close the door!" Desperately, Bonita pleaded, "You can't tell anyone about this! It's a matter of life and death!"

"Bonita, you're my friend. All we want to do is make sure you're okay and to help if we can."

Bonita looked at Jeremy. "You can't tell your father."

Jeremy, suddenly aware of the dilemma he found himself in, was silent.

Emily grabbed Jeremy by the arm. "Jeremy! This is Bonita. She needs us."

He looked first at Emily, then at the two young women waiting for his answer. "I know, but who's with Bonita, and why is she here?"

"Those are very good questions."

Startled, all four turned to see Father Barney step around the corner at the far end of the hallway.

***

"I was curious. I heard you drive up and saw you run around the back of the school." Father Barney had led the little group to the parsonage, and Father Jim had joined them as they were seated around the kitchen table of the parsonage. Hunger overruled anxiety, and Carla was scarfing down the second of two Big Macs, a meal improved by a large, cold glass of milk rather than a soda.

It took nearly an hour until they finally got to the truth. Clearly, Carla had been brutalized, but if the man in the nightclub's driveway remembered Bonita or her car, Bonita also could be in danger. "I can take care of myself."

"I'm sure you can, but extra caution and some help from your friends might be welcome. Right now, we need to find a safe place for your new friend and to get her some medical aid," Father Barney said.

"I did what I could for her knees."

"I can see that, but there may be additional medical needs."

Closing her eyes, Carla bowed her head and began to softly cry. It took a moment for Emily and Jeremy to determine what the Fathers knew was likely the case.

***

Considering the serious nature of the allegations, the call was remarkably brief. Jeremy and Emily drove through the rusty open gate and down the lane lined with day lily and hosta plants, past old oaks and pines, to park beside Father Barney's modest sedan. Bonita and Carla rode with Father Barney, and Carla's eyes had widened in amazement at the remarkable sight. She had never experienced up close such a beautiful house with lawn, flowers, and trees all prospering under a blue sky reflected by blue waters. Standing at the doorway of the grand old house were two women, one tall and slender and the other shorter, plumper, and with a joyful face. The tall woman recognized the guests' arrival with a nod, but the shorter woman was smiling and waving in greeting as they exited the vehicles.

Carla had not allowed herself to think of her own family, of how worried they would be. It was dangerous to think that way. She had set thoughts of them aside, focusing instead on day-to-day survival. But sometimes, late in the night when the abuse had paused, dreams of her loving family had crept in unintended, dreams that were swept away when she awoke to the sour desperation that crushed her faith in the future.

She had trusted in her familiarity with the priests, one older, a bit like her grandfather, and the younger priest, who had addressed her in Spanish. But with the sight of the two elderly women inviting her into their home, the despair that enveloped her, that had washed over her threatening to drown her in sorrow, was tempered by the slightest glimmer of hope. She was wary and deeply anxious, yet here were these people, caring and eager to help, inviting her in like a family she had yet to meet.

***

On the road outside the rusty gate, the driver of the silver pickup paused. His search was rewarded, but now he faced a new challenge. He had been careless, overly confident, and if he didn't take care of this business soon, he wouldn't be around to take care of it at all—or anything else.

Janneke's call the previous evening had morphed into a pleasant Saturday afternoon on the lake in *Frau Nägel*, and a shared pitcher of margaritas with chimichangas at a favorite Mexican restaurant, but the romantic evening walk by the lakeshore that followed was rudely abbreviated by a sudden thunderstorm.

Spurred on by several lightning strikes, they dashed up the steps from lakeside to the screened-in porch of Michael's home. Thoroughly soaked, they stood laughing. Stepping closer, Michael gave Janneke a hug and said, "I love your laugh." They shared a light, familiar kiss. Shivering from the coolness, Janneke looked up at Michael and smiled. "Maybe we should get out of these wet clothes."

To Michael's surprise and delight, Janneke spontaneously disrobed, dropped her soaked clothing on the outdoor carpet and only stopped at the doorway long enough to look back at Michael and say, "Well, come on!"

They had been distant, frozen in a remote friendship foreign to them both, unsure of the depth of harm to their relationship caused by the recent attempt on their lives. Now, whatever damage had been done was pushed aside by the exuberant celebration of a need for each other that surmounted and surpassed any lingering fears.

The bedroom window was open slightly, and the lace curtains fluttered gently in the breeze. The thunderstorm passed, replaced by something cool and renewing. The fragrance of damp air and earth mingled with the fragrance of their love-making as Michael and Janneke remained wrapped in each other's arms. Their heartbeats slowed and breathing softened even as the inner glow of desire for each other remained.

It was Michael who first spoke. "I missed you."

"And I missed you. Michael, I'm sorry. I've just been off balance since…You know."

"I knew we'd both need time, and I didn't want to be pushy."

"I appreciate that. I'm still not all the way back, but I'm glad to be this far."

Lost in each other, time interrupted, they luxuriated in their embrace. Janni stirred. Looking up into Michael's eyes, she said, "This may not be the time I had in mind, but I have something to tell you. It's not for me but something I promised to do for someone else. Please listen and don't judge."

Tipping his head to the side, Michael responded with a frown.

"What?"

"Nothing."

"Michael, when you make a face, it means something. What is it?"

"I'd rather not say."

Janneke opened her eyes wide in a marginal attempt to be coy. "Come on, you can tell me. I'll be nice."

Michael took a deep breath, then made an admission. "All right. When you ordered me to listen, it sounded like my sister, Madge."

"What? I didn't order you anything."

"Case in point."

With a large smile and mischievous intent, Janneke answered, "Well, I'd consider that a compliment if it wasn't for the fact that we're rolling around in bed together naked as babes in a nursery. Let me rephrase: Michael…"

"Yes."

"I have something important to share with you, and I would appreciate it if you would hold your opinion until I'm finished."

"My dear, I always try to let you finish before me."

"That's not what I meant, smartass, and thank you."

"You're welcome. Now what is it that you need speak and I must bear in reserve?"

"You've heard about the discovery of the missing FBI agent?"

"Am I to respond to questions when posed to me?"

"Yes, that is allowed."

"Okay, yes I've heard of the discovered FBI agent or the parts of the agent, if that's what you mean."

"That's not a very elegant point, but factually correct."

"What about it?"

"As you know, I was working with the Sandovals before our unfortunate event with Anthony, but since then, Lucia and I have become closer in business and in friendship. She is a remarkable woman. I have an informed opinion of my abilities, but I'm not sure I could deal with all the personal drama she has faced and still be successful in business."

"I would remind you of the personal drama you faced. You seem to be doing well."

"But I'm not responsible for a multi-million-dollar enterprise with employees depending on me and investors looking over my shoulder."

"Don't sell yourself short. So, Lucia and the Lodge are thriving?"

"So it seems."

"That sounds as if there's a caveat."

"Perhaps. It's about the FBI agent. How much do you know about the case?"

"Maybe more than I should. Sheriff Conrad and I have talked about it. Connie has a good relationship with other law enforcement agencies, but he's frustrated over interagency cooperation or lack thereof and a lack of progress in the investigation. The Dickinson County Sheriff's Office has jurisdiction and Connie called in the Iowa Division of Criminal Investigation for help. But since the case involves a retired FBI agent, a highly regarded FBI agent, the Federal Bureau of Investigation believes they should be involved. They haven't taken over, but Connie and I both believe the FBI is running a parallel investigation. The fact that the deceased agent and our governor were long-time friends complicates it even further. The governor is not pleased with the attention coming from the FBI, and his chief of staff calls Sheriff Conrad every day for an updated report. Connie's getting pressure from all sides, including the area chamber of commerce types who are afraid it will hurt business. The Des Moines Register had an article in last week's paper and now our local pamphleteer, Milo Leadbetter, seems to think he needs to get into the action by siccing his hotshot intern on the Sheriff."

"Has Sheriff Conrad asked for your help?"

At this, Michael hesitated. Having said more than he'd intended, he recognized a need to equivocate. "From Connie? No, not officially. He has more help than he needs. That's part of the problem."

"Good! Well, not so good for Connie, but maybe better for what I have to say."

"And that is?"

"The FBI has all but taken up residence in the Lodge. They are digging into every nook and cranny of the business. They've interviewed and reinterviewed the staff, harassed anyone who deals with the Lodge, and implied Lucia may be the mastermind behind some pernicious plot, perhaps to drain the lake and plant corn. According to their made-up theory, agent Smith got in the way of Lucia's plans and had to be eliminated. All these accusations are ridiculous. The investigation by the FBI is going nowhere, so they're churning up mud hoping something useful will be uncovered. It's distasteful and a waste of time."

Janneke paused. Her voice had grown heated with indignation. The moisture at the corners of her eyes and the flush of her face articulated the frustration she shared with Lucia.

Michael was still.

"I'm sorry. I really get upset thinking about this."

"Take your time. I'm not going anywhere."

Janneke forced a smile and continued. "Lucia has consulted her lawyer, or rather the lawyer for the Lodge. Nothing has officially been filed against her or the Lodge, but the FBI doesn't seem to be considering alternatives. Or if they are, they're not sharing them. Lucia is their prime suspect. You can imagine, she is nearly out of her mind with worry."

Janneke paused a second time. Locking eyes with Michael, she said, "Lucia and I talked about whether we should bring in our own investigator. I suggested I could ask if you would look into the case. She trusts you, and she believes in you. She understands how dogged you are. Sorry. I may have had a little influence on that last part. Lucia wants to cooperate and is willing to allow you access to anything you need. I know this is a big request, but will you at least consider helping?"

An interval of silence grew until, slowly, Michael nodded, a modest acquiescence to Janneke's plea. "I'll talk to Lucia. I may be able to give her advice, but I won't promise to investigate. It's complicated.

The FBI will not be pleased if I begin asking questions that challenge their theory. If I do, they will notice. Sheriff Conrad will not be thrilled. He has to work with multiple agencies as it is, and if the governor got word that I was batting for what he may believe to be the opposition, longtime family friends or not, it would become most unpleasant."

"Thank you, Michael. That will be of some comfort for Lucia, and, frankly, for me. I'll call her tomorrow and try to set up a time so the three of us may meet without drawing attention. And I have another very different request. I've been thinking a lot about this recently. I'd like to take you up on your promise to teach me to fly."

It may have been a ploy to deflect his lack of enthusiasm to meet with Lucia, but it was a promise he'd given this past spring, before the mess at the Lodge.

"I'd love to! How about Monday morning? I need to work on fall classes." It was a better excuse than explaining why he was investigating a missing woman. "But I would still have the afternoon and evening. I'll pick you up at eight, we'll do your first lesson, and then go for an early lunch, perhaps at the Lodge?"

"Monday morning it is! I'll see if Lucia can join us for lunch."

Tapping the end of Janni's nose with an index finger, Michael added, "Now, I have something to ask of you."

Before falling to sleep, it occurred to Michael that Janneke's willingness to renew their intimacy may be a subterfuge intended to enlist Michael's help, but he knew that would be unnecessary. While they were playful in their love, their relationship rested upon a fundamental trust in each other, though sometimes they did tend to get lost among the trees before reclaiming the forest. And, it might have motivated Janneke to agree to speak with Jeremy and Emily. Jeremy's call early that morning suggesting they meet at the church after mass the next day now seemed providential.

27

To most, if noticed at all, it may have appeared that Michael and Janni's arrival at mass together was a coincidence. After all, Janneke was one of the song leaders, and Michael was seated with family. Still, they had arrived in the same car. To Michael's sister, it was no coincidence. Seated next to one another in the family pew, Madge leaned over to him and asked, "Is there anything you might want to share?"

Michael felt the heat rise from his neck to his face. "No, and if I did, certainly not here and now."

The only other person to take notice was Gladys Simpson, parish scold and general music teacher for the local school district, who thought Janneke's performance was exceptionally bright and spirited this morning. Gladys thought the nearly incessant smile Janneke exhibited throughout the service was suspicious.

Standing outside following mass, Michael was rescued from Madge's impending inquisition by Jeremy. "Okay, Uncle Mike. Emily and I are ready if you are."

Michael smiled at his sister. "Duty calls, per your request," and felt a bit smug as he, Jeremy, and Emily stepped away, leaving Madge-sourced questions in their wake.

Walking around the church, past the overhanging branches of the fully leafed lilac bushes now devoid of spring blooms, they met Janneke at the steps leading to the sacristy. Addressing his nephew, he said, "Okay, now what?"

"Now we wait for Father Barney."

Nearly on cue, the door to the sacristy opened, and the smiling elderly priest made his way down the steps. "Hello, hello everyone! What a beautiful service! Janneke, I do believe your voice is more lovely each time I hear it. Come along, everyone, I believe Father Jim has coffee and some refreshments."

Michael looked at his nephew as if to ask what was happening, but Jeremy only smiled in return as the quartet followed Father Barney to the parsonage.

**

Father Jim and the aroma of coffee greeted them at the door, and all were soon seated around the massive dining room table, a gift from the estate of a grateful parishioner. Coffee was poured, pastries were passed around, and Father Barney's chitchat was pleasant, but the resultant delay only intensified Michael's curiosity. What was the plan, and why were they including Father Barney and Father Jim?

Finally, Michael had to ask. "The coffee is excellent, but what are we doing here? My understanding was that Janni and I were to visit with Jeremy and Emily."

Father Barney nodded his head, and with that, Father Jim stood, left the room, and promptly returned with Bonita.

Emily spoke up. "We know why we were supposed to meet, but Jeremy and I have something different we need to share with you and Janneke. We have a favor, maybe several favors, to ask. Father Barney and Father Jim have agreed to help. This is my friend Bonita, and to begin, we would like her to describe what has happened to her new friend, Carla."

Bonita's unease was obvious, but with encouragement from Emily and Jeremy and a few reminders that filled in the narrative, what had happened and the dilemmas presented were understood, perhaps better by Michael and Janneke than the youngest people in the drama.

Michael's discomfort grew throughout the long and detailed account. Considering the end was near, he spoke up. "Jeremy, have you shared any of this with your father? If not, Sheriff Conrad will be in a very awkward position."

It was Father Barney who replied. "Ah, well, that is my fault, Michael. I discovered Carla at the school. Father Jim and I consider Carla, Bonita's newfound friend, to be in the care of the church, in sanctum, or sanctuary, if you will. While this may seem problematic to you, it is less so for us. Protected by the church, she is in the care of a trusted family and will remain so until matters may be resolved."

"Legally, you are on shaky ground."

"That may be, but there it is."

Michael shook his head and turned to Bonita. "The FBI must be informed. The information you have will save many people as well as you and your friend from harm and may be critical to an investigation already playing out in the Lakes Area." Bonita recoiled, ready to bolt from the room.

Michael's tone of questioning had shifted into interrogation. Janni, knowing Michael's aggressive interviewing techniques, intervened. "Father Barney, Father Jim, I assume Carla remains in danger. I can appreciate the remarkable effort you are making to protect her, but how long can this continue, and how do you plan to protect everyone?" With a sweep of her hand, she asked, "How do you protect Bonita, Jeremy, Emily, and yourselves? What Bonita and her friend know is a threat to someone, and that someone cares little about the law, whether civil, legal, or theological."

Father Barney nodded in agreement. "And so, we are talking to you and Michael. We will consider Michael our legal counselor and expect confidentiality from you both. Father Jim and I hoped you could help us come to a compromise."

Michael asked, "Such as?"

"Bonita's friend shared what she knows. She explained it clearly, but in her own way. Father Jim is fluent in Spanish and is close to our immigrant community. It was his idea, with Bonita's help, to have Carla write everything out, in detail, in Spanish. Father Jim asked questions and guided her with suggestions that helped her. It was very difficult, but with Bonita's encouragement, Carla had much to say about where she comes from, her family, what she experienced at the hands of her traffickers, the deception, abduction, and forced prostitution, and finally, her escape. Father Jim translated what she wrote and checked to confirm the accuracy of his translation. It is incredible what Carla has endured. She and Bonita are both amazing young women. Father Jim, perhaps you'd like to explain further?"

Other than pleasantries over coffee, Father Jim had been silent, stoic but for an occasional nod of encouragement to Bonita. "Thank you, Father. Carla provided a great deal of information on the organization and people running it. Besides human trafficking, she knows what is taking place at the Ridge Top Nightclub—the drugs, gambling, prostitution, and what sounds to me like extortion. Carla was the favorite of an important client, someone called Big Man. She was told to be very good to him, a euphemism meaning do whatever he asked her to do. She and the other girls talked among themselves about the owner of the Ridge Top. His name is Farley, and his use of the nightclub and his boat, the *Maximilian*, as part of a plan to win a casino. I'm speculating, but the traffickers may be helping Farley's activities because they see a lucrative future if Farley is successful."

"What Carla provided is very detailed, but before it's turned over to law enforcement, we—and by 'we,' I mean all of us, including you, Michael and Janni—must insist upon protection and help for Carla and all the girls that were trafficked. If not, then none of this will be made available, and Father Barney and I will muddle along as best we can. After all, the Church does have an interest in such matters and a good deal of sway should it come to a showdown with the government."

Everyone sat quietly, waiting for Michael to speak. He appeared inscrutable except for a slight smile, less friendly and more like the approaching white shark. Finally, he said, "I can't promise anything, but I will speak with Connie. He's working closely with an FBI Special Agent, someone he respects. That may be our best way in. With their loss of Carla, the traffickers will be nervous. We'll have to act fast before something happens to Carla and all the other girls disappear. We'll relate to the FBI Agent that Father Barney found Carla in the school as you described, but we'll leave Bonita, Jeremy, and Emily out of it for now. If I may ask, where is Carla?"

Father Barney shook his head. "No, not yet. Speak with Connie and the FBI Agent. If they agree to protect and defend Carla and the other girls, we will turn over Carla's information. But we will not share Carla's location until there are assurances that the girls will be cared for. I would again emphasize that we do consider Bonita to be under sanctuary."

"That's not going to hold water."

"If we have to, we will have her remain within the church walls."

Janneke had a question. "Is there anything in what Carla had to say that implicates the Lodge or Lucia Sandoval?"

Both Fathers looked a bit surprised, and Father Jim answered. "No, neither the Lodge nor Sandoval were mentioned and there is nothing I can see that suggests involvement in any way."

"Thank you. That will be some comfort for Lucia."

"But remember, the girl's safety is paramount."

"Yes, I understand. Michael?"

"Understood. Yes, of course!"

**

Before leaving the parsonage, Michael called Connie and arranged to meet at the Courthouse that afternoon. It was easier than he had anticipated since Connie had assigned himself weekend duty. Unannounced to Connie, Father Barney agreed to take part in the meeting. Even with Father Jim's approval, Bonita felt uneasy with the deception to her family but agreed, for now, to maintain secrecy. Jeremy and Emily were relieved to have shared the burden, although "the conversation" with Janneke and Michael remained unspoken.

As Michael drove to her condo, Janni remained the calm in Michael's storm. "Connie's not going to be happy about any of this! This will put him in a hell of a fix. This is going to be a shitstorm beyond belief. The Feds are going to go ballistic. And wait until the governor hears about all this."

Michael's jaw was flexing and his hands so tight on the steering wheel, Janni was concerned he could lose control of the vehicle. "Take a breath, Michael! Maybe the governor already knows about the Ridge Top business. He probably knows a lot more than he has told you. You and Connie need to leave the entire matter of Carla and human trafficking with the FBI, and you need to stay focused on finding the missing woman."

"And what do I say when they ask how I came to know all of this?"

"That's obvious. You were told to investigate the missing student and, in the process, came across this information."

"That won't be enough for the Feds."

"I know, but for now, your sources are confidential."

Michael snorted. "Oh yeah? How long will that last?"

"Tell them if they need more, they are to talk to Father Barney and Father Jim. That should cramp their style. Oh, and by the way, I'd inform the governor before this afternoon's meeting."

Michael shook his head. "Crap. Could it get any worse?" The question hung there, the hum of tires on the road filling the silence, when suddenly he slammed a fist on the steering wheel.

"Damn! Yes, of course it can! The Lawery Sisters! Father Barney's first choice would be the Lawery Sisters!"

Janni reacted with enthusiasm. "That's a wonderful idea! She's safe with them. They'll take great care of her."

"Are you kidding? Great care of her? It would be easier for us if Barney had dropped her off on the Pope's doorstep! Heaven and hell combined won't move the Lawery Sisters from their determination to protect Carla! You accuse me of an overdeveloped sense of justice. Compared to Faethe and Hoepe, I'm a rookie! The Lawery Sisters are in a league of their own!"

Michael ground his teeth. Janni was quiet. She smiled, then giggled, then began to laugh out loud. Michael glanced at her, the corners of his mouth twitched, and finally, he could not hold back a raucous laugh. "Those poor Feds! Wait until Faethe takes a bite out of their collective asses and Hoepe bakes them cookies."

Janni let out a whoop. "Cookies! Oh my God, yes, cookies! Can I be there when they show up? Please, please, I've got to see this!"

"Are you kidding? We're both going to be there! We'll take pictures!"

"Pictures? I'm taking a video!"

With a broad smile, Michael looked over at Janni. She returned the look. "What?"

"You just reminded me"

"And that would be?"

"With you, I may be the luckiest man in the world."

Janni made no attempt to be coy. "Hah! You better believe it!" Sharp jabs with an index finger in his ribs punctuated the last six words. "No maybe about it, Michael Cain!"

28

He didn't need to ask. Upon his arrival, the weekend receptionist buzzed Michael into the Sheriff's Department. Michael made his way to Sheriff Conrad's office and knocked on the open door. Connie peered over a hefty pile of papers and waved him in. "Have a seat!"

Michael shut the door and plopped down into one of two heavily wooded chairs facing the Sheriff's desk. "I called your home first. Madge said you were here. I thought the Conrad family's Sundays were sacrosanct—Church and Family."

"True, but family extends to my people at the courthouse. This is one of those days I'm needed here. I'm glad you called. I don't know how much this helps, but I've got some news."

"So do I, but rank has its privileges. You first."

"We found the boys who took Agent Smith's, or rather the Sports Shop's, boat. They're college kids here on their own vacation, camping at Emerson Bay. They have a boat, but they saw Smith's drifting in the middle of the lake and thought it was abandoned. Two of the kids took it and drove it around until it ran out of gas. They called their friends to rescue them and left the boat adrift where it wound up in the slough near Willy's place. You already know Willy's part in this."

"Are you going to charge them?"

"Nah! It was a prank, not meant to be criminal. The Sports Shop is happy to have the boat returned undamaged, if and when our CSI and the FBI agree to release it. Nigel's not interested in pressing charges against anyone, especially considering what happened to the person who rented it. The FBI may not feel quite as sanguine, but the kids cooperated and helped fill in the timeline, and we, or rather the FBI, now have his phone. They've already confirmed his wife had been trying to reach him. They also confirmed Smith called Governor Dirksen several times. If they weren't aware before, they now know the Gov is involved."

"They probably knew about the Gov, anyway. So, you let the boys go?"

"For the time being. Now, why are we meeting, and why is Father Barney sitting in the lobby?"

***

Sheriff Conrad's natural inclination was to act, to attack a challenge, but to his credit, he exercised uncharacteristic patience as Father Barney recounted what he called "the situation" and chronicled the circumstances that had brought it about. He listened intently, took no notes, but focused entirely on Father Barney. Not for the first time, he appreciated how precisely Barney could articulate a line of reasoning and frame it in moral terms. Barney's thought processes and moral compass were unwavering, and as usual, he ignored any notion that "Caesar's Law" may take precedent. If necessary, it was left up to the listener to deal with any dissonance between God and the laws of man.

Nearing the end of his account, with the opinions and suggestions established, Father Barney drew a proverbial line in the sand. "There is one matter that Father Jim and I insist upon. We will share information with you, but know that Father Jim and I consider the victim to be in the care of the Church, in sanctum if you will. We will not reveal her name or location until there is a guarantee by all those concerned that she will be protected, and should she choose, be allowed to remain in country. We pray all the trafficked women will be recognized as victims and treated accordingly."

Connie remained silent, jaw set, dark intense eyes bright and blazing. The intelligence and instincts that made him a great lawman were about to be tested as rarely before. Michael broke into the silence.

"Janneke suggested something as we were driving to her condo. And I quote: 'Provide the information, let the FBI deal with it, and you and Connie get back to the governor's request to find his missing woman.'"

Connie glared at Michael. "I'm not sure the Feds will be so understanding."

Barney interceded. "Father Jim and I asked Michael for legal advice. Together, with his counsel, we agreed to pass the information on to you with the understanding you would provide the same to the FBI. The information is documented and extremely detailed. As Michael, or rather Janneke, intimated, you are only the messenger. I expect the FBI will question Father Jim and me, but as I said, we found the young woman on church grounds, and due to her circumstances, we consider her to be under the protection of the Church. The FBI may take it up with our bishop, but in the meantime, I cannot guarantee that the situation won't become public. That could be detrimental to their investigation."

"And I imagine that has been arranged?"

"Not officially, but others interested in finding her may ask questions, raise suspicions, and who knows? Maybe the purveyor of our local news sheet will take up the cause. You know how snoopy Milo can be."

Connie let out a huff and slowly smiled. "Milo? Wouldn't that be interesting? Doesn't take imagination to know how the area chambers of commerce and local business owners would react."

Father Barney remained calm and resolute while an apprehensive Michael watched Connie chew his bottom lip, nod several times to an inner voice, and finally say, "I'll call Special Agent Kaufmann to see if he can meet with us immediately. He's probably still in the building. The FBI is using one of our Law Center's conference rooms as an operations center and Kaufmann is practically living there."

***

Seated in the conference room, aka the FBI operations center, Father Barney calmly reiterated, nearly word for word, what had been shared in Sheriff Conrad's office. Unlike Sheriff Conrad, as FBI Special Agent Kaufmann listened, he scribbled notes on a legal pad. The further Father Barney worked into the narrative, the more frenzied the scribbles, with dark lines under some sentences interspersed with large question marks and further punctuation by arrows drawn to highlight whatever had struck him as important. The anxiety over the Agent's reaction to the news was tempered by his head nods, slight smiles, and a wave of a hand to encourage Father Barney to continue whenever he paused.

Special Agent Kaufmann ignored Father Barney's implications about bishops and news media, but when Father Barney appeared to be finished, he looked around at the little group and shocked them when he pumped a meaty fist and exclaimed through gritted teeth, "Yes! Yes!" And continued, "Hot damn! Hot *DAMN!* Sorry, Father." With a collection of dropped jaws and incredulous looks from his company, Kaufmann added one more fist pump and reiterated his exclamation.

Michael cleared his throat. "Okay. Now would you please explain? I must say, I wasn't aware that 'Hot Damn' was part of the official lexicon of the Bureau."

"Yes, of course. Sorry about that, but you don't know what a big development this is to our investigation. We'll need all the documentation, Father. That's critical, and I promise to do everything within my power to guarantee the woman's safety."

"And the other women?"

"Of course, if they cooperate,"

"Once they're safe, I'm sure they will."

Connie interjected, "Not to be a wet blanket, but that's a big commitment on the part of the FBI. What about the other agencies?"

"I can't give you all the details, but this is a big deal, a really big deal. Every agency involved is going to want a piece of this. Her information will save a tremendous amount of time on the ground. We have the big picture, and this could be the evidence needed to roll up an entire organization, from the bottom up. It may take a few days to organize, but you'll get your cooperation."

Michael asked, "And what of Fathers Barney and Jim?"

"Are you kidding? If this works out the way I think it should, I'll personally give them medals or recommend them to the Pope for sainthood!"

Father Barney was less enthusiastic, more concerned with the immediate needs of Carla and the other young women. "What do we do now?"

"Now, you repeat what you told me. I have a few questions and want to check my notes. I need to meet as soon as possible with Father Jim. Then I'll read the documentation, and if it holds up, make several phone calls. Then all hell will break loose." Kaufmann grinned and for a second time, pumped a big fist, "Hot damn! Oh, sorry again, Father. My father's Deutsch, so I blame me Irish mother!"

Father Barney smiled and blessed Special Agent Kaufmann and his mother.

A barely subdued but slightly embarrassed agent did the sign of the cross. "Thank you, Father."

Alex, on "first-call" for specific situations, had worked with the Boss Man and his organization before. A calculating and meticulous planner, she was good at the job and efficient, leaving nothing to connect her or the organization. She was not inclined to improvise. This job wasn't unusual, but she would have preferred more time to observe and prepare. Still, there was urgency and a couple of old biddies shouldn't pose a problem.

The Boss Man had made it clear the first priority was to recover the lost merchandise, a change in plan that did not please RV Man. But RV Man knew his place, and after a little initial unpleasantness, opted not to argue with Boss Man. If a successful recovery was questionable, then the original plan would be executed. The decisions of whether and how to act were left to Alex, a tribute to the confidence the Big Boss had in his favorite fixer.

A skilled, experienced pilot, Alex owned two airplanes, a twin Navaho and a Taylorcraft. The more modest Taylorcraft would attract less attention at a small airport and better suit her purpose. A passenger, sedated and shackled in the seat next to the pilot in a small cockpit would be secure and manageable, and the Taylorcraft would better negotiate the short landing strip where Alex would drop off the merchandise. A bonus: It should be a beautiful day for flying.

It was still dark when Alex departed and just after dawn when she landed at the airstrip near The Lodge on Okoboji. In the brief time parked at a sleepy little airport, no one would pay attention to a modest addition, nor would they notice the hastily altered numbers on the plane, numbers borrowed from a list of retired numbers from damaged private aircraft.

RV Man was there to meet her, and on the ride to the Ridge Top, Alex had time to study what little information was provided and check Google Earth for a view of the area around the target. She preferred to work solo, or at least minimize dependency on others, but with little time to prepare and the need for immediacy, RV Man would be helpful.

***

While Alex prepared for her mission, Michael picked up Janneke for the plane ride he'd promised her, the introduction to flying. Having flown many times commercial, she had never flown in a small private plane. Earning a pilot's license was on her bucket list, and Michael did promise last spring to help. Michael may have forgotten, but Janneke's reminder was holding him to it.

On the way to the airport, conversation was light, and in their personal fashion, teasing, although Janneke seemed chatty, suggesting some apprehension. A part-time perfectionist, if there was such a thing, Janneke's expectations held more for her own conduct rather than others', and she tended to compensate when facing the unknown.

Parking in the small airport lot, they went directly to the Cessna

172. Michael took little notice of the new arrival and dismissed a passing impression of something amiss about the Taylorcraft's appearance. He went through and explained to Janni the what and why of the preflight check, and once settled into the cockpit, ticked the last on the list.

Janneke was absorbed by all Michael was doing as they taxied for takeoff. Turning the plane into the wind, Michael increased the throttle, and the Cessna's Lycoming engine responded boldy, eager for flight. Janneke's response was less so, pushing back into her seat to resist whatever was about to happen and drawing deep breaths.

Gaining speed, the plane lifted lightly, released from the embrace of terra firma, and ascended. Michael glanced at Janneke and smiled. Her anxiety had faded, and her reaction transformed by a view expanded from narrow grass airstrip to surrounding environs and the amazing deep azure beauty of West Okoboji.

***

They would keep it simple. RV Man had appropriated a rather nondescript older model car whose owner was out of town. By the time the owner returned, the car would be back in the garage, wiped down, the odometer turned back to the original mileage, and no one would be any the wiser. Alex would use the car to drive to the target while RV Man would keep watch in his pickup truck a short distance down the road from the driveway to the target. Alex would acquire the merchandise for him, or not, but either way, she would drive directly back to the airport, leave the car for RV Man to pick up, and fly off, mission accomplished.

The card she carried verifying her medical expertise as a registered nurse was true but not under her name. An ID for a non-existent private service designating authority to evaluate and report on the state of a victim had been useful in the past and should allow access. Even if challenged, once in, only a few minutes were needed to do the job and quickly disappear.

Passing by the rusted, perpetually open iron gate, Alex slowly drove the lengthy flower and tree-lined drive and was relieved to see no vehicles parked in the set-aside. She paused to take in the grandeur of the fine old house. It was a mix of architectural styles, but she recognized the Queen Anne and the influence of what she had once read as a Farmhouse design. Rather than a mashup, the total effect was stunning. She rather wished she had more time to appreciate the house and grounds.

Reaching across to the passenger seat, she retrieved her medical bag. Inside was everything she needed to carry out her ruse and more. As she approached the broad extended porch, the great door opened and standing in the frame appeared a tall, aristocratic woman. "Ms. Lawery?"

"Faethe Lawery, yes. May I help you?"

Stepping onto the porch, "Hello, my name is Heidi Gustafson. I'm a registered nurse employed by an organization that works with law enforcement to provide outreach and an additional layer of protection for abuse victims. Here's my business card and a copy of my RN card. I've been directed to do a brief checkup on Carla Rodriguez."

Faethe Lawery carefully read the proffered cards. "I believe you have been misinformed, and I am not familiar with this organization."

"This is the home of Faethe and Hoepe Lawery?"

"Yes, but whatever gave you the impression anyone else resided here?"

"I understood Carla was temporarily under your care."

"Again, I believe you may be mistaken. Who did you say sent you?"

"My supervisor was contacted by someone from the Sheriff's

Department. If I may just take a quick check, I'll not use any more of your time."

"I know Sheriff Conrad very well. If the Dickinson County Sheriff's department were to make an arrangement for someone to come by our house for any reason, we would be informed in advance."

Challenged by this formidable lady, Alex decided on her own challenge. "I'm sure someone at the Sheriff's office will confirm my assignment. If I may, I'll wait by the door while you call."

Faethe stepped aside. "Wait here," she said and crossed the foyer to a portable phone resting next to a lovely silver bowl on the antique sideboard.

As she tapped in the number, Carla stepped into the hallway from the kitchen and called out, "Miss Faethe, Miss Hoepe says the cookies are done."

Alex immediately took advantage of Faethe's hesitation over whether to continue the call or step between Carla and this unverified visitor. Entering the open doorway, Alex quickly strode down the hall and extended a greeting. "Hola, Carla! My name is Heidi, and I'm here to be sure you are safe and well."

Carla backed into the kitchen.

"It's alright, Carla, I'm here to help," Heidi said, following Carla into the kitchen, "and you must be Hoepe Lawery. I'm so pleased to meet you, and the cookies smell wonderful."

Hoepe was gobsmacked by the sudden appearance of this stranger, but at the mention of cookies, she said, "They're just out of the oven, and we have fresh-brewed coffee. Have a seat, and I'll get you a cup."

Alex set down her bag and took a seat on one of the stools. "Thank you. Coffee would be appreciated. So, Carla, how are you doing?"

"What is this really about?" Faethe had finished a brief call and followed Alex to the kitchen.

"Just as I said. I'm here to check on Carla."

"I don't believe you. The receptionist knows nothing of your arrangement and will call me back after she checks with Sheriff Conrad. What's your real name?"

Now it was Alex's turn to be gobsmacked. Slowly, she reached down for her bag. Sliding open the zipper, she withdrew the 38 caliber Smith and Wessen LadySmith, her handgun of choice for an easy, intimate assignment such as this. "I don't want to hurt anyone, so if you would kindly remain calm, I'll take care of business and be on my way."

Faethe was quick to challenge her. "And what is your business?"

"There are some people very interested in Carla. It is my business to take her to them."

Hoepe tried to be helpful. "Would you like to take some cookies with you? I have a take-away cup for coffee." Hoepe turned to open the door of the cabinet behind her, and Alex fired a single shot into the wall next to the cabinet.

Carla screamed and ran into Faethe's arms. Hoepe slowly turned. "That was unnecessary! You frightened the poor child!"

30

Alex had to admire these strange elderly women. Admiration or not, she would deal with them. But killing would create greater problems. It would get messy.

Recognizing the dilemma she and Hoepe presented, and hoping for the better outcome, Faethe made a suggestion. "You know, if you harm us, the law be damned. There are people who will never rest until you and whoever you represent are dealt with. Perhaps it would be better to just lock us in the basement and go about your business. The key is hanging on a hook next to the door, and by the time someone finds us, you'll be long gone."

The intelligence behind the sharp eyes had spoken a truth. A sloppy killing and her value to the organization would be lost. More likely, the organization would have her eliminated. Alex was not their only employee for this sort of work.

It was an unwelcome and seldom experienced sensation, standing at the edge of indecision. Before she could act, her cell phone rang. It was RV Man.

"Get out of there."

"What?"

"You've got company. It's those dumb shits that work for Farley. Deal with Carla, and get out of there!"

Disconnecting, Alex glanced out the kitchen window and saw an old, brown, beat-up sedan pull in next to her car. "Damn!" She turned and pointed her gun at Carla.

In desperation, Faethe intervened. "Wait! There's no need to shoot anyone. I don't know who that is, but I'll send them away, and you can take care of business."

Seizing Carla by the arm, Alex said, "Get them to leave, or I'll shoot Carla."

Faethe nodded and at the sound of the doorbell, she strode with purpose down the hallway, paused to take a deep breath, and opened the great door, calmly looking and acting as though this was just a normal day in the neighborhood.

"Hello, ma'am. I noticed you have a lot of trees and plants around your place. Me and the boys are looking for work and wondered if you could use some help with trimming and mowing. We're cheap and do good work."

"That's kind of you, but we have someone who has worked for us many years. But you might try some of the other places down the road. Everyone's always talking about how hard it is to find good workers."

"Thank you, but I'd like to tell you more about what we could do for you and how much money you might save. If I could come in, it would only take a few minutes."

"That won't be necessary, but thank you again for your offer." And Faethe firmly shut and locked the door.

Alex watched from the window as Ralph walked back to his beat-up car and said something to the two men inside. Ralph reached in through an open window and drew out a large caliber, stainless steel revolver while the other two men stepped out. Both were armed, one with a short barreled tactical shotgun with an extended magazine and the other with a semi-automatic handgun.

"Where's the entrance to this basement?" Alex demanded.

Faethe pointed. "Just around here. The key is by the door."

Alex motioned with the gun. "Go!" Keeping her grip on Carla, she followed the sisters, watched them descend the stairs, then used the old skeleton key to lock the basement door. Dragging Carla behind her, Alex returned to the kitchen and tossed the key on the counter. Glancing out the window, she was alarmed to see one of the men approaching the outside door to the small mud room off the kitchen. Alex retrieved something from her bag and dragged Carla to the kitchen door. Opening the door, she ordered Carla not to move. "Stand here. When he comes in, let him see you. You do it right, and no one gets hurt."

As the outside door to the mud room opened, there was an astonished pause as the intruder couldn't believe his good fortune. As he stepped into the room, there was a slight motion from behind the opened door. Before he could react, he felt a sharp snap at his neck and dropped into a quivering lump on the floor.

She reached out for Carla's hand. "Come with me!"

Stepping over the lump on the floor, Alex dragged Carla outside, peered around the corner of the house, and watched Ralph as he began banging on the front door. "We know you're in there. Come out, or I'm breaking down the door!" Pausing, he nodded to his companion who raised the shotgun and blasted the lock. The door slowly swung open, as though it were stalling.

As both men burst into the house, Alex grabbed Carla, dragged her to the car and threw her into the back seat. "Get down! Stay put!" Alex leaped behind the wheel, started the engine, and executed a sharp 180. As she floored the underpowered sedan, the back window exploded from a shotgun blast. Ignoring the sharp stab to the back of her head, Alex sped around the drive's small curve only to be stunned by the appearance at the gate of a pickup truck painted in a dull primer coat. Slamming on the brakes, the car stopped inches short of a collision.

On an errand to deliver new clothes and personal items for Carla, Jeremy and Emily were as stunned as the sedan's driver. With the sudden stop, Carla did a hard bump into the back of the front seats. When she popped up to see what was the cause, she saw Jeremy's truck and Emily pointing. She couldn't hear, but she saw Emily exclaim to Jeremy, "It's Carla!"

Jeremy shifted into low and rammed his truck into the small sedan, shoving it backward into a long bed of hostas. As if on cue, Carla leaped out and began to run into the woods. In one smooth move, Alex threw open her car door and fired a single shot at Carla. Carla spun around, backed into a tree, and collapsed onto a soft bed of molded leaves and wildflowers. As Alex turned the gun toward the truck, Jeremy yelled to Emily, "Get down!" put the pedal to the metal, and rammed the truck into the sedan a second time.

Alex got off one wild shot as the sedan's door slammed against her arm. Struggling from the car she tucked the broken arm against her body. Reaching with her good hand for the fallen gun, another shotgun blast rocked the car.

There was no time to think, only react. Leaving the gun where it lay, Alex dove into the woods as another blast broke tree branches overhead. Alex could only glance at Carla's open eyes and still body as she ran by. Breaking out of the woods, she scrambled into the bed of RV Man's waiting truck. RV Man looked back into the wild eyes of Alex, who was screaming, "Go! Go! Go!"

By the time the shotgun's owner broke from the woods, RV

man's truck was already around the bend and out of sight. Approaching from the opposite direction came more bad news, the sound of sirens.

Ralph barely scraped by the abandoned sedan and slipped around Jeremy's truck. He slowed enough for the shotgun-wielding Tolly to jump into the back seat and join Joe, the still-confused victim of a stun gun attack.

RV Man didn't stop until he came to Highway 86. Alex rolled over the side of the box, and with some difficulty, jerked open the door. "Where the hell did those jerks come from?"

"Farley wanted to know where Carla was hidden. I told him not to worry about it. It was taken care of, but he insisted. I knew he was a screw-up, but I can't believe he was this stupid."

Glancing over at Alex, he shouted, "You're injured!"

"I'm fine. The job's done. Carla's dead! I shot and killed her. Forget about the car. Get me to the plane, now!"

RV Man turned onto the highway, but had to ask, "Can you fly like that?"

"I could fly barefoot with one arm tied behind my back."

"But you're bleeding."

Only then did Alex realize she'd been shot. "It's nothing. A little blood. It looks worse than it is. Get me to the plane. I'll fly out and everyone's home free. Go! Go!"

Janneke was a natural. While they spent time circling the Lakes Area, Michael explained the function of yoke, rudder pedals, ailerons, flaps, a little about the importance of angle of attack, and the most basic physics that allowed flight. He allowed Janni to lightly try the yoke and the rudder pedals. At each attempt, her enthusiasm grew, and questions came in a rush.

There was no other air traffic Michael was aware of, and radio communication was minimal, coming only from the airport's part-time manager, Don Cooper. Don's hours were flexible, often exceeding his paid time. He was retired from the military and had done a stint as a Dickinson County Supervisor. His part-time work for the airport was a labor of love, a job he would have done for free. He had come in later than usual, noticed that Michael's plane was gone, and was curious about the newcomer.

"This is manager Don Cooper at the Okoboji airport calling Cessna 56632. Hello, Michael Cain. Do you copy? Over."

"Good morning, Don. It's a beautiful day, and I'm giving my

best girl a flying lesson. Over."

"Copy that. Do you know anything about the Taylorcraft parked by the strip? I haven't seen it before, and I'm curious why some of the numbers appear to be altered. Over."

"No, I don't know anything about it other than it was there when we arrived around eight. Over."

"Just thought I'd ask. One more thing, I'm listening to the police scanner, and something big is going on. It sounds like someone attempted a kidnapping, and there were shots fired. There is an APB out for a brown, older model four-door sedan and a silver crew cab pick-up, both seen fleeing the area. Let me know if you see one of them. Over."

"Not likely from this altitude. We've been busy learning to fly. Over."

"Just yanking your chain. Enjoy your flight. Over."

"Will do, thank you. Over."

Michael was quiet.

"Michael?" Janni finally said.

"Oh, sorry. Who do we know who might be a target for kidnappers?"

"Carla? Oh God, no! The Lawerys!"

Banking sharply, Michael reduced altitude and began to fly across West Okoboji in the direction of the Lawerys' home, prominent from the air as well as the lake. Flying over the target, Michael was alarmed to see what appeared to be a fleet of police, emergency, and fire vehicles, all with lights flashing.

Janneke spoke first. "What is going on?"

"I don't know, but it doesn't look good."

Turning slowly to do another fly-over, Michael asked Janni to retrieve his mobile phone from his carry-on bag and to dial Faethe from his contacts list.

"Michael! Where are you?" Faethe said as soon as she picked up.

"I'm flying my Cessna over your place right now. What's going on down there?"

"A woman tried to kidnap Carla. Jeremy and Emily stopped the kidnapper, but Carla was shot and is on her way to the hospital. It doesn't look good. Everyone else is safe, but it is absolute bedlam down here. Fortunately, our neighbor heard the gunfire and called 911. He drove by to see what, if anything, was going on and reported a large silver pickup speeding down the road. He thought it was unusual for a woman to be riding in the truck bed. It sounded like it could have been the kidnapper."

"Stay safe. I'll be there as soon as I can."

"Thank you, Michael. Hoepe and I are quite capable, but there are others here who could use your help."

Disconnecting, Michael looked at Janni and had to shake his head. "Those Lawery sisters are really something."

"I want to go with you to the Lawerys'."

Michael made no attempt to argue. "Of course." He turned his Cessna toward the airport and opened up the throttle.

As he neared the airstrip, the radio crackled. "Hello, Cessna 56632. Michael? Over." It was Don Cooper.

"This is Cessna 56632. That you, Don? Over."

"Where are you? Over."

"I'm two or three minutes out. Over."

"I thought you'd want to know. A silver pickup like the one described in the APB just pulled up and dropped off a woman. The truck took off, fast, and she is heading for the Taylorcraft. Over."

"Call it in. I'll buzz the strip and see if I can distract her. Over."

"Already done. Copy that. Out."

Michael mumbled, "It was the numbers."

Janni looked at him. "What?"

"When we walked by the Taylorcraft, I thought something looked odd. It was the numbers. A couple of them were crooked, didn't quite fit, like someone had altered them."

"So?"

"Think about this. If you were a kidnapper or killer who knew how to fly, what better way would you have to escape than an innocuous little airplane at a lightly used airport?"

"You think that's the kidnapper?"

"I think it's likely."

"What are you going to do?"

"Try to stall her until the police arrive."

"Short of crashing into her, how do you intend to do that?"

"I don't know. I'll buzz her before she can take off and see what happens."

"Buzz her? Really? Like fly over the top of her? What if she's already taking off?"

"I don't know. I've never been in this situation before."

As Michael approached the airport, he allowed the Cessna to sideslip to lose altitude. Lining up with the grass air strip, he saw the smaller plane turning to face the wind, about to take off.

Michael realized he needed to land immediately. With little choice, he sharply altered his angle of attack and dropped the Cessna fast, passing just over the Taylorcraft. Cutting power and dropping the flaps, he pulled back on the yoke, and the Cessna bounced once before rolling to a stop. Turning the nose wheel and braking hard on the left pedal, he gunned the engine, snapped a sharp turn, rolled up to face the waiting Taylorcraft, and shut down his airplane.

He glanced over at his passenger, but Janneke was silent, gripping the sides of the seat, and glaring at the woman in the Taylorcraft. Like a slap to her face, Michael yelled, "Janni! Get out! Run! Get help!"

Janni bailed from the cockpit, but Michael knew he needed to stall for time to allow Janni to escape and law enforcement to arrive. Removing the keys from the ignition, Michael climbed out of the cockpit, took a few steps toward the smaller plane, stopped, and made a slashing motion across his throat. In response, Alex shut down her airplane's engine. Keeping her eyes on Michael and the keys he was dangling from his fingers, she reached under her seat and retrieved a small back-up handgun.

Michael stood silently watching as Alex struggled to step down from her plane. There was blood on her shoulders, a lot of blood, and something was wrong with her arm. He noticed she was holding the little semi-automatic in the wrong hand.

Michael spoke first. "There's nowhere to go."

She smiled. "There's always somewhere to go. We'll use your plane."

"Not going to happen." He threw the keys into the weeds along the strip.

"No!" She fired a wild shot at his feet. "Get the keys, or the next shot is between your eyes."

Her hand was shaking as she attempted to raise the gun. Stepping closer, she stumbled but regained her footing.

"I don't think you're in any shape to shoot or fly."

"I can shoot, and you'll fly. Now get the keys!" Her arm waved as she took another unsteady step closer. Suddenly, there was a honk, a loud blast followed by quick, repeated bursts. Janneke was in Michael's truck!

At the unexpected alarm, Alex spun, lost her footing, and collapsed. Dashing forward, Michael kicked the handgun away from her hand. Alex lay where she'd fallen, unmoving. She would no longer fly. She could no longer shoot. Buckshot from the shotgun had found their mark.

32

It was as if a great fog had descended on events at the Lawerys' and the airstrip. FBI Special Agent Kaufmann and his minions had sucked up all the information and surrounding oxygen. The FBI now had more than a parallel interest in an investigation into a missing retired FBI Agent.

Lunch with Lucia was forgotten, and Michael and Janneke endured a long afternoon of questions after which Janneke went home to nurse a monster headache and reconsider her interest in learning to fly. Michael, at Governor Dirksen's insistence, remained at the courthouse to sit in on the review of the day's events and an evening planning session. Present was a generous supply of FBI agents and several officials generally referred to as Homeland Security, their true provenance likely a medley of alphabet-referenced agencies. Connie and Detective Donahue were there accompanied by two agents from the DCI. Michael recognized and was not surprised that one of the agents was DCI's own specialist, Byron Nordlich. Recently, Agent Nordlich had been honored for his work with human trafficking, a recognition that reached all the way to Washington.

In spite of public assumptions, resources, even for the FBI, were limited and had to be prioritized. Once a peripheral activity, depending upon and monitoring the work of local and state authorities dealing with the expanding activities of a larger criminal organization interested in the Lakes Area, the FBI now claimed point on the investigation into human trafficking and a growing list of related felonies. With only the bare bones laid out, Michael was surprised by how quickly the investigation was expanding. Clearly, even prior to the disappearance of retired Agent Smith, the FBI had been more interested in the area than local and state law enforcement understood.

FBI Special Agent Kaufmann reviewed what was known and shared an overview of what needed to be done before moving forward. There were still some gaps, but the intelligence Carla had provided was a major breakthrough, and whether for the success of the operation or the need to rescue the trafficked girls, Kaufmann laid out in stark terms the imperative to act soon.

"Carla Rodriguez was the target of an attempted kidnapping at the home of Faethe and Hoepe Lawery. We know Carla had escaped from traffickers, was rescued by local priests, and her location with the Lawerys kept a secret, even from law enforcement. Carla was shot and seriously wounded in the kidnapping attempt and remains in the hospital attended by a small team of medical providers and heavily guarded by agents of the FBI. We don't know how the traffickers determined her location, but we must assume they are aware of our scrutiny and may pull out at any moment. To possibly delay this, we have publicized that Carla is deceased and little else is known. As part of this effort, information to media is limited and only sourced by Dickinson County Sheriff Conrad. This is his patch, he knows the local players, and for the time being, the less that's known about the federal investigators, the better. It is our belief that if the traffickers believe Carla was killed, they may think they have a small window of time to wrap up business before they disappear. They have time and money invested and hope for a big pay-off. They will be reluctant to let it go."

At this point, Kaufmann paused. "Any questions so far?"

His audience was stone still until Michael raised a hand.

"Yes. Please identify yourself and ask your question."

"My name is Michael Cain. I represent Iowa Governor Dirksen. Is there anything to suggest how much time we have before the traffickers, as you indicated, may disappear?"

"Nothing definite. I'll include it in a potential timeline. I will say it may be connected to the upcoming decision by the Iowa Racing and Gaming Commission whether to establish a casino in the Iowa Great Lakes Region. We have identified one board member we believe is directing the commission to award the casino license to Bart Farley and his organization, Free To Play. We don't know how or to what degree Farley and this board member are tied to the human traffickers, but we do have evidence of collaboration. Which leads to my next point.

"In addition to the usual prostitution, drugs, and extortion, we believe this is an attempt by a major criminal organization to establish and control a casino in the Lakes Area. It would be to their advantage to make this a part of their enterprise. The opportunity to expand operations would be exponential. Relative to that, we know retired Agent Smith became interested in the activities of Bart Farley, the owner of the Ridge Top Nightclub and the excursion boat *Maximilian*. Farley and the owner of The Lodge on Okoboji are competing for the casino license. While there was nothing conclusive, like a good investigator, Agent Smith took interest in anything he learned that could in any way help in his search for a missing young Asian woman. In the process, he seems to have posed a potential threat which may have led to his death. The autopsies on body parts as they have appeared were done by the State of Iowa's Pathologist Laboratory in Ankeny. We are waiting for further evidence, if there is any, from the lab. Although still in the care of the Iowa pathologist, Agent Smith's remains will eventually, if necessary, be sent to our federal facility."

Michael again raised his hand.

"Yes, Mr. Cain."

"I've been privileged to have access to Agent Smith's investigative notes, and while there is competition between Farley and the Lodge for the casino license, I've found nothing to implicate the Lodge in anything illegal. Do you have any information that suggests the Lodge was involved in Agent Smith's death or the attempt to kidnap Carla Rodriguez?"

Special Agent Kaufmann frowned. His jaw muscles popped as he clenched his teeth, and he gave a non-answer. "Concerning the Lodge, nothing more is forthcoming at this time. Now, if I may continue, the assassin, known to the FBI as Alex, was a free agent but associated on a basis of need with an organization we have been watching for some time. During the attempt by Alex to retrieve or dispose of Carla, three men arrived who we believe were on the same mission independent of Alex. During gunfire that ensued, Alex was injured, and in the confusion, Carla attempted an escape and was shot by Alex. Alex then fled the scene in a large, silver pickup truck, driver unknown, and subsequently died of her injury at the Okoboji airstrip while attempting to escape using her personal airplane."

"The three men have disappeared, but we know who they are and have issued an APB for them and the car they were driving. As with Alex, we do not know how they came to know of Carla's location, but after an investigation into a body found at a junkyard in the city of Spencer, we believe they have a connection to Bart Farley."

At this point, Agent Kaufmann paused, but no hands were raised.

"Good. Let's take a short break. Plan to meet back here in fifteen minutes."

Before he could step out, Kaufmann approached Michael. "Mr. Cain, a word?"

Drawing Michael to a corner of the room away from others, Kaufmann stepped in close, noses nearly touching. "Your governor must have hot red lines to the State Department and our FBI Director. I've been instructed to inform you that you may continue your investigation into the disappearance of the missing Chinese woman but with the understanding you will not involve yourself in the larger investigation by the FBI. However, if you incidentally find evidence that may relate to our investigation, you are to inform me immediately. Understood?"

Besides the noticeable pulse at his temples and his need for a breath mint, Michael considered that FBI Special Agent Kaufmann was having difficulty dealing with being less in charge than his position implied. "I understand. I will, of course, keep the governor informed at all times of my progress."

Kaufmann stared hard, jaw muscles clenching, but knowing he had little recourse under the circumstances dealt to him by the Director of the FBI, he nodded. "Agreed."

33

It was late afternoon, and Big Man remained at his desk, suffering a massive headache, a consequence of the weekend's debauchery. Pinching the bridge of his nose, he had to smile, thinking aloud, "No such thing as too much partying!"

He had arrived home late Sunday evening, slept a few hours, and had been at his desk since mid-morning. The vote on the casino license would be Thursday afternoon, and the announcement of the result made public by Thursday evening. Between now and then, much remained to be done. Foremost was keeping all the votes for Farley and his organization, Free To Play, in line and then reassuring Farley and his people. Beyond that, Farley could screw himself. Big Man was more concerned about the people bankrolling the project. Farley was all swagger and bluster, but with the money and resources invested, the people behind him had to be dangerous. It was odd. Farley didn't get it. He really thought he was in charge.

Big Man planned to personally announce the result of the Gaming Commission's vote to the media and the competing parties as part of a celebration aboard the *Maximilian*. The vote would be close but certain, and he was composing a little speech, not that he'd need it. It was a small detail, but he did not want it to niggle at him the rest of the evening as he relaxed over highballs, dinner, and an early bedtime. Bless his wife's heart. She was so caring and understanding considering all the time he had committed to this project and his frequent trips to Northwest Iowa. She was clueless. Strangely, he did not revel in this knowledge. Somewhere in his psyche, there remained a faint scrap of decency.

Setting the finished notes for his speech aside, he leaned back in his oversized executive chair, stretched, and pushed away from the large desk. He took a moment to turn and admire, as he often did, the considerable array of plaques and photos of him with prominent people. Smiling, he was reassured he could obliterate any challenge he faced, including Fart Barley. He chuckled at the minor vulgarity.

Rising, he felt shaky. Speaking aloud, he admonished himself, "Man, I am tired. Time to get out of here."

But as he stepped around the desk, the burner phone rang—Farley's private connection. Retrieving it from his suit coat, he glared at the offending number. His first impulse was to throw it against the wall. He answered on the fourth ring.

"What?"

"Big Man?"

"Who else? What the hell do you want now?"

There was a pause. "I assume from your manner that you haven't heard the news?"

"What news?"

"The news about your favorite girlfriend."

While Farley broke the bad news, Big Man could hardly contain his fury! How could the situation have gotten so out of control? Farley was a total screw-up. Why hadn't he let the RV People take care of the missing girl? Farley's boys had totally screwed the pooch, and now the Big Man could be next pooch!

Farley hammered home the point. "We don't need video. We'll bury you so deep in her death, you'll never dig out. Anything you say about our involvement is circumstantial. You wanted a girl, and the RV People provided a service. Something went wrong, and you arranged to have her killed. I knew nothing about any of it. End of story."

Farley was ecstatic to reassert control over the Big Man. He waited, but there was no reaction, so he continued. "As for a casino in the Lakes Area? I applied and competed with the Lodge but had no idea if or why you might have manipulated the vote. Maybe you were helping the Lodge and it went south. Maybe you thought to extort me. It doesn't matter. Granted, there may be a slight problem with prostitution, but that's contained. Small price to avoid bigger issues. You're the one who will answer to murder, extortion, and prostitution."

The Big Man let all the bile wash over him. His only response was: "So what now?"

"Now, you do as we planned. Deliver the casino to me and all your problems go away. You may even get the benefits I promised. Carla, your favorite Latina, and your young Asian girl are both dead. The assassin sent to eliminate Carla is dead and my buddies have disappeared. No direct connections to you need to be known unless I let them be known." He paused, then said, in a flat, cold tone, "No one else needs to die."

His implication lingered as though it were over an open grave.

"You'll get your casino. The vote is Thursday, and I plan to be aboard your *Maximilian* for the big announcement."

"You deliver, everything is good."

And that was it. What had seemed a simple straightforward scheme, a promise of big money and satisfaction for his indulgences, was now a fucking time bomb. If an assassin and two working girls were only collateral, what was he? Dead, rotting meat.

Big Man did not reflect long. Pulling up the contact list in his phone, he punched in the personal number for FBI Agent Kaufmann.

He had met Kaufmann at a workshop on gambling and the influence of organized crime provided by the FBI to the Iowa Racing and Gaming Commission. Big Man had been impressed, had asked several questions, and later, had met privately with Agent Kaufmann. The meeting was useful. Big Man understood how the state of Iowa worked to prevent the criminal element from penetrating the casino business, but talking with Agent Kaufmann took it to another level. If Big Man was to excavate himself from this mess, Kaufmann could be the man with the shovel. Agent Kaufmann was strict FBI and could be trusted to follow a procedure which, with Big Man's cooperation, might provide a lifeline. Kaufmann was a talent ascending in the FBI. It would be a great career boost to an agent who could break open a case of human trafficking and solve multiple murders.

This could not wait. He would meet with Agent Kaufmann and rather than a casino, Big Man would see to it that Farley got what he deserved!

***

The Big Boss was calling from his office in Chicago, "Did you talk to Farley?"

RV Man was expecting the call. "Just now."

"And?"

"Farley's Big Man is scared shitless. He'll do anything we say to avoid going down for murder."

"I get that, but what about the casino vote?"

"The votes are in the bag. The Gaming Commission votes Thursday, and the announcement is Thursday evening. We need to lay low until then."

"How's Farley holding up?"

"Arrogant and ignorant, as usual. He believes he's the boss, like he's some sort of criminal mastermind."

"Okay. Let him think that, but we may need to deal with Mr. Farley sooner than we thought."

"I agree. Any thoughts on how? It's not my area of expertise, but I'm so sick of the bastard, I might enjoy doing it myself, like maybe a little accident falling off his own boat, late at night, in the middle of the lake."

"I like the irony, but don't get ahead of the plan. What about Farley's boys?"

"What about them? Farley's boys don't know or at least can't prove anything. Once Farley is gone, they're a non-issue. They'll probably do their best to disappear."

Big Boss persisted. "What if they're caught?"

"It's all on Farley. We deny, and they can't prove anything. Right after the announcement Thursday night, we'll move the girls. Any sign of prostitution or trafficking disappears."

"And Big Man?"

"He shouldn't be a problem. He has too much to lose and is connected to the death of the two underage girls.

"He's still a loose end, but we'll do what is necessary when necessary. You take care of your business, and I'll take care of the rest. Now tell me about this guy who's investigating some missing girl."

"What guy?"

"That guy you told me about. Cain. The lawyer who keeps sniffing around!"

"Sorry. I didn't think that was a problem. There's a lot going on, so for now, I'm ignoring him."

Big Boss was becoming impatient. "Really? What if he turns out to be a problem?"

"Look, the word I got is he's spinning his wheels. He's trying to help the sheriff's office in some way, but Loren Price, our guy at the Lodge, says he's asking the same questions about a missing woman and hasn't gotten any farther than the retired FBI guy. It's a dead end. Look, no one knows for certain how the agent died. It may have been an accident and there is no connection between Cain or the dead FBI guy to the Ridge Top, the *Maximilian*, or our interests."

"And the girl, Carla Rodriguez?"

"She's dead. It doesn't matter what she told the priests who found her or the women who were hiding her. Anything she said is now circumstantial or at best arguable. If asked, she must have been an illegal alien who ran away from her family. We had nothing to do with her, and all our other girls will have disappeared. Everyone else will keep their mouths shut, or else. It's all on Farley. But it is puzzling."

"Why do you think that?"

"Her death will lead to questions about the Ridge Top, but other than Farley, there is nothing other than conjecture that connects us to the plan for a casino. And if the agent hadn't been killed, we probably wouldn't have the FBI crawling all over the place."

RV Man could hear the clink of ice dropping into a glass. "Okay. We're close to the finish. We'll stay with the plan. But be ready to pull the girls, and don't ignore Cain. He has a reputation for causing trouble."

"Got it, but we may cause more trouble than necessary if we mess with him. As you said, we can clean up loose ends after Thursday's announcement."

With the call ended, Boss Man sat staring at his cell phone, lost in thought. Drawing a deep breath, he nodded his head, an affirmation of an important decision. He valued loyalty above all else and trusted his employees. But his trust in their competence only extended so far. He punched in the number, and his call was answered on the first ring.

"Hello, brother, what can I do for you?"

"Jimmy, I'd like you to arrange a field trip for me by car to depart Thursday morning and return that night, very discreet, of course."

"Of course. Anyone besides you and the driver?"

"Two of our better people—a man, for brawn, and a woman, for brains."

"Can do."

"Have them pick me up at the office at 8 a.m. Oh, and have them all, even the driver, be equipped for contingencies."

"Understood. Thursday, 8 a.m., at your office. Good hunting!"

It was settled. He would personally oversee the final stage in his far-reaching plan from the Ridge Top Nightclub.

34

This was one of the more enduring of Michael's favorite times and places: early morning on the broad, screened-in front porch of the family home, overlooking the changing moods of West Okoboji and allowing the effect to wash over him. From day to day and hour to hour, the lake provided a kaleidoscopic array of personalities if only one took the opportunity to notice. On a quiet morning as this, the whisper of waves kissing the shore and the sigh of sand relenting as waves receded were both a singular moment in life, yet timeless. A kind of eternity. To Michael's sensibilities, it was a reminder of opportunities offered, then ceded—his own story, at least in part, in recent years.

But here and now, before the heat of the day could swell along with water moved by freshened breeze and watercraft, before the man-made sounds could intrude then overtake the calm as the nightly shroud was shed, he found contentment. For a moment, the unpleasantness of the previous day was forbidden. It was a time for peace, reflection, and memories. A ghost of the swimmer's float where

Michael and Janni had first... Michael smiled. He closed his eyes and inhaled slowly, drawing on the scent of lake and memory of their first night.

Sipping hot coffee, Michael shivered in the light lakeside breeze and watched a large pontoon boat far out on the lake bludgeon its way over dark waters and through prescient waves. *Marv's Marina is up early*, he thought. Less than handsome, the craft was useful for setting and removing docks and provided for a variety of necessary tasks on this watery playground. It did not disrupt his mood but was a reminder that the day had begun.

The night before, in a short conversation with Connie after an interview with Detective Donahue and FBI Special Agent Kaufmann, Michael agreed to refocus on the investigation into the missing Chinese woman. He soon would be back at ILCC, and if Michael was to be of any help to the missing woman and the governor, it would have to happen this week. As promised, if he did come across anything of interest to the FBI, incidentally of course, he would pass it along, but otherwise, he would keep his nose out of the Fed's business.

Arriving home late and unable to sleep, Michael had sat at his desk, reinforced by a small Glenfiddich, and reviewed the information he'd been given on the disappearance of the young woman.

Iowa Department of Criminal Investigation Agents had interviewed her family and the host family. Little was learned. Her week at Okoboji was fun but uneventful, some sightseeing and socializing, with nothing that suggested risk to her safety. At the end of the visit, she was to be given a ride home by her host, but when called to rise and shine for breakfast before the drive back to Ames, she was already gone, as were a few clothes and personal items. A handwritten note remained on her pillow: *Don't worry, I'm safe, and I'll be back soon. Luv you guys!* Shocked and totally surprised, neither her family nor her host could shed any light on the disappearance.

A search of social media was unhelpful, even bland, perhaps due to some sense of propriety for her family's status. But since the time of disappearance that morning, her use of social media was nonexistent, and her phone untraceable, notable in that both likely denoted the hard beginning of a timeline.

Restraint, a consequence of secrecy, may have justified the brevity of the DCI report. The only conclusion provided was the young lady likely disappeared voluntarily. Why and whether in the company of someone else was unknown. So much for the official efforts to investigate!

Considering the short time he had been in the area, Agent Smith had made a good start, and his journal, as downloaded from the cloud, was detailed. Helen Smith had explained her husband was a bit old-school. He always carried a notebook and would write down information, then transfer his notes to the computer. For security, he saved the digital version in the cloud, deleted it from his computer, and destroyed the hand-written notes. As an adherent of redundancy, he provided his wife access to his cloud account. All of Smith's notes had been downloaded and included in the governor's information.

Smith had spoken with the host family and drilled down hard, specifically about people, but the family, aided by their daughter, had nothing to add to the list of people and places they provided the DCI Agents. He did note the family clearly was distraught and discounted them as suspects, however, he added, *Does the daughter know something without understanding the significance?*

His detailed notes varied but were comprehensive and included casual conversations and general observations, much of which did not seem to contribute much to the investigation. Michael considered this approach "brain spinach." An investigator may not know the significance of a detail at the time, but sometimes a seemingly unrelated conversation or observation could, on review, nourish a lead to something or someone significant in the investigation. Several people seemed to have been interviewed in more detail, and in addition to notes, Smith had recorded some interviews and had taken pictures. A short list of people and random ideas required follow-up.

In comparison to Agent Smith's detail, Michael's own account was brief. True, the governor's request was only a few days old, and after all, there had been a good deal of activity since, but Michael should be further along in his efforts. Consequently, he had composed two lists, the longer was of Smith's interviews and sources yet to be contacted or to be repeated, and the shorter list, prioritized, included his own thoughts, some of which were tangent—more brain spinach—yet typical of the thoroughness Michael brought to the beginning of an investigation.

Smith had taken a ride on the *Maximilian* and had written a short paragraph about a hostess named Linda, who, when asked and shown her picture, had tentatively identified the missing Chinese woman as a passenger. She had said the young lady was with a group, perhaps six in all. The hostess did not know any of their names but admitted the woman in question seemed interested in one of the men, and Smith had written a quote: *"A bit clingy, you know?"* She also shared that it was cool out on the water and the young man had taken off his jacket and given it to the young woman to wear. Again, Smith had quoted the hostess, *"It seemed odd, like incongruent."* A cryptic note followed. *Check the recording.*

He'd taken the recording on a cell phone and saved it in the cloud. A transcription had been sent as part of a report to the governor. Michael paged through the packet of information until he found the transcription.

"How do you mean incongruent?"

"It was a nice jacket. Satin, I think, and it had a motorcycle on the back, really nice embroidery, like custom-made. Above the motorcycle

it said, 'My car is' and below, it said, 'an Indian,' which is weird."

"Why is it weird?"

"You know, because it should have said, 'My other car is a Harley.'"

"Why do you think that?"

"Everyone knows that, besides I used to date a guy with a Harley, and he had a bumper sticker on his pickup that said, 'My other car is a Harley.' Every guy at the Spokes and Suds probably had the same bumper sticker. Some of the women, too."

"Was there anything else, about the people she was with?"

"No. They all seemed normal, happy, and you know, chatty."

"Anything else about the young man? Maybe something unusual besides the jacket?"

"Not really. He was fairly tall, slender, with shoulder-length blond hair, about the same age as the others. Although now that you ask, there was one thing."

"Yes?"

"Well, not to be judgmental, but he was sorta feminine, ya know?"

"Feminine? In what way?"

"I don't know. He looked delicate. Odd if he was a biker. Just an impression, ya know?"

The picture of Linda that accompanied the transcript was of a college-age woman, average size, dark hair, attractive (in Michael's opinion), and wearing a t-shirt emblazoned with "To the Max!" on the front. Michael added the name of the hostess to his list.

On the same ride, Smith had spoken to Farley, had shown him a picture of the missing woman and had asked if he'd seen her, but Farley had blown him off. There was a blurry picture of Farley, likely taken surreptitiously. Smith wrote that his gut instinct told him Farley was off in some way, besides acting like a jerk. Smith had a memo to "Deep-dive Bart Farley!" and Michael added Farley to his list of names.

Continuing on, Michael read about Smith's visit to the Spokes and Suds bar where he'd spoken with the owner Shirley McGaven. When shown her picture, Shirley recognized the girl and confirmed she had been at the bar with friends but was not sure about a boyfriend. However, when suggested, she did remember the satin jacket.

"Nice embroidery, and the cliché? A bit unusual, but clever. There are a few of the old Indian motorcycles around. My impression was that was his ride."

Though it was a long shot, Smith had a reminder to follow up with authorities and on social media for an Indian motorcycle and to revisit the Spokes and Suds. Michael would need to do the same and revisit Shirley.

What remained in Smith's notes mostly eliminated leads or possibilities that had occurred to the investigator, but Michael thought a reference in Smith's notes about Dr. Charles Chen was curious. Identified as a part-time maintenance engineer on the *Maximilian*, no other information was provided, but Michael wondered whether Agent Smith thought there may be a connection to the missing girl. Both Asian? Meaningless and xenophobic on Michael's part. Michael would speak with Dr. Chen. Besides, after the brawl between Weird Willy and Charley, Michael's innate sense of curiosity needed a mend. Satiated with his lists and priorities written on a fresh legal pad, Michael had finally been able to sleep.

Reluctantly, Michael left the shade and serenity of the porch to go inside, recharge the coffee mug, and return to his desk for a quick review of the lists composed the night before.

The *Maximilian* was high on the list. He opened his computer to learn if there was a website that listed a schedule of departures and arrivals for *Max*. He would take a ride in the belly of the beast, and if she was available, talk to the hostess.

But first, he would take a long run to clear his mind, enjoy a shower, eat a light breakfast, and thus fortified for a busy day, start from the top of his personal list of names by making several phone calls. It was time to tap into his expansive group of friends and colleagues known as Michael's Marauders!

***

FBI Special Agent Kaufmann had not slept. In the midst of the frantic response by his small team and the sheriff's deputies to the kidnap attempt of Carla Rodriguez and its chaotic aftermath, he could have ignored the incoming call, but he recognized the name. It was Big Man.

The brief prelude Big Man provided was all the explanation needed for Kaufmann to understand how critical the information and explosive the impact would be on his investigation. Instructing his agents to cooperate and support the deputies and DCI agents as best they could as they worked the scenes and witnesses, he made a flurry of phone calls as he drove faster than allowed, lights flashing, to Des Moines.

Unlike Michael or Agent Kaufmann, Janneke slept well. Arriving home the evening before, drained from the lengthy interrogation, she called Luke, her former husband and abiding partner in business, to say she would be not be in to work, took Tylenol, and went right to bed. Up early, her headache was gone. After an early morning jog, she showered, dressed, and indulged in a large breakfast. She was famished. Then she turned her concern to Michael and her curiosity of any news he may have.

She called the landline, as she usually did if calling early or late. The phone rang until the ancient answering machine he had inherited from his mother responded to her call.

"Hello, Sweetie! Either you're still in bed, or the game is afoot! My headache is gone, I've recovered from the enforcers' inquisition, and I'm reveling in having saved your sweet little buns from the nasty assassin. Now I want to hear all about your interview and any gossip you picked up from our local constable-in-chief! I'm looking forward to our next flying lesson, something quiet, maybe a fighter jet with rockets! Call me!"

"Wait! I'm here!"

"Why didn't you pick up?"

"I just did!"

"I meant sooner!"

"Sorry. I know. I just got back from my run and was unlocking the door when the phone rang."

"You lock your door to go out and run?"

"After the bonk to the noggin I took this spring, I've been more cautious. Besides, yesterday's events suggested caution may be warranted."

"Don't be such a wuss! So, what are we doing today?"

"What do you mean?"

"I mean, my dear Michael, by now you probably have a ream of lists, and I am ready and willing to contribute my considerable talents to your flailing efforts. Besides, I'm dying—sorry, poor choice of words—to know if there have been any developments since last night."

"Well, listen up, Lady! I'm no wuss, ya hear me? I'm a big-shot investigator on the hot trail of a missing girl! And maybe what I know is private! What do you think of that?"

"Okay, big-shot. So what is the governor going to say when you have nothing to report? I bet you're getting ready to call in the Marauders. Am I right, or am I right?"

"Well, you got me there. Let me make a few calls, and I'll get back to you."

"Good. I'll call Lucia and see if she can meet with us today."

"Us?"

"Yes, us! Admit it, you need your Watson, Sherlock! You're smiling, aren't you?"

"Guilty as charged." Michael was still smiling as they ended the call.

***

After a quick shower and breakfast, he was back at his desk, ready to call and solicit help from some of his Marauders, when his cell phone pinged. The text message was from Janni. *Lunch with Lucia at 12:30, in her suite. Be there! Ciao!*

Knowing better than to grouse, he sent a reply: *See you at 12:30.* Then, as an afterthought, he wrote, *Plan to take a ride on the Maximilian. Care to join me?* She responded immediately, *When pigs fly! Once was enough. No way will I again set foot on that boat!* Several nasty emojis followed.

Michael laughed, then sent, *LOL. Just thought I'd ask. See you at the Lodge.*

The first call on his list was to long-time friend and quasi-colleague, Iowa State University Chief of Police Barry Seward.

As a prosecutor, Michael had worked with and advised Barry on several cases involving students at ISU. Most recently, Barry and his devoted PA, Mavis, had been helpful with the investigation into a murdered ISU student, a young woman from Okoboji. Mavis was plugged into nearly every department and office on campus. The intelligence, opinions, and gossip she was able to glean through her network of fellow personal assistants were an important contribution to the information that flowed daily across Barry's desk. It was Barry who nicknamed Mavis, "The Maven of Marvel" and who called her university-wide connections, "The Legion of Peers."

It was Mavis who answered, "Hello, Michael."

"Hello, Mavis. How are you, and how are the wonderful folks in ISU law enforcement?"

"We are well and continue to soldier on. Barry just got off the phone. I'll ring you through."

There was a brief pause, then Barry picked up. "Michael! How are you?"

"I'm fine, but as usual, I'm up to my ears in bears and alligators."

"I understand. Blame Governor Dirksen. Everything is hush-hush, but I get a call for an update from his man every day! I heard you had a little visit from our esteemed Governor. Are you making progress in the search for our absconded Chinese student?"

"Not yet. It's only been a few days since the Governor showed up on my doorstep—big surprise—and since then, it's become more complicated which may or may not be related to the missing girl."

"So I heard. According to the local news media, the Okoboji Area is having quite a little crime spree. Keep it up, and you'll be on national TV."

"I'm not surprised, but there's nothing in the media about the missing woman, is there?"

"No, but it's like a ticking time bomb. Sooner or later, someone is going to start asking very public questions."

"Speaking of, I have some questions for you. Governor Dirksen left me everything he had on the investigation by Agent Smith and the DCI, but I want to hear your perspective."

"Well, I have nothing, and I mean absolutely nothing, more to report than what I told the DCI and FBI. The FBI made it known that the ISU Police Department would not question the girl's family and the FBI and DCI would share—I'm doing air quotes—what they learned. You probably have more information than I do."

"If what I was given is all the FBI and DCI have, they have a big problem. I bet there's someone up the chain of command composing a variety of announcements to cover their ass when this becomes public."

"Michael, the best I can give you, which should be no surprise, is Mavis. She was not questioned, and considering that what she may know is based on gossip and conjecture, I did not suggest her name.

She and I have talked it over, and as usual, she has her own opinions and insights. I don't know how it would help find the girl, and if there was something definitive, I would have acted on it. But you never know. Hold for a moment, and I'll check with her."

Mavis's voice came on seconds later. "Michael?"

"Hello again."

"Barry asked me if I would share with you any thoughts or information I may have about our missing girl, and of course, I want to do everything I can do to help a student. Just remember, this is not, as our ISU researchers would state it, based upon empirical evidence, but it still may help fill in a few blanks."

"Mavis, anything you have to say will be treated in confidence and is much appreciated."

"Very well. I do a tai chi class with her mother and have gotten to know her casually. Also, one of my dearest friends is on the faculty, a professor of Chinese language and literature. I take lessons from her on Chinese and with her encouragement, I've started volunteering at the church to help ESL learners."

"The missing girl's father is a researcher on a shared project between the USDA and the equivalent Chinese agency. It would be, perhaps, inconvenient for everyone concerned if this matter should become public, something the young lady may understand but chose to ignore, most inconvenient. Her mother is a stay-at-home mom but is an active volunteer in the ISU Chinese community. She is a registered nurse and helps on occasion at the ISU student health center when someone with her nursing and language skills are needed. The boy is ten years old, and I understand he's an exceptional student, a pianist, and loves to play soccer.

"I can say with confidence that her family is well-respected and the parents love, even dote, on their daughter and her younger brother. The father is strict—not unusual—but she is unusually independent.

This is not the first time she has fallen off the radar, so to speak, although only briefly, and never before like this. She is very bright, social, personable, media-skilled, and fluent in English. The sense of it, as I've been told by my friend, is that the young lady is excited to be living in the United States and curious to learn and experience as much as she can. On this occasion, it may have promoted poor choices and placed her at risk. Of course, it also means she is putting her family and their future at risk. That's pretty much everything, Michael."

But Michael knew that was not quite everything. "And your opinion, Mavis?"

"Yes, well, if you want my opinion, I think there's nothing malicious in the young lady's intent, but her hyper-enthusiasm and naivete may have contributed to a questionable decision. She must be with someone, someone who is a unicorn, that is, unscripted. If she is fortunate, this someone is benevolent and trustworthy. If unfortunate, someone may do her harm. I suspect the consequence will reveal itself in spite of efforts by law enforcement. Of course, we still must try."

After thanking Mavis and then Barry for their help, Michael sat quietly at his desk, better informed about the family but knowing nothing more to help in his search for the errant young woman. Only Mavis's edict remained. *Of course, we still must try.*

The rest of the morning went quickly. Michael called and spoke with Joan Eckhart, the wife of the local family who had hosted the missing Chinese woman. Michael was careful to explain the Cain family was a long-time friend of Governor Dirksen, and the Governor had personally met with Michael to ask him to quietly review the investigation into the missing woman. He added the Governor had expressed a personal interest and wanted the case solved quickly with as little publicity as possible. Mrs. Eckhart said she shared the Governor's sentiment, and her family had no desire to draw unwanted attention to themselves. She explained that her husband, as the high school principal of the Okoboji Community Schools, felt more distressed for the possible loss of someone under his care. Mrs. Eckhart assured Michael her husband, Bill, and their daughter, Kaye Eckhart, Lei Ming's roommate, would be available and eager to assist Michael by answering his questions. She offered, and Michael agreed, to meet the next day.

Next, Michael called and spoke with Dr. Chen, the maintenance engineer for the *Maximilian*. After explaining why he would like to meet, Dr. Chen's response was, "Of course, I'd be happy to do whatever may help. We can have coffee or tea and visit. If you have time, my wife may give you a tour of the gardens. Morning would be best. Our gardens are lovely in the morning."

One arrangement remained. He called Pam Schneider. Michael had substituted for Pam while she was on maternity leave from Iowa Lakes Community College. Pam was the proverbial calm in the storm and a counterbalance to Michael's tendency to turn an interview into an interrogation. On good advice, he had asked her to accompany him on a sensitive interview with a witness in a previous case. Pam's rapport with the witness and subsequent insights proved to be critical to the investigation. Now, again called upon to assist, she enthusiastically agreed to be, as she phrased it, his girl Friday or any other day.

Finishing with a quick review of any ILCC duties, he locked up and descended the nineteen steps from house to shore, lowered *Frau Nägel* from the lift, and in minutes, was on his way to the Lodge.

36

As suggested, they met in Lucia's private quarters. In spite of a self-promoted day off and role as Michael's "Watson," a call from the Sports Shop owner, Nigel Waterford, had hijacked Janneke's plan to join them for lunch. Her call to Lucia was brief. "No promises," she'd said, "but if I can, I'll try to be there for dessert."

Greeted by his gracious hostess, Michael accompanied her to a small intimate table set by the window overlooking the lake. He helped her be seated (an attempt at chivalry), took his chair, and their server laid before each a small, chilled dinner salad topped with bay shrimp and Roquefort dressing (a favorite of Michael's) on the side. The entree that followed was thinly sliced, rare prime rib served open-faced on lightly toasted Italian bread accompanied by the Lodge's own creamy horseradish sauce, and a peach compote to soften the horseradish. The meal was accompanied by a young pinot noir. Dessert was a slice of Black Forest cake with raspberry glaze accompanied by strong black coffee. Michael thought, *Compared to my usual, this is decadent!*

Talk was relaxed, tangent to what would come, but with the dishes cleared and a second cup poured, it was time to get serious.

"Thank you, Lucia, for a lovely lunch."

"You're very welcome, Michael."

"Janneke told me some of your concerns following the discovery of retired FBI Agent Smith. I'm not sure what I can do, but I will try. How may I be of assistance?"

Lucia drew a deep breath. "The investigation by the FBI is widening, and I don't know how or why, but the effect seems to be pulling the Lodge into a downward spiral."

"Different agencies have questioned the staff repeatedly and have gone through all of our personnel records, even copied them! I know it sounds on the fringe, but there seems to be a conspiracy to discourage visitors to the Lodge. We've had an unusual number of cancellations, and the local traffic for our restaurants has dropped off the edge. The news media has not been helpful. They keep reporting an ongoing investigation of an unidentified nature. I don't know how to change the perception that we at the Lodge are doing something illegal or immoral."

"Immoral? What is that about?"

"One example of why I need you. I hope you can separate fact from rumor and help me navigate the FBI and any other agencies, especially federal agencies, which have turned our business on its head. We were doing so well, even recovered from the mess this spring, and now this. Please, I would be so grateful for anything you can do."

"I'll try, but within limits that I'm not free to explain. I can say the investigation into Agent Smith is now in the hands of the FBI."

"I thought Agent Smith was on vacation. What was he doing, and what's all this cloak and dagger stuff?"

"Agent Smith was investigating the disappearance of a young woman. He may have come across information having nothing to do with his investigation but which put him at risk."

"But it's so intrusive! I'm afraid the FBI has decided the Lodge is responsible in some way and now just looking for a way to prove their theory."

"The FBI is thorough. They are looking at everything that may relate even remotely to their investigation. Agent Smith was staying at the Lodge, so naturally, that's a focal point. I know how difficult it is to accept, but I would advise patience."

Michael paused to observe her reaction. Lucia was silent, eyes downcast. Recognizing a possible stalemate, he made a decision.

"I assume you've heard of the shootings at the home of the Lawery Sisters and at the local airport?"

Lucia looked up and stared directly into Michael's eyes. "Yes."

"It has to do with a much broader investigation by the FBI. I'm not privy to the details, but when it's complete, it is highly likely it will show there is no connection between the Lodge and Agent Smith. Please trust me on this."

"Does it involve the decision on the casino license?"

Michael paused, thinking, *nothing gets past her!* "It may but to what degree, I have no idea. My opinion?"

"Yes, please!"

"The FBI is close to concluding their investigation. In spite of your concerns, continue to work as if everything is normal. Do not question or change your mind about the casino license. It would not alter anything as far as the FBI is concerned but to the public, it may look suspicious. Stay the course. You and the Lodge will come out at the end a bit bruised but cleared from any involvement in this sordid mess."

"From your lips to God's ear!"

"Less than God's ear, although the FBI may appear to assume."

At that, Lucia smiled, took another deep breath, then added, "Thank you, Michael. But how can I ever truly thank you?"

"No need, but maybe save Janneke a slice of that wonderful cake?"

This time, Lucia laughed. "Maybe a whole cake?"

It was a good ending, a compliment to an excellent lunch. Lucia felt better. Their meeting might not immediately solve any problems at the Lodge, but Michael's words were encouraging, and the opportunity to share concerns and hear advice from someone she admired was welcome. Besides, it had been a long time since she'd had private time with a man she found desirable.

***

She answered the call from Supervisor Bland, aka "The Owl," on the second ring. His first reply was, "It is as I suspected."

"And?"

"Any threat posed has been neutralized, and Mr. Price is in time out, so to speak, until we can use him for any countermeasure."

"You're sure?"

"Yes. He's deep in gambling debt to some very bad people who leveraged his place at the Lodge for intel, but we can connect him as a co-conspirator in the disappearance of the retired FBI Agent."

"Connect him how?"

"This fellow, Farley is his name, called Mr. Price to say he had arranged to have someone pretend to be the wife of Agent Smith, and Price, as the registration manager, was to facilitate her arrival and provide access to Smith's room. When Price asked what would happen if Agent Smith showed up, Farley laughed. He said Agent Smith just met *Max* and would not be returning. By the way, with Price's help, I identified the first woman claiming to be Smith's wife. Her name is Pauline, or Pauly for short. I've seen her chauffeuring guests between the Lodge and the Ridge Top. But I digress. When I spoke with Mr. Price, it was made clear that should he cooperate with us, we would protect him, for now. Otherwise, he had a choice: FBI or the organization's enforcers. When I explained that to him, he was only too eager to cooperate."

"Very good. And my daughter?"

"Stressed, as you can imagine, but holding up well. Lucia has support from a good friend, the Sanderson woman, and she met with the former prosecutor I told you about. I'm not sure what transpired, but in my opinion, he should be considered an asset, not a threat. He's deeply loyal to friends and family and has a keen—again in my opinion—over-developed sense for seeking justice. Under the present circumstances, that's useful."

"As usual, I'll trust your judgement. And the Lodge?"

"Attendance is down but will improve whenever the FBI completes their investigation."

"When will that be?"

"Indefinite, but our flipped informant says the fix is in, and after Farley's group 'Free To Play' is awarded the license, they will either make nice or attempt to take over business at the Lodge, likely by extortion. Whichever they determine is to their advantage."

"The casino would be an incredible asset, but it was not part of our original business plan. It could become a liability. We will do well without it, provided there is no outside interference."

"I understand. How do you want to proceed?"

There was a slight hesitation. "When will the casino license be awarded?"

"The Gaming Commission is expected to vote, and then the award will be announced later this week."

"If there are no surprises, leave things as they stand until the decision is announced, then we'll deal with what remains. I'm sorry to leave Lucia twisting in the wind, so to speak, but pre-emptive action on our part could be harmful rather than helpful."

"I agree, but don't worry about Lucia. She's resilient, determined, and a remarkable business person. The staff and guests love her, and in spite of fierce headwinds, she's having amazing success. Frankly, she is better off without that scoundrel. Whoever blasted him to hell did her a favor."

"She loved him."

"Yes, but not as much as he loved himself."

"We spoke of this before, and perhaps I should have listened, but it's past and we remain focused on the future. Keep me apprised, and as usual, I am deeply grateful to you."

"I will. It's my honor, madam."

He hung up and took a moment to reflect, as he usually did after their conversations, on the affect, even arousal, elicited by the low, silky voice of this remarkable woman. Very Marlena Dietrich! An aficionado of film noir, Dietrich was one of his favorite actresses.

37

Michael drove *Frau Nägel* at top speed across the lake from the Lodge to where the *Maximilian* was about to depart. The vintage runabout responded with enthusiasm, slicing easily through the waves, spray adding a sheen to the craft's fine patina. Even at that, Michael barely made the 2 p.m. launch from the West Village Resort. He smiled, remembering Janneke's tart refusal to join him for an investigative cruise.

Last to board, Michael was greeted by a young woman whose name tag identified her as "Hostess Linda." Returning her greeting, he flashed his finest smile, but in deference to her immediate duties, he postponed questions. As he stepped aboard, he watched her, assisted by a burly deckhand who could have doubled as a bouncer at a nightclub, draw up and stow the gangplank.

This time of day, the trip would take them directly to the State Pier at Arnolds Park to drop off afternoon workers and passengers who wished to spend the day at the park and to board passengers, mostly tourists, for the hour-long cruise of the lake. Less interested in tourism, Michael would have time to wander and learn what he could about the boat and interview the hostess.

What he'd been told and what he'd seen from afar was true, the *Maximilian* was a strange beast. Oversized in width compared to length, three decks, the first with a slightly raised ceiling complete with a squat chandelier—hopefully plastic and not glass teardrops—a modest raised platform, ostensibly for live entertainment, and a truncated bar well-stocked with both standard and up-scale brands. Behind the bar, with a pass-through window, was a small kitchen.

There were several permanent booths around the perimeter, but most of the floor space was open to accommodate a variety of needs. The high wrap-around windows and wide sliding door aft provided an open and airy sense to the space. Narrow sliding doors gave easy access to an outer walkway crowned by a broad overhang from the second deck providing the first deck shade and protection from the elements.

The spacious second deck was accessible by exterior staircases port and starboard and a narrow interior stairway passing by the bar and kitchen area. Deck two was dedicated to viewers with its rows of benches and a few small tables and chairs near the back. There was no bar or other amenities as there was on deck one, but seating extended to include the overhang area, and to Michael, it seemed awkward, out-of-balance. He wondered what the effect would have on stability with large waves or in a strong wind storm.

A single stairway led to the third deck and pilot house. There was space enough for a few benches and high guardrails to protect the overcurious. The pilot house itself took up a generous portion of the deck, and Michael noted with approval the display of radar, radio, and various instruments dedicated to communication and the safe navigation of the craft. Though not as broad as decks one and two, it also seemed overbuilt for its purpose, leading Michael to further question the boat's stability.

With the boat underway, the captain's main concern was to avoid other boaters. The fishing and speedboats were less a problem than sailboats and personal watercraft like kayaks and the occasional canoe. Michael tapped on the door to get the captain's attention and asked if he could ask a few questions.

"Captain Billy at your service. And you are?"

"Hello, Captain Billy. I'm Michael Cain."

"I thought so. You made the news last spring."

"Yeah, I'm trying to forget."

"I thought it was impressive. So, are you here as an investigator or as a tourist?"

"Well, a bit of both."

"What can I do to help? By the way, Captain Billy is not my real name, but the boss thinks it sounds nautical."

"I understand." Taking a picture from his pocket, Michael asked, "Have you seen this young woman, or do you recognize her?"

Taking the picture from Michael's hand, Captain Billy removed his sunglasses and put on the reading glasses hanging from a lanyard around his neck. Squinting in the sunlight, he tipped his head back until his eyes focused, then shook his head. "No, sorry. I haven't seen her or recognize her. Should I know her?"

"Not necessarily. She was a passenger with some friends a week or so ago."

"Other than the PA system, I rarely interact with the passengers. You'd be better advised talking to Linda."

"I'll do that. Would you mind if we talked about the *Maximilian*?"

"Sure. What would you like to know?"

"Well, first, I assume you really are a licensed captain?"

"I am."

"And you have experience piloting various watercraft?"

"Yes. Over twenty-five years and counting, though I'm semi-retired. I do seasonal work, mostly for lake resorts up north in the summer and Florida coastal resorts in the winter."

"Good. If I may ask, strictly off the record, what do you think of the *Maximilian*? I wouldn't ask, but it may help in an investigation." Michael didn't consider it necessary to explain how or which investigation it would be.

"Strictly off the record?"

"Yes."

"If we survive the summer, we will have Lady Luck and Dr. Chen to thank."

"Dr. Chen?"

"The retired engineer from ISU. He's the one who keeps *Max* running. Without him, we'd be done in a week."

"Should I talk to him?"

"I'd recommend it if you really want to know about *Max*, but be sure to set aside enough time. He loves to talk about anything mechanical or fishing."

"I'll keep that in mind. What about your boss? Farley, is it?"

"Yes. What about him?"

"What can you tell me about him, again, off the record?"

"He pays well, well enough I don't quit. He's not licensed but insists on piloting the boat himself once a week, usually early in the morning, before the start of business. He says he needs to maintain a feel for how *Max* is performing. Nobody's complained, and it's his boat, so I don't argue. He goes alone except for Charley who's below deck fine-tuning the engine and steering system. Farley and I get along, but when we finish the season, I'm done with him."

"Why's that if he pays well?"

"He can be a jerk. No people skills. And all he talks about is this casino license he expects to win. If what he says is true, and the people from the Gaming Commission he keeps bringing onboard are representative, he's got it sewed up."

"Who on the Gaming Commission?"

"I don't know them, but there is one guy, he calls him Big Man, who's his ringer on the commission. Big Man's here nearly every weekend. Farley says it's for research. I think most of his research is with booze and the ladies at the Ridge Top. Just my opinion. Now, if you'll excuse me, I need to dock at the State Pier. It's not easy, and steering this beast takes all my concentration."

"Thanks. I appreciate it."

"You're welcome."

As Michael turned to leave, Captain Billy called out, "Enjoy the boat ride, and if you make the paper again, please don't mention my name."

Michael laughed. "You got it. Thanks again!"

Back on the main deck, Michael tried to order a beer and chat up the bartender. "Sorry, I've got to restock the bar. My supplier is on the pier. Come back after we sail, and the booze crowd thins."

***

With the exchange of passengers and resupply of the bar and kitchen complete, the *Maximilian* began its cumbersome withdrawal from the pier. Multiple wakes from passing boats nearly pushed the slow-turning craft back against the pier. A powerful thrust from the twin props eliminated the peril but nearly knocked over standing passengers. *Max* settled into a steady, throbbing pulse, and other than a few questions and comments, her passengers disbursed about the boat.

With the craft underway, Michael watched until he thought Hostess Linda's initial duties were done. He caught up with her before she could move on. "Hello, Linda! My name is Michael Cain. I know you're busy, but I'm looking for a missing person and would greatly appreciate it if you could answer a few questions. It will only take a few minutes."

Mildly startled by Michael's abrupt appearance blocking her way to deck two, Linda recovered quickly enough to appreciate the strikingly handsome man she had appraised as he had come onboard. She thought to herself, *He really is gorgeous! A bit old for me, but still...*

"Linda?"

"Oh, sorry. You surprised me. Yes, a few questions, then I need to check passengers on the upper decks."

Hostess Linda did remember the young woman in the picture, the satin jacket, and several of the people she was with, but in the end, she only reinforced what Agent Smith had reported. She knew nothing about the Big Man or visitors from the Gaming Commission but did add that Dr. Chen and Bart Farley were not onboard today.

"Farley likes to pilot the boat at least once each week. He claims he's hands-on and likes to get the feel of the boat. I agree he likes to feel. I make sure to stay away from him. Dr. Chen usually rides several times a week and is on call whenever Captain Billy thinks there's a need. He's a nice man, and our deckhands agree with our Captain, without Dr. Chen, we'd probably be at the bottom of the lake."

Michael smiled, thanked and assured her what she told him was important. She sighed and bit her bottom lip as she watched him move on to question the bartender. *He's even lovely from behind!*

Michael got his beer, but the bartender was of no help. Shown the picture, all Michael learned was, "Nah, I probably had the day off."

FBI Special Agent Kaufmann was running on adrenaline and coffee. The aborted murder of Carla Rodriguez meant the FBI needed to act soon. The bad guys would be on edge and could disappear at any moment. Any unnecessary delay could jeopardize the entire operation. But the stunning call and subsequent interrogation of the Big Man increased the urgency. They would move up the raid of the Ridge Top from Saturday to Thursday evening during the cruise on the *Maximilian* and before the planned announcement of the result of the Iowa Gaming Commissioners' vote on a casino for the Iowa Great Lakes.

His superior agreed, saying, "If you wait any longer, the goose will have flown the pen." Kaufmann had smiled at the misquote knowing his boss was a city boy and likely had never set foot on a farmyard.

The warrants were being tendered and requisite personnel would be on hand by tomorrow. He would meet with his team and local leaders later today. Kaufmann knew from experience the quality of support by local law enforcement could be uneven, but he was especially impressed with Sheriff Conrad and his people at the courthouse. He could rely on them to play a role critical for the success of a complicated operation.

The Ridge Top Nightclub, motel, and cafe were accessed, thus isolated, by a single entrance, but a review was taking place with Google Earth, a video by drone flyover, and an in-person team to reconnoiter the area. While not likely, there was the chance someone in desperation may try escaping through the fields and cropland that surrounded the target. Kaufmann intended to block every possible avenue of escape. It was a total lockdown; no one was going to get away.

***

Sheriff Conrad did not like the news. A call from the PM nurse charged with caring for Carla reported Milo Leadbetter's hotshot intern, Stevie Carson, was sniffing around the hospital and asking a lot of questions. Something needed to be done.

At Connie's request, Dr. Matt conferred with Carla's surgeon and called back to say he and the surgeon agreed. Under the circumstances, Carla could be moved to a safe house, provided someone was on hand around the clock to care for her and she was within minutes of the hospital.

With Dr. Matt's help, they would covertly move her from the hospital, the change of shift would be a good time, but Connie puzzled over where he would find a nearby safe house. *Who do I know?* He had the answer and better fortune than Michael reaching Janneke.

Janneke made one call, then answered Connie's request. "The Lawerys will take her back in. They are isolated enough from neighbors, and anyone snooping would be obvious. The bad guys wouldn't expect Carla to be back with the Aunties, and it would be easy to protect the home from land and lakeside. I'll move in, and the Lawery

Sisters and I can care for Carla until it's safe to go public. Dr. Matt can arrange to provide a confidential nurse, and I'm sure Matt would agree to be on call."

By noon, Agent Kaufmann, exhausted but up to speed, called Sheriff Conrad to share the breaking news about the Big Man. Subsequently, he outlined preparations and set a time to meet with area officials including Sheriff Conrad, Dickinson County Deputies, and Department of Natural Resources officers later in the day.

"We'll gather in the conference room at the Sheriff's office at 7 p.m. I'll arrange for the Iowa DNR to assign some of their local people to do lake patrol, but with extra attention to the Lawery property. I'll leave it up to you to choose someone from Lake Patrol to attend the meeting."

"I know just the DNR Officer to call, and I'll suggest my off-duty deputies arrive in their personal cars. We don't want it to look like a cop convention."

"Good! On Wednesday, my team and I will meet at the Dickinson County Courthouse again with you and leaders of all branches of participating enforcement—Feds, State, County, and local. My team will arrange the meet with the federal and state people, and I'll rely on you to bring on the local police chiefs, the selected DNR Officer, and any deputy you consider in a key leadership role. The local police departments will not be directly involved unless something goes very wrong, but they need to be apprised and available if needed. We'll have an update at our final meeting Thursday afternoon before we stage everyone in place to hit the Ridge Top. We'll execute our raid Thursday, at 1900 hours local time."

Sheriff Conrad remained silent, took notes during Kaufmann's outline of preparations and when asked he said, "No questions at this time, but I do have something else to run by you."

Sheriff Conrad then explained what and why they needed to move Carla. Kaufmann approved the plan, provided two FBI agents would be a part of the protection team. In addition, Sheriff Conrad would assign a deputy to stay at the Lawerys'.

"Thank you for making the arrangements. You have good people in place. I do have a request. We need one of our people on the *Maximilian* while everything is going down. I just want an observer and a contact on board in the event something gets wonky."

Connie smiled. "Well, I think I know exactly who to call. I'll let you know what I arrange."

"Excellent. I'll see you in a few hours."

***

As the morning shift exchanged with afternoon, and while a guard remained outside the door of Carla's room, a gurney slipped surreptitiously down the hall to the elevator. With no stops between, the gurney united with a van emblazoned with only "Plumbing Service" in the utility area of a lot vacant of the usual employees due to a manufactured emergency on the hospital roof.

***

Docking *Frau Nägel* late in the afternoon, Michael reclaimed the nineteen steps and paused on his screened-in porch to call Janni. He had tried calling while on Max, but as before, his call went straight to voicemail. Before sending another text, he thought, *Check the answering machine.*

There was both success and disappointment. "Sorry, Michael. Several things came up I cannot ignore. Sorry, sorry, sorry! I was so looking forward to today. I'll call later to explain."

Michael punched the button and listened again. He was incredulous. This was so unlike Janneke. "So much for my Watson!"

Reheated mac and cheese, a bratwurst sandwich, potato chips, all washed down with a Heineken, did little to lift his spirits. Talking aloud to himself and whatever spirits were lingering, he said, "What a lot of wasted motion! I'm no further along than I was this morning."

Discouraged or not, he would stay with the plan he'd sketched earlier that day. Checking his wrist watch, he said, "Should be a good time to hit the Spokes and Suds. Maybe Shirley will remember something more."

In spite of the establishment's spurious reputation, Michael was impressed by its well-kept, even tidy, appearance. He knew the owner-manager's attitude was that if the place looked neat, it cut down on the number of disturbances perpetrated by some of the clientele. And, considering the clientele, it was a smart policy.

His timing was good, early evening, the dinner crowd was satiated and had gone its way, and the drinking crowd was yet to arrive. As he entered, a tall, lanky figure bussing tables looked up, and upon seeing Michael, broke into a toothy smile that splintered cracks across his weather-beaten face. Setting down the tray, he charged across the room and nearly crushed Michael's hand in a large, enthusiastic handshake while loudly calling to the attractive, middle-aged woman behind the bar, "Now, Shirl, be on your best behavior. This here is Michael Cain, my personal lawyer. He and I solve crimes together."

"Let him be, you old fool! If anyone needs a lawyer, you do. Hey, Michael! Good to see you!" This was encouraging. Talking to Willy was a challenge, but with Shirley by his side, Willy-jabber could be moderated.

Agent Smith had been to the Spokes and Suds and had spoken with Shirley but had made no mention of Willy in his notes. Shirley shared, "Willy was fishing. We needed a few walleyes for some special customers at our Friday night fish fry. You should try it. We'll keep a fresh walleye for you."

Not sure how to respond to what was intended to be thoughtful but likely illegal, Michael mumbled, "Thanks. I like fish." It felt like a stupid reply, but it seemed to get him off the hook, so to speak, and what followed more than compensated.

Shirley confirmed to Michael that Smith had shown her a picture of a young Asian woman that may have been to the bar. "I told him she was here with a young man about her age. They were nice, kept to themselves, had appetizers and a few beers, and left. That was about it. I was busy in the kitchen and I didn't think to tell Smith to come back some time when Willy was here. Willy waited on them. The guy was a biker, and Willy even went out to see his motorcycle."

Michael stared at Willy. "You waited on them?"

"I did."

"Do you remember our agreement? You left out a few details."

"We talked about the agent, not a motorcycle."

"I'm looking for the same missing woman Agent Smith was asking about. You didn't think to say anything about seeing her with the biker or about the biker's motorcycle?"

"Didn't seem important. Probably wasn't even your missing woman. Besides, you know how it is. Keep an ace up your sleeve, just in case."

"That's not an ace. It's a royal flush!"

Willy's face went dark. He closed into Michael's personal space. "Get this straight. What I told you was true. Our deal was for anything more that I learned about your agent, and I didn't learn anything more. I wasn't here when this retired agent came in. Besides, I was protecting Shirley. Neither of us had anything to do with your agent and sure as hell didn't need the FBI scaring away all the bar's best customers."

"You tell him about the motorcycle, Willy, but make it quick. I've got to get back to the kitchen, and remember, you're tending bar, not just spinning BS."

Willy did an epic eye roll.

"What about the motorcycle?"

"It was an Indian!"

"A what?"

"An Indian, a motorcycle, the Classic! It was beautiful. I know because I almost bought one myself when I was sixteen, but my buddy tried it out and said the frame was damaged. He called it a suicide bike. Still wish I'd bought it though." Willy began to ramble. "This one was a beautiful restoration job, not entirely original, but whoever did it knew what they were doing. It had a great paint job, powder blue, and a custom sidecar, more recent than the bike, but the bike and sidecar fit like they were made for one another. The bike was too small for a big man. I sat on it and my long legs and big feet were awkward on the frame and clutch pedal."

Shirley yelled from the kitchen. "Show him your pictures!"

"You have pictures?"

"Well, yeah. It was a beautiful, like a piece of art. You know how it is."

Willy had several pictures on his phone, one of which was of Lei Ming standing behind the bike while its owner straddled the motorcycle. Michael's sarcasm was wasted. "Anything else you can remember, like maybe a name or the license plate?"

"Willy! Bar!"

"Sorry. Be right back. Here, look at these while I take care of business."

Willy handed Michael his phone open to a stream of photos of a motorcycle, powder blue and clearly from another era. The photos featured the bike and sidecar from different angles, some with the missing woman and a young, tall willowy figure wearing a biker's jacket, and one of Willy standing beside the motorcycle. As he scrolled through the gallery dedicated to a beautiful artifact, one picture stood out. The young Asian woman was standing beside the bike, wearing a helmet. Looking closer, Michael was stunned to see a partial of the plate peeking out from behind her leg. Trying to absorb the importance of what he was seeing, Michael had a sense there was something else he should notice. Then he saw it. A second helmet perched on the seat of the bike!

"Hey, Michael! Earth to Michael!"

The flood of possibilities rushing through his mind was interrupted only when Willy finally reached out to shake his shoulder. "I thought I lost you there for a moment."

"Oh, sorry. Willy, do you remember this photo, the one where the girl is wearing the helmet and the bike's license plate is partially visible?"

"Sure. I remember them all."

"I see two numbers. Do you remember the rest of the plate?"

Taking back his phone to check the picture, he said, "No, sorry. He did say he planned to register the bike as an antique but changed his mind when he found out driving registered antique vehicles, including antique motorbikes, was restricted to weekends and holidays."

"Can you send me the pictures?"

"You bet."

Within seconds, Michael's phone pinged. Willy may be retro in his ways and opinions, but he was skilled at using a smartphone with the latest technology.

"Got it," Michael said. "Thank you." Without the sarcasm, he repeated his earlier question. "Anything else you remember, like maybe the biker's name?"

"Oh, sure. He said he was Bobby Joe and was from Tennessee."

Michael blinked. "Bobby Joe?"

"Yup. That's what he said. From Tennessee."

Michael shook his head. "Okay, Willy. Let's try this again. Please, is there anything, and I mean anything, else you can remember that may help my search for this girl?"

"Nah, that's it. I was too busy admiring the bike."

"Yeah, that's not all he admired." Shirley made her point from the kitchen.

"Now, Shirl, you know it's all about the bike."

"Right. I was more impressed by his jacket."

It had taken two beers—on the house, though Michael left a large tip— and less than an hour for Michael to learn more about how to find the missing girl than in all the previous interviews he and Smith had done. As he left Spokes and Suds, the party drinkers were beginning to arrive, mostly young people or older people trying to feel young. The serious boozers would come later.

***

The gathering at the Courthouse was impressive. Sheriff Conrad had rarely been part of an operation with such a collection of law agencies. Numbers favored the FBI, and state and local agencies were heavily represented, but he hadn't anticipated officers from ICE and Homeland Security. And while he could not claim similar demographics for local law enforcement, the improvement to diversify the federal ranks was noteworthy.

Kaufmann appeared to have aged a decade since Conrad had

seen him the day before, but he introduced everyone without stumble or referring to notes. His team members passed out packets containing diagrams, pictures, and operational information while Kaufmann explained in a crisp, efficient manner the game plan and everyone's duties. The tactics were straightforward, and success dependent upon secrecy, stealth, and speed.

"Everyone in our path will be scooped up and thoroughly interrogated. Certain targets, you have their pictures and bios in your packets, will be arrested on sight. Anything even remotely relevant as evidence will be seized for processing."

"Our primary goal is to bring down this criminal organization and their business in the Lakes Area. As important as that is, remember that the young women they are using are victims of human trafficking. It is critical to rescue them safely. We will overwhelm the target, and once the site is secured, remove the women and deliver them to the local hospital for physical and psychological examination. Following this, they will be assigned appropriate care for rehabilitation. ICE will be on hand to assist with identification and outreach to families of any victims who are aliens."

As he paused, several hands shot up. Kaufmann ignored them. "Take a short break, then go to your assigned small groups. Check your packet to learn which group you are in and where to meet. You have sixty minutes, including personal time. When you return, I'll take questions and give you tomorrow's schedule."

Connie finally began to appreciate the scope and cause for the FBI's presence on his home turf. The planning was not something improvised in a few days. It had to have been preceded by much spade work over time. The loss of retired Agent Smith and the information given by Carla Rodriguez was not a beginning, it was provocation and confirmation to act.

As people rose to use the restrooms and get coffee or water,

Kaufmann called out, "Sheriff Conrad, a moment please."

***

It was a long shot, but it was worth the effort. If he could find the bike, he might find the biker, and if he found the biker, maybe the missing woman. Time again for the Marauders! Before leaving the Spokes and Suds parking lot, he called Glen Novak.

"Hey, Michael. How's the truck? Still intact?"

Michael laughed. "Yes, still intact and looking sweet, thanks to you."

"My pleasure. By the way, if you see your nephew, remind him to bring in his truck. He still needs to have it painted. I know he's excited, but if he keeps driving it around with primer only, we may need to re-prime before painting."

"If I don't see Jeremy, I'll be sure to tell Connie. On another matter, how much do you know about antique or at least old, restored motorcycles?"

"Not a lot. I worked on a couple old Harleys, but nothing I'd call an antique."

"Is there a source where I might be able to find the owner of a rebuilt Indian Classic? Maybe a club, a website, anything?"

"Google Indian Motorcycle and work from there. Some owners register and post pictures on the different websites devoted to Indian Motorcycles. Also, do an internet search for Antique Motorcycles and try the Antique Motorcycle Club of America. Tell you what, I'll do a search and call the Indian Motorcycle factory here in Spirit Lake. They may have a lead. I'll email you what I find. Is there something specific you're looking for?"

"I'm trying to locate a young man who was in the Lakes Area recently and riding a rebuilt powder-blue Indian Classic with a sidecar.

I have several pictures. Would that help?"

"You bet!"

"I'm on my way home. When I get there, I'll download the pictures from my phone and email them to you."

"Excellent. I'll do some research and see what I can turn up."

Arriving home, Michael sent the pictures to Glen, excited to think he was finally making progress. The rest of the evening on the internet was of no help, but Michael remained optimistic. Tomorrow would bring answers! He would find the missing woman! Exhausted from lack of sleep and a long day, he called it a night and slept soundly, dreaming of powder-blue motorcycles with sidecars.

40

"Sure, I can do that. I'll get back to you later today. Anything else I should look for?"

Michael's first call of the day was to Terry the Tech at the Dickinson County Courthouse with a request to do an internet search for anything he may be able to find on the unknown biker and Indian motorcycle. He emailed Terry everything he knew including a possible name—Bobby Joe—and what he'd found in his internet search the night before, which was inconclusive.

"I thought I was onto something with the antique thing but didn't find much that was helpful. I called Glen Novak to see what he knew, but motorcycles are not part of his business. He emailed this morning, and he didn't find anything more than what I'd learned."

"It shouldn't take long. As law enforcement, I have a lot more resources than you. I'll email you the results."

"That would be great, Terry. Muchas gracias, mi amigo!"

"You betcha!"

***

He was nearly late picking up Pam Schneider. Having seen Charley in action and knowing nothing of his wife, Michael was unsure what to expect and was grateful to have Pam's assistance. He also knew the interview with the host family and their daughter would be touchy, and Pam's empathy could be critical to any success.

The Chen's home was located off a hardtop road a few miles south of the town of Spirit Lake. It was a beautiful sunny morning, cooler, thanks to a high-pressure front that had moved in overnight. Fields of tasseled corn and canopied soybeans with an abundance of pods already formed, swayed in the light breeze. A sign posted at the entrance declared: *Paradise Acres, the Largest Small Ranch in Iowa.*

The gravel driveway led to a modest farmyard that included a fenced-in lot attached to a small barn, a chicken coop, and directly ahead, a work or storage shed. In the lot could be seen a small herd of goats, all with ears raised and eyes directed at the newly arrived interest. A good many chickens wandered about, more outside than in the coop. An older but attractive farmhouse with a long wrap-around porch, was set back in a small grove. The rest of what Michael estimated to be about a total of ten acres was filled with flowers, vegetables, and an orchard. Michael thought, *Paradise? A case of one man's paradise, another man's hard work.*

Michael had learned from the ISU Website that retired Professor of Engineering, Dr. Charles Chen, and his wife, retired Professor of Horticulture, Dr. Lily Chen, were second-generation Chinese, whose parents were well-educated by Chinese standards of the time and who had survived the ravages wrought on their country by World War II. In the aftermath of the war, the family was able to emigrate to the United States, earn permanent status, and avoid being subsumed by the advance of Communism.

During Michael's call, it was Iowa State University Chief of Police Barry Seward who suggested, and Mavis agreed, that an interview with the Chens might be useful as background information. Barry had described the Chens as highly respected University academics, acknowledged as devoted educators and researchers and greatly appreciated for their work with the Chinese community within the University. They were sensitive and skilled in assisting new arrivals learn and deal with, for many, a different but temporary life in America while respecting the reality they would face on their return to China. Barry had forewarned Michael of the reluctance the couple may have to express more than general assumptions concerning Chinese nationals and their families.

Mrs. Chen was watering pots of flowers when they pulled in. She topped off a gorgeous hanging basket exploding with a profusion of colors as her husband stepped around the corner of the house, coffee cup in hand.

Waving to them as they disembarked, Charley called out, "Hello, Michael. Lily, this is the gentleman I was telling you about who was there, and helpful, when Weird Willy tried to force me to walk on water."

"Hello, Michael. So pleased to meet you, and take my word for it, that would not have been the first time the esteemed Dr. Charles Chen had attempted to walk on water!"

Everyone laughed, including Charley, who may have laughed the loudest. "And who is this lovely lady?"

With greetings and introductions complete, they made their way around to the kitchen door and sat at a handsome maple table. The immaculate kitchen was filled with aromas suggestive of spices, herbs and, thankfully for Michael, freshly brewed coffee.

"Would you like coffee, or do you prefer tea. We've got some oolong." Michael and Charley had coffee, and Lily was delighted to share her taste for tea with Pam. Lily set a platter of little cakes, similar to petit fours, on the middle of the table, passed out plates and silverware, and invited them to serve themselves.

Michael was surprised when Lily expressed her condolences over the loss of Ginny Lawery. "I was saddened to learn of her death. She was a lovely young woman and so interested in gardening. She would always stop by my booth at the Farmers Market, and we'd talk about what was in season and about food in general. Sometimes she'd have that unusual young man following her around. I guess they were friends, but they made an odd couple. I read where you solved the mystery of her murder."

"I was one of several people involved in the investigation, and now I'm hoping for help to prevent losing another young woman, this time a woman from a prominent Chinese family in residence at ISU."

Charley and Lily looked at each other. Both stiffened, and there was a slight but notable change, a coolness, in their expressions.

Michael had explained to Pam the reluctance the Chens may hold in discussing the missing woman's family, and Pam interceded. "Whatever is said of our missing woman and her family is confidential."

"Pam is correct. I spoke with Barry Seward and his PA Mavis, and they both encouraged us to speak with you, but they emphasized, and we are hyper-aware of the sensitivity of the situation. As Pam said, everything is in the strictest confidence, and if you prefer, when we finish, this conversation never happened."

Charley nodded, and Lily replied, "Who is missing, and how is it we may help?"

Neither Michael nor Pam were surprised by the initial reticence, but after assurances of confidence and the need to help a missing Chinese woman, both Charley and Lily began to open up.

Charley was the first to respond to Michael's queries. "We've met the young woman's family but don't know them well. They arrived at university after we moved to Okoboji. We heard they are well-respected in the ISU community, and the extended family has ties within the Chinese government. But there could be serious consequences should a negative issue arise while they are in this country."

Lily continued, "Some of our friends agree it is a nice family, but we think the girl is trouble. Keep in mind what may be viewed as 'trouble' in a Chinese family may be considered minor in many American families. You might consider the culture shock such a young person experiences when they first come to this country. Usually, these differences are sorted out quickly, but this young woman's behavior is unusual. Her parents have reason to be alarmed."

Rather than an interview, time with Charley and Lily became a conversation which lasted through pots of coffee and tea, then for Pam, a tour of the flower and vegetable gardens with Lily while Michael and Charley talked about fishing. Charley said little about his work on the *Maximilian* other than that he considered it a strange contraption whose future on the lake was questionable. But his enthusiasm for and knowledge of fishing was impressive.

Finally thanking Charley and Lily for their time and advice, Michael and Pam drove the blacktop to West Okoboji, crossing the bridge between East Okoboji and Lake Minnewashta, and made their way to Lyle's Deli. It was a bit early for lunch, and they had no trouble finding a booth. The usual long line for takeout was just forming. The food was outstanding, and like most customers, they paid little attention to the cracked floor tile, the questionable sheen to the painted walls, and the taped repairs to the vinyl booths.

They ordered the special of the day—fish and chips with coleslaw. With food quickly served, Pam dipped several chips into ketchup, and between bites, she asked, "So do you want my usual?"

"Yes, please."

"It's clear why the governor wants to keep this quiet. With the public attention on the FBI agent, it's amazing the media hasn't gotten onto this. I don't envy your position."

"Thanks, I think. The Chens were more forthcoming than I thought they'd be, and they confirmed some of what I knew, but I can't say I learned anything new. Did anything stand out to you?"

"About the missing Chinese girl, or rather, woman? Not really. I didn't hear anything to point us in the right direction, or any direction for that matter. I did hear more about veggies and flowers than I could absorb. And although he helps, it seems Charley does not share her enthusiasm for gardening. Lily didn't complain, but she's worried. She thinks Charley doesn't know how to retire. He's used to working hard and needs something to do, a major project or a second career.

She said he follows her around some days until she tells him to go fishing. Fishing is the one thing besides the engineer in him that he loves to do, but he keeps getting calls to fix that big, dumb boat."

"Something to keep in mind if you ever get your kids and your husband raised and decide you want to retire."

"Hah! Like I'll ever get Darrell to finish growing to adulthood! That man really keeps things interesting."

Michael had to laugh. He had learned through the ILCC grapevine about the unlikely pair, so different and yet so deeply in love. It occurred to Michael that if Pam and Darrell could be that happy, perhaps there was still hope for him.

***

This was it. The vote on a casino for the Lakes Region, for Farley's casino, would take place tomorrow afternoon via teleconference. The Big Man had called only to say the result would be made public tomorrow evening, and he promised it would be worthy of a celebration.

Anticipating his win, Farley had arranged a gala cruise on the *Maximilian* for supportive big-shots from the area, members of the Gaming Commission, and, of course, the Big Man. Big Man had agreed the high point of the cruise would be his announcement of the result of the vote by the Commissioners.

It was arrogant and maybe risky, but Farley could not resist inviting Lucia Sandoval. Under the guise of "may the best offer win," he had called and suggested she bring a guest.

"The result of the Commisioners' vote is to be made public tomorrow evening, and whatever the result, I wanted you to know there are no hard feelings. I know this has been a trying time for us both, but perhaps we can even find ourselves working together some time in the future."

Farley paused for Lucia's response but only heard soft, rapid breaths and thought, *She's going to cry!*

"I would be appreciative if you could be with us on the *Maximilian*. I've been informed that the public announcement will be made during our little cruise. I know you and Mr. Cain have become very close. Perhaps he'd like to be your escort. And, of course, Janneke Sanderson may join in, make it a threesome."

Farley was enjoying this. Sandoval must understand the double entendre implied in his words, and even if she didn't, he did. But he was surprised with her reaction.

"Mr. Farley, as challenging as it has been, I am indebted to you for the opportunity provided by our competition. This has been a time to reevaluate the potential of The Lodge on Okoboji and for Sandoval Enterprises. I am now even more optimistic about the future. I would be happy to be a part of your cruise and will extend your invitation to Mr. Cain and Ms. Sanderson. What time do you depart?"

Farley paused to consider another possible jab but came up blank. Instead, he said, "Please be dockside at the West Shore Resort by 7 p.m." Almost an afterthought, he added, "There will be light refreshments, free drinks, and a live combo if that interests you."

"That sounds like a pleasant evening. We'll plan to be there. Thank you."

Lucia disconnected, and Farley replied, "Pleasant for someone!" Through gritted teeth, he snarled, "It sure as hell won't be you!"

***

Michael knew the interview with Lei Ming's host family, Bill and Joan Eckhart, and their daughter, Kaye, would be touchy, but Pam established an immediate rapport by expressing concern for the family and inquiring as to their well-being. As a result, the interview became cordial, and answers to questions were brief, to the point, and absent of embellishment. Like the morning's visit with Charley and Lily, most of what was known was reinforced, and nothing new was learned. Kaye Eckhart confirmed she had seen the powder-blue motorcycle and its rider, but had nothing more to add. The Eckharts did reveal that Lei Ming was allowed freedom to explore on her own and may have concealed her intentions. As a result, something she did not expect, something very bad, may have happened to her.

The visit took little time. There was no coffee, tea, or tour of gardens.

On the drive back to Pam's home, Michael asked, "So do you think their daughter is telling the truth, or does she know more than she's telling?"

"I believe her. I think she feels responsible, even guilty, for her friend gone missing and doesn't know how she should act. She doesn't strike me as subtle or familiar with the art of deception."

"I'll trust your judgement. I can be a bit dense when it comes to understanding young women."

"Just young women?"

They both laughed.

As they stopped in her driveway, Pam hesitated.

"Did we forget something?"

Pam looked at Michael. "You know, we might be overthinking this. It could be as it appears. She took off on a whim and will turn up on her own."

"I can only hope, but hope won't pay the piper, or the governor for that matter. In the meantime, thank you again for your help."

"Any time."

"Say hi to Darrell for me."

"Will do. Let me know when you find her."

Michael watched as Pam was greeted at the door by kids and

dogs. Was there a touch of envy, a small ache for the road not taken?

***

Terry the Tech was disappointed. He was sure the right motorcycle was among several he found on different websites, but none were a match to the name Michael had provided.

"Terry, come back to earth!" It was Delores, Sheriff Conrad's PA.

"Oh, sorry! I'm just stuck on some research for Michael Cain."

"Did you finish running those plates I sent you?"

"I sure did."

"Did you send Sheriff Conrad the results?"

"Ah, let me check. Okay. The list came in a few minutes ago, and I just sent it to Sheriff Conrad."

"Terry, Terry, Terry. What are we going to do with you? If you weren't so darn good, you'd be in trouble."

"Again, I'm sorry. When I get in the zone, I'm on a different planet."

"What planet were you on this time?"

"I'm trying to trace the owner of a motorcycle. I have pictures of the bike, a partial plate number, and possible first and middle names of the owner. I've found several bikes that match the description, but none that match the name I was given. I even trolled for a driver's permit, but none of the permits have a match for a Bobby Joe. I tried Robert Joseph, Roberto Joseph, and any variation I could think of, but no hits. I'm so close, it's frustrating."

Looking over Terry's shoulder at the computer screen and the most recent result of his frustration, she said, "May I suggest something?"

"Sure."

Given Delores's suggestion, Terry served up several key strokes and hit return. "I'll be damned!"

Delores smiled. "I certainly hope not! And you're welcome."

Michael snarfed a burger and fries on his way home. Pulling into his driveway, he had a brief sense of *déjà vu*. A few months earlier, he had been assaulted when first arriving home.

"Screw that! This is my home, and I'm safe!" But he keyed in the code and reached into the compartment welded to the floor, a little upgrade by Glen when the truck was repaired, and removed his Beretta.

Unlocking the back door, he did a quick and very self-conscious sweep of his house. It was clear, and there was no warning whisper from Gabriel. Relaxing but feeling foolish, he was startled when his cell phone began to vibrate.

"Hey, Connie."

There was no greeting. Connie went right to business. "I have a favor to ask."

"Name it."

"The FBI just received new intel. The Big Man, the guy on the Racing and Gaming Commission working for Farley and his organization, had a lucid moment and decided it was healthier for him to call a friend in the FBI rather than become a loose end to be tidied up by some very bad people. I guess from what Kaufmann said, the guy is really a piece of work. The Feds planned to hit the Ridge Top this Saturday but have moved up their timetable. They're executing the raid tomorrow evening, just before the public announcement on the casino license for the Lakes. Everything is in place. With the army of law enforcement we have, this is probably the safest place in Iowa."

"Great news! What can I do?"

"That's my ask. The Big Man will make the casino announcement tomorrow during the evening cruise on Farley's excursion boat. The raid on the Ridge Top will go down during the cruise. Farley's planning a big bash on the *Maximilian*. He thinks it's all wrapped up in his favor. The Feds want to keep an eye on Big Man and Farley but don't want to tip their hand by putting agents on board. Can you find a way to get on the *Maximilian* for the cruise?"

"I'll call Janni. She won't like it, but she can wrangle a way on, and we can go together."

"You may need to consider an alternative. Janneke is not available."

"Why not?"

"She is on duty, so to speak."

"Is that why I can't reach her?"

"Probably. When was the last time you tried to call her?"

"Yesterday."

"You may have better luck calling her now. She can explain the situation. Would Lucia Sandoval be willing to go with you? It would be logical she would be there for the big announcement and you would be her escort. Sorry, poor choice of words."

"That makes sense, but I want to check with Janneke first."

"I'll leave it up to you, but take care of it by tonight. Let me know what you arrange, and I'll pass it along to Kaufmann."

"Got it. I'll start calling right now. It may take some time to reach Lucia. Stragglers will be checking in at the Lodge, and there will be a big crowd for supper. I'll get back to you as soon as I confirm."

"Good, and a word of advice. Touch base with the Gov. He knows the plan but is even more worried that the investigation into our young woman of interest will be further derailed. Any progress on that front?"

"Maybe. I have your tech following up on a hunch for me. It depends on what he finds."

"Check your email. Delores says he was going bonkers over something he found. Whatever it was, he sent it to you. He should have checked out for the day, but he's still in his office. I think he's waiting to hear from you."

"I'll call him. The poor guy needs to get away from those computers."

"Maybe, but we need his skills. No one else around here can begin to do what he does, and without him, we'd be blind to social media. Keep me up to date and again, please call the governor. My impression is he's against the wall, and the wall is about to fall. If that happens, it won't be pleasant for any of us."

"Good or bad, I'll give him an update this evening."

"Call me later. I'll be at the office till at least nine. After that, call me at home."

***

Janneke answered his call on the third ring. Michael's greeting was, "There you are. I've been trying to reach you."

Michael was unsure if Janneke's response was meant to be critical or teasing. "Well, my dear, how should I begin? Is it guns, planes, boats, trucks, or you just have a pernicious attitude to any challenge?"

Michael stared at his phone. "What the hell are you talking about?"

"There seems to be this risky element in our relationship. I enjoy entertainment as much as the next girl, but there are limits. I'm safe, and I'm helping to protect the client. I'm not going to explain. We'll have a grand time after this is over. Have you spoken to Connie?"

"Yes."

"Then you know what this is about."

"Generally, yes."

"Generally is enough for now."

"If you say so."

"I do, and call Lucia."

"What?"

"I spoke with her a short time ago, and that jerk Farley called to gloat and invite her to the celebration aboard the *Maximilian* tomorrow night. She needs someone to accompany her, and I can't go. She expects you at 6:30, so don't be late. Do tidy up, maybe bring a rose or small corsage, and be your charming self, not your shark persona."

"Wow!"

"Wow, what?"

"Just another reminder of my perpetual state of affairs when it comes to women—clueless"

"That's part of your charm, Michael. Call her. Lucia is confidant and capable, so don't be Mr. Heavy. Be pleasant, even loquacious. You like to talk. Mingle. Have a nice time."

"I will. Connie asked me to find a way to get onboard. The FBI doesn't want to tip their hand but wants someone to keep an eye on the Big Man and Farley."

"You and Lucia will be a natural."

"That's what Connie implied."

There was an awkward pause, then Michael said, "I miss you. Is there anything else I can do?"

He could hear, nearly feel, Janneke's breath. "I miss you, too, Michael. Be careful. I have some great ideas about what we can do for each other, but I need you alive and intact."

"I'll be fine. Just a boat ride. I'll call tomorrow night after the big round-up. You be careful."

"Don't worry. There's lots of help, and I have my pink lady."

"Pink lady?"

"Remember the little Ruger you recommended after the debacle last spring? I got it in pink, and thanks to the Dickinson County Sheriff's Department, I have training and a carry permit! Bye, bye, Lover Boy!"

The line went silent, and Michael stared at his phone. "Pink lady?"

***

"Terry, I just read your email and think you need a new title. How about Terry the Terrific?"

"You like what I found?"

"Like? Terry, if I had my way, I'd give you a gold shield and call you detective first grade! How did you do it?"

"Well, I had help. I was frustrated, and Delores suggested that Bobby Joe may be Roberta Josephine. I tried it and it popped right up. Roberta Josephine Dalton, aka Bobbi Jo, from Tennessee."

Michael had opened Terry's email and found a document with Bobbi Jo's home address and phone number followed by a link to her Facebook page. He clicked on Facebook, and there she was, or rather they were. The biker was obvious; the passenger less so. Lei Ming was wearing the helmet Michael had noted earlier. Her face was obscured, and unless someone knew who they were looking for, she would be unrecognizable. Below the picture was a text: *Last day of a great week with my new best friend. Say our good byes tomorrow at Okoboji, then I'm home to Tennessee.*

"Can you access Bobbi Jo's Facebook page and leave a message?"

"No problem. What do you want it to say?"

"Just write: *Hello Bobbi Jo! Please drop your new best friend at The Lodge on Okoboji and ask her to tell the receptionist that the owner, Lucia Sandoval, made her a reservation. There's room for two if you wish to stay over.*"

"Consider it done."

"Thanks again."

"You betcha."

Before going further, Michael needed to confirm the accuracy of Terry's discovery. He called Bobbi Jo's listed telephone number. The call was answered on the second ring. "Mrs. Dalton?"

Next, he dialed Lucia's cell. Confirming arrangements for Thursday evening's boat ride, he added, "I have a favor to ask. It's about a young woman who was thought to be missing but will arrive at the Lodge sometime tomorrow. She may be with a friend."

Michael's call to Governor Dirksen was transferred directly to the Governor. "Good news, sir. We've located the missing woman, Lei Ming. She is safe and will be back to Okoboji sometime tomorrow. An APB is unnecessary and would only draw unwanted attention. I'll inform Sheriff Conrad to have a deputy on hand to greet her. If you would inform the family of the good news, you may tell them a reservation has been made for them and for their daughter at The Lodge on Okoboji under the name of the owner, Lucia Sandoval."

And finally, a short call back to Connie. "We found the missing girl! She'll return some time tomorrow. You might assign a deputy to the registration desk to meet her or have the receptionist call your office when she arrives. Lucia arranged reservations for Lei Ming, Lei Ming's family, and if necessary, her motorcycle buddy, Bobbi Jo. The biker's full name is Roberta Josephine Dalton. I just informed Governor

Dirksen of the good news and arrangements at the Lodge. He's probably on the phone right now with the family. We owe Terry and Delores a big thank you, and maybe a free ride on the *Maximilian!*"

"Very funny. That would be a hard no thank you!"

"Sorry, but they should be recognized for their help."

"They will be. I'll think of something appropriate. What about you and Lucia?"

"Lucia and I will be aboard the Maximilian tomorrow evening."

"I'll inform Kaufmann. And Michael? This should be simple. No need to be the hero. Stay safe."

"You, too. Thank you. Good hunting!"

Disconnecting, Michael was suddenly aware of the fire of intense anticipation in his mind and body. There was so much, so critical, and until it all came together, tomorrow would pass at a rate commensurate to the formation of the Iowa Great Lakes—glacial!

Farley was ebullient as he greeted guests dockside. He noticed but gave no significance that all five of the committee members, including the Big Man, were accompanied by their spouses—their own, he assumed. There were murmurs and heads turned as Lucia and her escort Michael Cain arrived. He had to admire Sandoval's moxie. Lucia was stunning in a bright red cocktail dress and matching ankle strap heels. A glittering golden necklace studded with ebony stones drew attention to deep cleavage atop a jaw-dropping curvaceous figure. Her long, lightly tossed dark hair framed a face dominated by large, brown eyes and accentuated by full ruby lips.

Even Farley had a major touch of jealously as he took in her beauty, and the near match of her handsome companion wearing a classic dinner jacket. Indeed, those of the feminine persuasion, as well as Donald, the bartender, admired the gentleman who so complimented the woman lightly gripping his arm.

"Welcome! Welcome, Lucia, Michael!" Farley exchanged a brief icy hug with Lucia, and nearly winced by the force of Michael's handshake. "Oh, and where is Ms. Sanderson?"

Michael's tight smile was more grimace than social. "Sorry, but Ms. Sanderson was unavailable."

"Unfortunate, but please, come aboard. Have a drink."

Already the deck was crowded and the musical combo was playing. Making their way to the bar, Michael recognized and nodded to several people he knew and thought might be considered area movers and shakers. Over the din of excited voices, Michael leaned across the bar to be heard and ordered a Dewar's on ice and white wine for Lucia. Turning, he was startled to find himself nearly nose-to-nose with Big Man. "Michael Cain! Finally, we meet. Don't worry, in spite of what others say, I think you're okay." Taking a step back he barked his loud laugh and gave Michael a solid slap on the shoulder.

"And Ms. Sandoval! So nice to see you again. Please, let me introduce my wife, Irene."

Michael stood with his mouth open, searching for the right words, any words. In contrast, Lucia, flashing her dazzling smile, stepped forward and reached out with both hands. "Hello, Irene. So very nice to meet you."

Nonplussed, Irene took Lucia's hands in hers, and with a generous smile, she said, "Thank you, and it's so nice to meet you."

Given the moment by Lucia to recover, Michael considered that Big Man's wife was much more attractive than Big Man deserved. Michael smiled and extended a hand. "Good to meet you, Irene."

Taking his hand, Irene's expression changed. The smile vanished, and she stared hard into his eyes. "And you, Michael."

Michael blinked. Irene had a curious way about her, chameleon-like but poised, as if she knew all the answers. Before he could consider any more, the Big Man continued true to form.

"Well! It's a grand night for the big announcement. Regardless of the result, I want to express my appreciation to you, Ms. Sandoval, for the fine work you did with the Gaming Commission. I know it will be a relief for everyone to learn the result. I know it will be for me!" Once more, he laughed loudly. Irene stared at the floor and frowned.

Not quite finished, Big Man leaned forward, again nearly touching Michael, nose-to-nose. Then turning his face toward Lucia, with breath heavily pickled in booze, added, "Pardon me for saying so, but not everyone will be happy with the vote."

He paused, unsmiling, with an odd expression on his face, as if recognizing only what he could see. Then a remarkable thing happened. Irene moved close to her husband, smiled, whispered in his ear, and gave him a soft kiss on the cheek. Big Man smiled, moisture forming in his eyes. Without looking, Big Man handed Michael his drink, took the drink from his wife's hand, and passed it to Lucia. Wrapping an arm around his wife's waist, he pulled her close, and Michael could just make out his words. "Let's see if that combo will play our song." He smooched her ear, and she actually giggled!

He took his wife by the arm, and they made their way to the bandstand. A moment later they were dancing, staring into each other's eyes. Big Man kissed his wife lightly on the forehead. She drew him closer and placed her head on his shoulder. Then it hit Michael. The music, their song, was *"The Way We Were!"*

***

Little was spared to celebrate the occasion, and as *Max* left the dock, a generous champagne fountain was rolled out, and the musical combo struck up "Anchors Away!"

There was a slight overcast, but the light breeze complemented the smooth ride of the *Maximilian*. Although rain and wind were forecast for later in the evening, conditions would pose no difficulty for the large excursion boat. Waves and rain would have little effect, and the interior would be cozy, protected by closing the large sliding windows.

Assured of the comfort and entertainment of the guests, Farley made his way up the stairs to the pilot house. Captain Billy was easing the craft out onto the main lake. Everything appeared normal, but the captain seemed uneasy.

"The guests are enjoying the cruise so far. Is everything good up here?"

"Yes, sir. Everything is under control, although..."

"Is there a problem?"

"Not yet but I've been monitoring the weather radio, and the storm front approaching may become a bigger event than forecast."

"Like what?"

"The weather folks aren't sure, but they just issued a tornado watch for this part of Iowa."

From the pilot house's wrap-around windows, Farley could see the broad, dark bank of storm clouds off to the southwest.

"It looks to me to be far off. If there is bad weather, we'll be back at the dock before it arrives. Besides, *Max* can take whatever nature hands out." He thought, *No one, neither God nor Nature, is going to ruin my triumph!*

***

Farley's optimism would have dissolved had he known what was taking place at the Ridge Top. Late that afternoon, law enforcement officers from participating agencies met in the maintenance building adjacent to the courthouse to receive final instructions. The nervous anticipation only sharpened the focus and cool professionalism of the assembled personnel.

By early evening, FBI, DCI, State Troopers, DNR, and Sheriff Conrad's Strike Team were pre-positioned to cover any point of nexus that would be critical to the scene. Command control was in a black, non-nondescript van and on order from the FBI, the Dickinson County Deputies and State Troopers rushed to secure the restaurant and motel at the base of the hill while a large swarm of DCI and FBI agents stormed up the winding drive to overwhelm the Ridge Top Nightclub.

It was over in minutes. The only resistance was the fruitless attempt by RV Man and Pauline to force the large silver pickup truck past several police vehicles. Steering sharply into the deep ditch to drive past the roadblock at the bottom of the hill, the truck slammed into the far side of the ditch and flopped over onto its side. The operation was well-executed, and the initial stage successfully completed. Collecting evidence and processing the people ensnared at the nightclub and motel to sort the innocent from criminal would take longer, with one noticeable exception.

Seven young women were found huddled in the large RV parked behind the nightclub. The abuse the women had endured was as of yet unspoken, but they and the hardcore law officers who first found them were emotionally overwhelmed, moved to tears by the successful, and to the women, miraculous, rescue.

The party onboard the *Maximilian* was in full swing. The combo was hot, and the booze was cool. Several couples had joined Big Man and his wife on the dance floor, most guests mingled, chatting loudly, and except for a few who had gone outside to stand along the railing, were unaware of the change in the weather. The gentle southerly breeze had freshened, and scattered early evening clouds had coalesced into a dark mass, filtering the sunset into a sickly amalgamation of green and yellow. A light drizzle had begun to fall with the promise of more to come.

While a crew member went around sliding the windows shut, Farley asked the singer to assure the guests that a little rain and wind were no match for, as the singer expressed it, *"Mad Max,"* and the combo transitioned into a rather marginal rendition of "Singin' in the Rain." The tune and the singer's stab at humor were only slightly reassuring, and the crowd became subdued when the captain called over the boat's PA with a request that Mr. Farley come to the pilot's house.

For the first time this evening, anxiety intruded on Farley's sense of casino entitlement. Once out of sight of the guests, he dashed up the stairs. "Now what the hell is the problem?"

If the outburst was unsettling, the anger in Farley's face exaggerated by the glow of the red night light overhead conveyed to the boat's captain that his call to update Farley on the appending storm might have been better done some way other than over the PA system. Momentarily speechless, Captain Billy pointed to the weather radio.

"What?"

"Sorry, sir. I thought you should know that the National Weather Service has issued a severe storm warning. I called to check with the engineer at KICD in Spencer, and he just upgraded the tornado watch to a tornado warning. It's your call, but we are advised to return to the pier and get everyone into shelter."

Farley glared at the captain in disbelief. He wanted to scream, to punch him, to throw him overboard. Anything to seize control from the captain and the weather. With clenched teeth and lips drawn back into a sneer, he stepped up face-to-face with Captain Billy. "Let me make this clear. You will not return to the pier until the Commissioners' decision is announced and I can celebrate my moment of success. Until then, maintain course."

"Yes sir. Ah… May I make a suggestion that might help?"

Farley spat out, "What?"

"Right now, the wind is from the south-southwest. It may be better if we slow our speed, move with the wind to the nearest bay, and follow the shoreline. It should be smoother for the passengers, and when we return to the dock, it would be safer to steer into the wind."

Exasperated, Farley agreed. "Fine. Do what you need to do, but stay with the plan. This is a celebration, and nothing is going to interfere. Understood?"

"Yes, sir."

With that settled, Farley stomped back down the stairs, paused to take a deep breath, and affecting a smile, rejoined his guests just as the Big Man took over the microphone.

Big Man's face was flushed from booze, and his hands were noticeably shaking as he tightly gripped the microphone. On his signal, the combo played a short, boisterous fanfare, and those few guests who were outside came in to hear the news.

"Ladies and gentlemen, if I may have your attention, please. The moment we've all been waiting for has come! But before I make the big announcement, let's have a big round of applause for our host, Bart Farley. Come on up here, Bart."

Caught up in the anticipation, the crowd loudly clapped and cheered as a recharged Farley confidently strode up to the Big Man. "And Ms. Sandoval, where are you? Come on up here and join us."

There was a smattering of applause as Lucia reluctantly stepped forward but remained within an arm's reach of Michael.

"I also would invite you to give a grand round of applause for the members of the Racing and Gaming Commission who are with us this evening."

There was another more energized response from the gathering for the commission members, most of whom seemed a bit discomforted by the attention. Reluctantly, they raised their hands, nodded in the direction of the Big Man, then refocused on their drinks.

"I want to thank the members of the commission for their diligence and hard work as we studied the applicants' petitions and considered the copious amount of input from individuals and organizations who had an interest in this project." He paused, pleased with himself for using the word "copious" to describe what he earlier had referred to the commission members as a "shitstorm."

Farley noticed the Big Man was uncharacteristically nervous. Maybe he was over-excited or over-boozed, but he was swaying and sweating profusely. Loudly clearing his throat, he said, "I'd like to compliment Mr. Farley and Ms. Sandoval for their spirited competition and outstanding informed presentations and thank them for their patience as the commission painstakingly executed their duties. And so, as this evening's representative for the members of the commission, it is my pleasure to announce that by a slim margin of only one vote, the decision is...There will be no casino license for Okoboji and the Iowa Great Lakes Region."

As if choreographed, the dead silence that followed was ruptured by a stunning flash of lightning and explosion of thunder. The announcement was shocking, but with the thunder and lightning, attention suddenly shifted to the previously ignored and now rapidly gathering storm.

The Big Man leaned in close, and with spittle spraying from his fat lips hissed into Farley's ear, "The vote was a tie, and I broke the tie. I'll see you in hell, you miserable little bloodsucker! I voted against your fucking casino!" Leaning back, he roared in laughter and gave Farley a staggering slap on the back.

"Oh, and something else, the FBI has a welcoming party for you back at the pier. I made a deal. You're screwed! It should be interesting to see who gets to you first, the Feds or the investors."

Wild-eyed, the Big Man laughed again and swayed his way back to the bar.

**

Michael was as surprised by the announcement as everyone else, but when his phone began to vibrate, he stepped outside and found some shelter partially protected from the elements by the overhang of *Max's* second deck. The call was from Sheriff Conrad.

"There's a lot to clean up, but the plan went off without a hitch, and we hit the jackpot! We've rounded up everyone of interest including the Big Boss Man, the brains of the organization. We also rescued seven young women, all victims of trafficking. They are safe and being transported to the Spirit Lake Hospital. We're just starting the process of collecting and removing the computers and the digital and paper evidence and taking it all to the courthouse for documentation. The Feds hit the Boss Man's office and home at the same time we executed our raid. Between what they found and what we have, they will be able to roll up the entire organization! How are things on the *Maximilian*?"

"Did you hear the public announcement? Approval for a casino license was denied. There will be no casino in the Lakes Region."

"No, hadn't heard that. We've been a little busy. What was the reaction on the boat?"

"Most were shocked, especially Farley. I think Lucia was relieved. She and Janneke had plans that did not include a casino. Speaking of whom, is Janneke safe?"

"Yes. I think we need to start calling her 'Janni Oakley.'"

"What?"

"I told Janneke that Bonita, Carla, and the Lawrey Sisters would be secure at the Lawerys' home while we carried out our operation and she should shelter at her own home with a couple of deputies for protection. She said, 'Nuts to you!' and informed me that she was going to stay with the Lawery sisters until we were done. I had my deputies check on her, and she confronted them at the Lawerys' front door with what she calls her pink lady, apparently. She advised them that no one was getting to Bonita and Carla. Man, if you two ever stay together, the bad guys won't have a chance."

As he listened to Connie, there was a scream, and Michael turned to see Farley dragging Lucia by the arm toward the stern of the boat. "No! Farley's got Lucia!" Michael shoved his phone into a pocket and ran for the stern.

***

At first, Farley could not move, could not speak, his brain burned with the revelation, the humiliation, the utter failure. Everyone looked away, embarrassed to meet his eyes, everyone except for one. Lucia Sandoval stood tall and straight, head back slightly, smiling and staring directly at him. Smiling! All his fury shifted to Lucia!

In a fit of rage, Farley strode across the floor, grabbed Lucia by the arm, and pulled her outside, dragging her toward the stern. "You bitch! You conniving bitch! I don't know how you did it, but it's your fault I didn't get my casino. You're going to pay for this."

With a wild swing, he backhanded Lucia across the side of her face. Dazed, Lucia staggered back, then instinctively attacked him with fists and nails and fury. Stunned, Farley violently shoved Lucia away when suddenly, a powerful hand gripped his shoulder and spun him around. A crashing right hook knocked Farley flat on his back.

Michael seized Lucia's hand, and together, they struggled on the wet deck to make their way back to the safety of the crowd. Farley, gripping the railing, managed to pull himself to his feet. Dazed and consumed by a fog of rage, he lurched toward the retreating couple. As the boat rocked in the rising waves, Farley reached out to steady himself and found his hand on a fire extinguisher that hung from the wall. Ripping it free of its frame, Farley bolted forward and smashed it down onto Michael's head. Dropping the extinguisher, Farley caught Michael's slumping body and lifted him overside.

"No! Michael! No!" Looking over the railing, Lucia watched Michael's inert form as it bobbed in the wake. Enraged, Lucia turned on Farley, but before she could act, he seized her hard by the shoulders, shoving her against the railing. His face was a demonic sneer, and in a voice venomous with hate, he said, "There goes your hero. But don't worry, you get to join him!" Her scream was choked off as she hit the water. Farley watched as she bobbed to the surface, the bright red dress billowing around her like a pool of blood.

As he turned to make his way to the pilot house, he noticed one of Lucia's shoes lying near where he had struck her. Picking it up, he stared at it, smiled, then threw it as far out into the water as he could.

Scooping up the fire extinguisher, Farley strode to the back stairs, took two steps at a time, and arrived at the pilot's house breathless and unaware of the blood that dripped from the corner of his mouth. Turning to meet him, Captain Billy was startled by Farley's appearance. "Sir? Is everything alright?"

"Yes, everything is fine. Carry on."

"Yes, sir. If you say so."

As the captain turned, he had only the slightest warning in the window's reflection before the fire extinguisher struck his head.

45

With the pilot house secure of witnesses, Farley shut off all exterior lights except those required for navigation at night and attempted to turn the boat around. In spite of *Max's* multi-hull design intended for stability, at three decks above water level, the pilot house swayed violently, the pronounced effect of the increase in wind and waves. He knew how to steer the boat, but his experience was considerably less than Captain Billy's, and Farley struggled with the twin drive controls. *Max* responded to Farley's attempt to turn about but was sluggish, battling waves and wind that battered against the high profile of the boat.

With the heavy drizzle and lake mist, everyone remained inside. Without the aid of exterior lights, Farley knew it would be difficult for someone to see anything beyond the boat's railing through the fogged-up windows. Donning the night vision goggles kept on the shelf above the radio, the two targets struggling in the water immediately popped into view.

They were less than 200 yards directly ahead. They were struggling but still thrashing for shore. He was surprised how far they had managed to swim.

Max was closer to the shore than he liked, but Farley doubted anyone would be out in this weather. The guests inside would not hear any shouts for help or alarm as he approached the target, and they would not be able to see over the bow as the victims got sucked under the boat. The irony of lights from The Lodge on Okoboji, barely visible through the haze, was lost on him. Adjusting the helm, he set the boat on a path dead on to the objective.

The combo was playing a medley honoring several military veterans on board, and the musicians' repeat of Anchor's Away was a cynical accompaniment to the unfolding drama. The driving beat from bass and drums became a tattoo recalling the overboard couple. Farley gradually increased power from leisurely cruise to something he once joked to be "ramming speed!"

Lucia had lost her other shoe, had squirmed out of her cocktail dress, and had swum to Michael as fast as she could. She lifted his head from the water. He coughed and spit lake water, but he was conscious.

It took all her remaining effort to keep them afloat. Michael was able to discard his jacket, but their combined frantic attempts to kick themselves to shore, even aided by following waves, were becoming ineffectual. Pausing to look back, Michael despaired at what he saw. The boat had turned and was headed directly toward them.

The lack of exterior lights and the brightly lit interior presented the eerie sight of party goers hovering over the inky space below. Unseen by the occupants, but clear to Michael, the contrast of white froth pushed by the boat's bows demarcated the border to their destruction. Even at this distance, he could feel the pulse of the engine and the thump of the twin screws as the aqua-borne reaper bore down on them.

As the *Maximilian* drew close, Michael suddenly and inexplicably experienced that odd calm that overcame him at times in his life when impending violence should have rendered inappropriate the logic for any sense of peace. He had considered it in the past, but now he spoke to it aloud. "If you are with me, this would be a good time to help."

Misunderstanding, Lucia, in gasps, responded, "I'm trying... I'm trying!" She raised her head to look back and exclaimed, "Oh, no! No, No, No! Oh, God! Please help us!"

With the wave of calm, Michael stopped kicking, and as he waited for the inevitable, there came a great bong, as if a giant bell had been struck by Thor's hammer, the sound resonating through the water. The boat began to veer away, the bow redirected toward the shore.

Neither Lucia nor Michael could believe their eyes. The destroyer passed them by, a ghost ship drifting on unholy waters, crossing the River Styx, or in this case, Lake Styx, stealing through a misty gauze with illuminated guests inside its belly, drinking and dancing as if they were ghouls excited to feast on corpses floating alongside.

I am here. Michael was not sure who had spoken. He looked at Lucia, who was staring at him. Michael reached out, pulled his companion close, and together they watched as the *Maximilian* sailed aimlessly toward shore.

***

"What the hell?" The loud clang of something *Maximilian* had struck, reverberated through the boat and was instantly translated into a violent vibration as one of the screws struggled to regain purchase in the water. The immediate result was a sharp move to port as the mate to the stressed screw redirected the boat toward the nearby shore and away from its previous focus.

The engine struggled, at risk of damage. Shifting the boat's gears to neutral, Farley shut down the engine, grabbed the microphone from its bracket, and nearly breathless in panic, did his best to quiet everyone on board. "Please remain calm. We're perfectly safe, and everything is fine. We will be back underway in just a moment. Crew members, remain in place. Guests, please have another drink on the house!"

Ripping off the night goggles, Farley grabbed the head lamp kept on the hook above the console. As he dashed from the cockpit, inexplicably, he picked up and yanked on Captain Billy's blood-stained nautical hat and nearly stumbled as he plunged down the stairs.

Sprinting to the stern, Farley added the head lamp over the captain's hat, switched the lamp on, and stared into the inky water. A frayed strand of rope in the shape of a question mark floated below. Reaching under the rail, he removed a landing gaff from its place and leaning as far as he could, hooked and hauled up a length of the tattered fibers. Looping a ragged end about his forearm, he tugged until the cord drew tight. He muttered to himself. "Damn. It must be wrapped around the propeller shaft."

With a steady pull, Farley gained on the resistance and was surprised when a large silver chunk of metal scraped out from under the hull. Floating around it was a semblance of loose skin, a dark illusion, as if a rippling manta ray had emerged.

It took several attempts with the gaff, but he was able to snag the metal object through a gaping hole. Yet, as much as he tried, he was unable to wrench it away from the boat. In frustration, he stabbed and gave the surrounding debris several hard jerks. In response, the mass rolled over and the beam from his head lamp was reflected from a single large eye.

Startled, Farley stepped back as the cyclops and surrounding amorphous detritus undulated in the water. Freaked out, he remained aware of the urgent need to be freed from whatever this was and return his attention to the two people swimming for shore. Bending back over the rail, he repeatedly jabbed the gaff at the form until he was able to draw more of the aggregation from under the boat.

Farley plunged the hook further into the water. He had it now. There was some resistance, but as he continued to pull, he could feel the mass begin to float free. He still could succeed!

One more thrust, and he had the last of what held his boat in its grip. In a state of desperation, he gave a great heave and watched an arm-like appendage rise up from the black mass. Dangling from the appendage hung a long-battered metal shaft.

As he fiercely shook the gaff free, Farley was briefly aware of the twang, the sound of powerful elastic bands at their release. He was profoundly aware of the penetration through his throat and of his body rising as the lance from the deceased diver's spear gun drove him upward, the lance point burying itself in the deck overhead. Illuminated by the headlamp, Bart Farley watched his blood and life flow over the boat's stern to join the mangled corpse of retired FBI Agent Howard Smith in the dark water below.

The sound of *Maximilian's* hull scraping across sand and rocks was a death rattle, an anguished cry for absolution. Burdened by Farley's spear-impaled body and the remains of retired FBI agent Smith alongside, *Maximilian* listed sharply, relented in hope for clemency, and came to rest on the shore, an exculpated implement of death.

If clemency was granted to anyone, it came to Lucia and Michael in the form of suddenly diminished wind. Thankfully, the storm was passing. Gentler waves began to lift Michael and Lucia as they battled their way toward shore, until finally they found themselves at the water's edge. Fatigued beyond endurance, they took turns helping each other crawl onto the sand beach, then collapse, oblivious of the arrival of rescuers by water and land.

First to the rescue was a determined DNR Officer, Richard

Piccard. Unable to reach Michael after Michael's terse cry that Farley had Lucia, an anxious Sheriff Conrad had called and alerted Piccard that something had gone wrong on the *Maximilian*. In position to assist the FBI should someone try to escape by boat, Piccard's response was immediate. He turned loose all 115 horses of the outboard motor and blasted his boat through the raging waters, hell-bent for the far shore. Blazing spotlights from his boat raked the shoreline as he approached the beached *Maximilian*, and there, on the edge of illumination, was an amazing sight. Michael and Lucia were tangled together, bobbing in the ebb and flow of waves as they crawled onto the shore.

Epilogue

Exhausted and suffering from hypothermia, Lucia and Michael were tended to by EMTs, rushed to Spirit Lake Hospital, and admitted overnight for observation. Recollections in the following hours were fuzzy, but by the next morning, Michael awoke clearer of mind and overjoyed to find Janneke at his bedside. As he began to stir, she bent over and lightly kissed him.

While Michael waited for breakfast and dismissal from the hospital, Janneke related events, or non-events in the case of the Lawerys, since there had been no attempt to invade their domain after all.

"Carla is back at the hospital. I checked on her and on Lucia this morning, and they both are doing well. Connie has deputies assigned to the Lawerys until the FBI gives the all-clear, and the Aunties are not happy about it. But I'm sure by now the deputies are stuffed with Hoepe's cookies, and Faethe has clarified the parameters of their duties."

"Cookies sound good!"

A rather disheveled and very bleary-eyed sheriff stood in the doorway. "Sorry. I didn't mean to intrude, but Deputy Donahue and an agent from the FBI will be here soon to question you. I'm on my way home for a shower and fresh clothes before returning to the office and thought I'd check on you. How are you doing?"

"Big headache, but otherwise fine. Tell me how it all went down. I don't remember much after going in the water."

Connie reported passengers, musicians, crew, and the captain had been safely removed from the body of *Maximilian*. Most were shaken, a few bruised, the captain concussed, and everyone onboard was being interviewed by law enforcement agencies. Governor Dirksen already was hellbent to very publicly take to task anyone he considered responsible for the casino fiasco, with a special dictate for the Iowa Racing and Gaming Commission.

Lucia awoke at the hospital to a warm hug from a surprise guest—her mother, Sophia, who had flown overnight from Arizona by private jet. After a few mother-daughter moments, Sophia introduced the family lawyer who had Lucia relate the events of the prior evening, asked several pointed questions, and provided suggestions.

"We want the events of last night clear in your mind before the FBI questions you. If you don't remember, say so, and do not agree to attempts by investigators to fill in the blanks for you. I will be with you during any and all interviews."

Later that morning, with the FBI meeting complete and the permission of her doctors, Lucia was dismissed to the indulgent, loving care of her mother.

***

Although the investigation and prosecution of the criminal

organization's members would continue for many months, more immediate needs were resolved sooner.

The remains of former FBI Agent Howard Smith were recovered and sent to the forensics lab in Ankeny before release to his family. His life was lost while serving in a capacity similar to his time with the FBI, and though he was retired, his duty and sacrifice would be recognized on the FBI Wall of Honor.

Reminiscent of an earlier era in maritime history and a warning to would-be pirates should there be any like-minded individuals in the Lakes Area, the neck-pierced body of the late Bart Farley remained suspended from the overhang of the *Maximilian's* second deck throughout the following day. Only after all evidence was gathered and photos taken was his corpse unceremoniously dumped into a body bag to be transported to the state lab in Ankeny for autopsy. No one claimed the body.

The *Maximilian* was pulled from a potential grave site, thanks to Marv's Marina, and anchored in the bay off from the Lodge, awaiting the cutting torch. It had been seized by the Feds and would be sold to a well-to-do entrepreneur from Missouri who intended to have it cut into manageable parts, shipped to his home on the Lake of the Ozarks, and a more modest version reconstructed for his company's use as a party boat.

Due to his cooperation, Big Man would do less time at a tolerable facility for fraud but still awaited a charge of manslaughter for his part in the death of the young Asian woman. She had been identified, but her name and origin had been withheld pending notification of her family and confirmation by the Chinese government. Her cause of death had been determined as due to an overdose of drugs. The Big Man's wife promised to wait for him. He was no longer a member of the gaming commission. There were more openings on the commission due to sudden resignations.

As for Ralphy and his boys, the last members of the thoroughly defunct motorcycle club, it was thought they were hiding somewhere in Arizona, likely near enough to the Mexican border should another move be required. If they persisted on telling and retelling everyone at their new watering hole about the dreaded hound from hell, a move to Mexico might not be optional.

Junkyard Sam remained protective of his beautiful daughter, and his wife continued to pamper Percy, but Percy would not approach the misused crusher. Pete, the connoisseur of weed, remained clueless, and Sam's brother-in-law was no longer in service to the junkyard.

***

Considering the responsible manner in which Jeremy and Emily had conducted themselves under trying circumstances, it was agreed by all parties that the discussion with Michael and Janni was unnecessary and future encouragement would remain with the parents. Janni and Michael were relieved, while Emily and Jeremy remained unfazed. Jeremy was more grateful to find his truck unscathed but for a slight dent in the front bumper, and Janni, considering her recent experience, decided to postpone and possibly eliminate future flying lessons with Michael as the instructor.

***

Nigel Waterford was pleased with the result of his call to Ms. Janneke Sanderson, and due to her suggestion, Charley Chen was now the co-owner of the newly christened Sports Emporium, formerly known as the Sports Shop. The compatibility between the two men and their shared interest in fishing held promise for a prosperous future, with less time and stress on Nigel. Assistant manager Jerry

Strand was agreeable, and was even relieved with the change.

Bonita was safe, looking forward to a girls' day out and attending Iowa State University in the fall. She, as well as Emily and Jeremy, had become local celebrities, much appreciated by family and community for their courage and cool judgement in the face of danger. Nigel and even Jerry Strand practically doted on Bonita.

A great deal of work remained to heal and reunite the trafficked girls with their families and for each who requested, to provide them with a path to citizenship. Carla's new journey would remain long but less dark owing to her new-found friends. During the search for her family, she remained in the care of the Lawery sisters and under the guardianship of two pertinacious priests. Her incredible courage in the face of desperation was becoming legendary in the area Latino community. She was the focus of more love and support than she would have ever dreamed.

It was a tearful reunion when Bonita, with the permission of Special Agent Kaufmann, reunited Carla with her mother's lost rosary. Found hanging from the mirror of his pickup, RV Man explained he had found it on the road near where Carla was struck by Bonita's car. He considered it a talisman with the intent of bringing him success in recovering Carla, the "lost property."

***

The request by the Governor of Michael to solve the mystery of the missing Chinese student from ISU was resolved, inexplicably to some but anticipated by Michael, when she arrived at the Lodge wearing a satin jacket embroidered with an Indian motorcycle, a gift from her new friend. She accepted the reserved room and called her mother in Ames, yet unaware about everything that her disappearance had triggered. With her identity verified, she was questioned by Sergeant

Weisser, followed by a representative for several interested agencies. She enthusiastically shared the adventures of her summer hiatus with her friend Bobbi Jo, aka Roberta Josephine, from Tennessee. It was her first, and likely last, experience with that degree of freedom.

Bobbi Jo was questioned, signed a non-disclosure statement, and was released. All trace of Lei Ming's experience was scrubbed from Bobbi Jo's social media.

Thanks to Delores's suggestion and information provided by Terry the Tech, Michael had spoken to Bobbi Jo's mother, who explained her daughter was doing a ride-about before beginning medical school this fall. It was supposed to be a final call for a hoorah until she completed her studies. She shared that the Indian motorcycle was a gift from Bobbi's late father. Together, they had rebuilt the bike from the frame up, and despite her father's advice, Bobbi had insisted upon painting it powder blue. The sidecar was a last-minute custom add-on in the event she needed room for a passenger or other needs. She had confirmed her daughter was on her way home. "She called me to say she needed to drop off her new friend at Okoboji."

Later, when he told the story to Janneke, Michael expressed his opinion that, "Governor Dirksen and Connie were practically ecstatic when I confirmed for them that Lei Ming was safe, nearly finished with her freedom ride-about, and would be back at Okoboji the next day."

Listening to this, Janneke had smiled, recalling her mother's admonition regarding what she described as Janneke's "summer of whoopie." Lei Ming's experience may have differed from the original description, but Janneke still had trouble visualizing her prim and proper mother experiencing such a diversion.

Since Lei Ming was of legal age, had left voluntarily, and had returned unharmed, there were no charges. The State Department, relieved with her return and concerned about a possible leak of information, had scrubbed the missing persons case. Thus, there was no circumstance of any international concern. The entire matter was promoted as a misunderstanding due to unintentionally conflated, misdirected, and discredited use of social media. Although not directly responsible for Agent Smith's demise, Lei Ming remained the reason for his presence in the Lakes Area, and the consequences would weigh on her future and that of her family. It was a thankful but somber reunion when Lei Ming's family arrived at the Lodge.

***

Lucia and her mother had invited Michael and Janneke to a quiet celebration over dinner in Lucia's private suite. It was an opportunity to express appreciation for survival and to share what each knew of recent events. The future of the Sandoval enterprise, and more subtly, the relationships among those present, were open for consideration.

The FBI had cleared The Lodge on Okoboji of any malfeasance, and a lukewarm apology by some faceless entity within the web of federal agencies was issued. Perhaps more important was a very public apology and thank you from Governor Dirksen to the owner and manager of the Lodge in appreciation for the understanding and cooperation extended to law enforcement and the people of Iowa that resulted in the breakup of a criminal organization and the arrest of its perpetrators. On a related note, the Governor announced there would be enhanced oversight and a review of the regulations which guided the work of the Iowa Racing and Gaming Commission.

In appreciation, the Lodge, or rather its board of directors, had agreed to not press the intended lawsuit for slander and request for an independent criminal investigation into the Iowa Racing and Gaming Commission. The board of directors had, for the second time within the calendar year, unanimously voted confidence in the owner-manager, Lucia Sandoval. The Lodge on Okoboji once again sailed forth with Lucia the victorious commodore of this latest battle, if not the war.

Having turned down the request to remain as assistant manager, Tom Bland, aka "the Owl," his work complete, had moved on to his next assignment—the location and subject of the assignment was not shared. According to what was told to the staff of the Lodge, "One night, the Owl simply flew away." Still, there remained a grudging respect around the Lodge for his work ethic and help during a trying time.

Sofia had explained to Lucia who "the Owl" really was and why she had arranged for him to work at the Lodge. "It was not a lack of confidence in you, Lucia. Without Anthony, you had to do the work of two. But with the shock of Anthony's death and discovery of his criminal activity, I wanted to know of and prevent any residual outside influence. At my request, our long-time family friend, Tom Bland, was hired to be a firewall between you and any attempts to interfere with the future of the Lodge. Thanks to his help, we learned that one of our employees, Loren Price, was a spy working on behalf of the opposition. Tom was able to neutralize Mr. Price before handing him over to the FBI."

***

Michael had received private but profuse thanks from Governor Dirksen, but if Michael thought this latest task on behalf of the Governor was to be his the last, he was in for a surprise. As a part of an ongoing conversation among interested parties, a Chinese investigator experienced in human trafficking and who had worked with Interpol, was invited by Governor Dirksen to Iowa. The importance of and security for Chinese nationals researching or studying at Iowa universities was recognized and appreciated by both countries. Possible risks and potential unintended consequences were revealed with the death of the trafficked young Chinese woman, and the sudden self-determined independence of the young Chinese woman from an important family.

Rather than so-called "chaperones," some of which smacked of spycraft, there was a shared decision that a small, limited group would be responsible for studying and reducing the potential risk of exploitation to members within Chinese national communities and to the families of any foreign nationals who were studying or working in the United States. Iowa would serve as one part of an international effort to monitor and disrupt any possible related human trafficking that might threaten academics and students from other countries. The Governor needed a point man.

Michael's cell phone rang. "Hello, Governor Dirksen. This is a surprise."

"Hello, Michael. I have a request for you."

Acknowledgments

I am humbly grateful to former students, colleagues, long-time friends, and new friends, who have reached out to share how much they enjoyed my first novel, *The Girl In the Net*. With their support and support from business owners. librarians, and area journalists, I've found a community committed to the joy of reading books.

In *Sin and Sanctum*, a newly launched excursion boat whose size is a threat to the ecology of Lake Okoboji, symbolizes the greed and unbridled criminality of its owner. My sincere thanks to Mary Kennedy, curator of the Iowa Great Lakes Maritime Museum, for reviewing my descriptions and confirming the risks posed by such an oversized craft. (Mary and her late husband, Steve Kennedy, brought the Queen II to Lake Okoboji.) Michael Cain returns as the principal protagonist and is given another opportunity to demonstrate his piloting skills. Michael and I thank Lief Wilson, bush pilot and co-owner of 40-Mile Air in Tok, Alaska, for the information needed to keep Michael's Cessna 172 aloft.

With heartfelt thanks, I want to recognize my wife Vicki, my first of all readers, for her support and whose adherence to logic helps me to keep my writing on point. I also thank my daughter-in-law, Dena Gross, for help with Spanglish and all my family for their encouragement and many positive comments. I am indebted to and thank Dr. Zora Zimmerman, my first of editors, whose advice and suggestions I depend on from start to finish. And finally, my sincere thanks to Dr. Anthony Paustian and the remarkable staff at Bookpress Publishing, for this amazing partnership of "authors helping authors."

As a musician, I learned early on that composing, practicing, and performing a musical selection, in itself, is insufficient. The process of creativity and artistry expressed in performance also requires an audience of listeners. So too, with a novel. While the experience of writing is rewarding, it is the readers who give meaning to the creative process. I want to express my deep appreciation to readers who have shared in this performance and who helped to complete my creative process.